ALSO BY KATHERINE TAYLOR

Rules for Saying Goodbye

VALLEY FEVER

VALLEY FEVER

KATHERINE TAYLOR

FARRAR, STRAUS AND GIROUX

NEW YORK

•

Farrar, Straus and Giroux
18 West 18th Street, New York 10011

Copyright © 2015 by Katherine Taylor
All rights reserved
Printed in the United States of America
First edition, 2015

Library of Congress Cataloging-in-Publication Data
Taylor, Katherine, 1973–
    Valley fever / Katherine Taylor. — First edition.
        pages ;   cm
    ISBN 978-0-374-29914-9 (hardback) — ISBN 978-0-374-71381-2 (e-book)
    I. Title.

PS3620.A947 V35 2015
813'.6—dc23

2014044645

Designed by Abby Kagan

Farrar, Straus and Giroux books may be purchased for educational, business,
or promotional use. For information on bulk purchases, please contact the
Macmillan Corporate and Premium Sales Department at 1-800-221-7945,
extension 5442, or write to specialmarkets@macmillan.com.

www.fsgbooks.com
www.twitter.com/fsgbooks • www.facebook.com/fsgbooks

1   3   5   7   9   10   8   6   4   2

The author is especially grateful to Dewey Belli and June Donny for their help
in research, and to the Parents Taylor for their unrelenting support.

For Russel

VALLEY FEVER

1. I don't return to places I've lived. I avoid my high school dorm by not going back to all of Massachusetts. In London, I'll avoid Holland Park so as not to be reminded of the basement flat on Addison Road. The furnished two-bedroom on Via Annia in Rome, the bright studio in the white brick building on West Eighty-fourth Street with floor-to-ceiling bookshelves, the two-bedroom in Prenzlauer Berg I shared with a publishing-heiress insomniac who would speak only Russian: some of those places were good for a while. Still, whole neighborhoods, whole cities, can be ruined by the reasons you left.

"This entire thing has gone off the rails."

"Come home," Anne said.

"Home where?"

"At least you don't have a dog."

"Annie, I could kill you with a fucking pencil."

"Stop swearing," she said. Then she said, "I have soft-shell crabs."

I have made so many calls from airports, and so many times I have been crying. Here's what I like about airports: no one's surprised to see you cry. In airports and closets and hospitals, cry as much as you like.

"Well, I have lots of wine. Let's drink our way through Charlie's wine cellar, okay?"

"I don't have anywhere to go."

"Charlie wants you to come over here and drink your way through his wine cellar."

"Did you ask him that?"

"Charlie, do you want Ingrid to come over and drink her way through your cellar?"

"I'm taking a different flight."

"He does."

"It's going to be late."

Something else I like about airports is that you have no choice but to eat french fries and peanut M&M's. At the airport in Denver toward the end of the small C concourse, there's a mom-and-pop greasy spoon where you can get grilled cheeses cooked in shortening.

I said to the employee behind the airline counter in the lounge, "He says he doesn't love me as much as he thought he did."

Her name was Gloria and she had enormously coiffed blond hair and coral-pink lipstick that bled into the tiny lines around her mouth. "You're very brave," she said as she changed my ticket. Crying will get your ticket changed without a fee. "I was married for twelve years to a man who didn't love me."

On the flight from Denver to Los Angeles, I drank four glasses of wine. Gloria had upgraded my ticket to business.

It was not the first time Anne had rescued me heartbroken from an airport, or restaurant, or apartment, or football game, but it was the first time I really had no place at all to go. Ten months earlier, I had quit my job as a personal assistant to an aging news anchor and moved from New York to live with Howard in Los Angeles. Then, now, on the forty-five-minute flight from Aspen to Denver, Howard had told me, "This isn't what I thought I wanted."

"What did you think you wanted?"

"I thought I wanted you," he said.

We had spent an awful week with his awful father, a blank and stupid congressman from Nebraska who never, in two years, had spoken to me directly. On the way to the Aspen airport, we had stopped for bacon sandwiches at Jerry's. Howard was always introducing me to things I never would have considered, like Vietnamese fish-head soup or the Jerry's bacon sandwich, with sprouts and avocados and cream cheese and sunflower seeds. He knew things like where to get the best sushi in Little Tokyo and the best barbecue in Inglewood. One of the several terrible things about that flight from DEN to LAX was the delicious bacon sandwich that wouldn't get eaten.

"What changed?" I said.

"Nothing. Nothing changed."

"Something changed your mind."

"Maybe I changed."

"Is this because I don't have a job?"

"No, Ingrid. It's not like that."

"Because I wear my sunglasses indoors."

"No, no."

"They're prescription!"

"I know, Ingrid."

"Your father hates me."

"Why do you always say that?"

I said, "How is it, then? What happened?"

Howard said, because someone had to say it, "I think I only love you when I'm drunk."

———

By the time I landed at LAX, my hands throbbed with anxiety, as if something in my veins was trying to push its way out.

"You look adorable," Anne said. "You always look adorable." She took the small suitcase our parents had given me when I was thirteen, when I left for school. It said IPP on it. It was a floral tapestry, now covered in grime. "For someone who's just been demolished, you look fantastic."

Her car smelled new. Her posture was straight, her hair mussed but clipped back with a tortoiseshell barrette. Anne made everything in the world seem clean and fresh and obvious.

"Aspen will be ruined for you now," Anne said.

"Ruined for you, too," I said.

"Well, we already paid for the rooms at New Year's. Has he ruined all of Colorado? Can you still fly into Denver?"

"Thank you for coming to get me," I said, flattened.

"I will always come and get you." She tugged on a clump of my hair. "I'm saving up for when you have to come and get me."

Los Angeles was dark and wet and cold as it is every June, but this June the rain relieved a thirteen-month drought.

"They'll say one hard rain makes no difference," Anne said. This was not true, we knew. Every bit of water mattered. Even the smallest rain could make or ruin you.

"It's beautiful, though, isn't it?"

The windshield wipers went back and forth like a conversation. It was late. By morning, the gutterless streets would fill and overflow and potholes the size of platters would sink into Hollywood Boulevard. Anne and Charlie had held dinner. Back at their white clapboard house with the green shutters, Anne gave me wool socks and her shearling slippers and we kept the windows open so we could hear and see and smell the rain.

"The paint is going to bubble," Charlie said.

"It will be my fault," Anne said.

"Of course it's your fault."

She said, "He'll blame me for the peeling windowsills and for everything." The windowsills were already peeling. The windowsills in Anne's house peeled perfectly, the paint coming off in full strips.

Charlie fried wiggly, still-snapping soft-shell crabs in mustard and butter and we drank a bottle of malbec so rich and viscous, you couldn't see your fingers on the other side of the glass.

"Aren't you supposed to kill those first?" Anne suggested.

"I have done this before," he said, shaking the pan with the crab curling up in it. Just outside, under the eaves, Charlie had spears of sweet potatoes frying in a lobster pot over the barbecue, and he turned to check on them.

"All right, lovey. I am just trying to help." Anne's wavy hair and neat clothes and straight posture could make you hostile to her advice. "You'd think you would just want to kill it quick," she said, half to me and half to Charlie.

"You want me to cook some fritters?" I said.

She said, "We don't have any squash. Don't try to do anything tonight, Ingrid. You got off the plane drunk."

Outside the window, rain poured out of the storm drain like a faucet. We finished the first bottle of wine and opened a second.

Charlie said, "If you can't tell the difference between this and the malbec, then next time I'm going to serve you this."

I said, "I can tell the difference, Charlie."

When Anne and I were teenagers, Miguel caught us drinking Blue Nun in the vineyard. Dad was so angry, he sold Anne's car and forced us both to work in the packing shed for the rest of the summer. "This punishment is not for drinking," Dad said.

"This punishment is for drinking Blue Nun." Charlie has latched on to this story and to the idea of me and Anne as drinkers of German plonk.

Anne said, "Do you want to talk about it, Inky, or do you want to talk about other things?"

"Have you spoken to Mom?" I said.

"I spoke to her, but I didn't give her any details."

"You didn't have any details to give her," Charlie said from underneath the eaves. He used long metal tongs to lift the sweet potato fries out of the pot.

"I don't want to talk about it, anyway," I said. I never give Anne any real details. Keeping secrets is not one of Anne's specialties. In fact, Anne's specialty is using your secrets against you.

"I guess we'll cancel December," Charlie said.

Anne said, "You don't have to cancel the whole month. December exists."

"We can go to Wyoming instead," I said.

Charlie said, "I put the deposit down on Aspen." He emphasized the word *deposit*.

He filled my plate with wilted greens and slipped a perfect crunchy crab on top, straight from the pan.

"I can't go back to Aspen," I said.

Charlie said, "You're crossing a lot of places off your list, Ingrid."

"Are you going to let him keep Aspen?" Anne said.

"We'll see how I feel in December." The soft-shell crabs were crunchy and golden and tangy with mustard, but I couldn't eat more than their crispy little claws.

"You and I could go, Anne," said Charlie.

Anne picked at her wilted greens, eating them one by one. "I don't really want to go with just you."

The rain slowed down. You could hear each separate drop

hit the flat leaves of the palms. The rain, like everything, was temporary.

Anne gave me soft cotton pinstripe pajamas and a carafe with water. I opened the wide windows to let the rain splash in but the rain had stopped. There were leftover irregular drops from the rooftop. Beside the guest room I could hear Anne in the kitchen, drying the Saint-Louis and setting them back in the cupboard. Anne doesn't let anyone else wash her expensive glasses. I smelled the smoke from Charlie's weed, outside. Charlie liked to smoke and Anne didn't. I didn't either. Weed could make me suicidally depressed. Charlie used to say, "That's because you only smoke when you've been drinking." Charlie's marijuana came in a pharmaceutical bottle. It was an anti-anxiety prescription. One morning after dinner at Anne's and a late-night smoke with Charlie, I woke certain that if I did not immediately flush all my Lunesta and Vicodin and all my Tylenol PM down the toilet, I'd swallow pill by pill with bourbon. This is why I don't own a gun. Everyone else in my family owns a gun, including Anne. What would I do with a gun besides shoot myself?

The night birds started. I formed half the comforter into the shape of a person. Charlie tapped on his phone outside the open window. I lay there thinking and my head felt swollen and then all right and then swollen again. I tried to cry but didn't feel like crying. What a shocking day. Ten months ago I had a sunny loft on Avenue B and a job with a kind, elderly news anchor who wore bow ties and demanded very little. I had an enormous mirrored armoire with a secret compartment on the bottom and a set of white dishes and twelve matching coffee cups with delicate handles. Stupidly, I had put nothing in storage. I'd sold the armoire for three thousand dollars and given everything else to the nuns who set up apartments for homeless people. Ha.

Outside, I heard Charlie pour another bourbon into his glass. I wondered what he'd given up. I knew he'd given up paying tuition at Yale for a full ride to USC's film school. But then he had not made films, he'd become an entertainment lawyer. Charlie was the most successful compromiser I'd met in my life so far. One had to be a great compromiser to be married to Anne.

Anne had never given up anything at all. She'd won every argument and every raffle she'd ever entered. If Anne could see her losing position, she abandoned the enterprise entirely. But Anne was too lucky to fail at much. One summer during college she bought a scratch-off lottery ticket at the gas station on Blackstone and Gettysburg and won $100,000.

My head swelled and the room seemed to tilt and then I knew I was going to throw up.

In the morning, Anne and I drove down the hill to Howard's house to retrieve my things. He'd left the shades open, and I could see his coffee cup on the kitchen island before we even got out of the car. Howard never rinsed out his coffee cups. Thank goodness I would never have to rinse another of Howard's coffee cups. The house was still warm with his shower, his cologne, the smell of his dry cleaning and rosemary shampoo that already felt repellent to me.

"I hate these sofas," Anne said. Ample light came in through the south and the skylights. Anne flicked on the lights. "They really are the ugliest sofas. Why do these sofas have to be so ugly?"

"They're awful sofas."

Howard had chosen these huge sofas for watching the Saturday-afternoon Duke football to which he was devoted. They were deep and soft and feather-filled. I had, previously, appreciated these awful sofas because they were good for naps and for eating guacamole while lying down. But now Howard's love had hit its limit, and he had very bad taste in design and these brown chenille sofas.

"We both should have known a man with these sofas could not be trusted with anything of value," Anne said.

For a while in New York I had a photographer friend called Gil who, when he was seven, had found his mother in her bedroom with her face blown off and the gun still in her hand. How he had discovered his mother's suicide was one of the first things Gil would tell you about himself. It was years into our friendship that Gil told me the story of his college girlfriend, how she'd been sleeping with someone else on the men's tennis team. We were in Los Angeles on a work assignment, catching a showing of Baz Luhrmann's *Romeo + Juliet*, eating Milk Duds in the bright pre-movie space of the Beverly Cinema. I asked him, "Did she break your heart?"

He laughed. He shook his head and showed me his fingernails, with the yellow growth underneath them he'd had since he was eight, shortly after he'd found his mother. "My heart was already broken," he said.

When my heart is broken, like that first day of shock after Howard told me he didn't love me, I start to think about what happened with George Sweet. Through high school and college and for the year after college we lived together in New York, I had loved George plainly and completely, and he loved me back. But my mother forbade my marrying him. She feared he was lazy and she called his mother an "opportunist." She may have been right, at least about George being lazy. At any rate, I let her get right into the central artery of George and me, thinking, then, like a child does, that plain and complete love is easy to find. I always think, when I think about it, after each bad breakup, "My heart was already broken."

Anne said, "And I have always hated this house. Don't you hate this house?"

"Do you think I should take the brandy we bought in France?"

"It's a bachelor pad, Ingrid. There's a bicycle in the guest room."

"We were going to fix the guest room."

"I don't know how he thought he could live here with you. I don't know how you thought you could live here with him."

"I'm taking the brandy. It was my idea to get the brandy, anyway."

"You were the event in this relationship," she said, perched on the edge of an ottoman. "I mean, I like Howard and everything, but I sure am glad I'm on your side."

"You're my sister," I said.

"That has nothing to do with it."

"You were born on my side."

"I'll bet Howard's friends wish they were on your side."

When I bent over to put a stack of sweaters into my suitcase, I threw up the toast I had eaten for breakfast.

"We're not in a hurry," Anne said. "Let's sit." Anne made a cup of chamomile tea, but I threw that up, too. "It would be fun if we had to go to the hospital because of a broken heart," she said. "It would be dramatic."

I agreed it would be exceptional if I had to check myself into the emergency room. "I think I'm just hungover," I said.

"Keep puking," Anne said. "Then I can call Howard at work and tell him you're at the hospital."

We sat on the bathroom floor. "I might have to go to the hospital just so I have someplace to stay."

"You'll stay with me," Anne said.

"I can't stay with you indefinitely."

"Yes you can. Where else will you go?"

"I'll check myself into the hospital."

"Stay with me and Charlie."

"Too many sisters in one house."

"Two too many."

"I overwhelmed him last night."

"No, I did. Charlie, you know. Charlie has a thing."

"About too many Palamedes in one house?"

"He says we become very Central Valley when we're together."

"What's very Central Valley?"

"Don't worry about Charlie."

But I did. And Anne, them both. I worried about Anne and Charlie like I worried about my parents: always concerned that someone was about to tip something over, to break something valuable.

"I think I want to go home," I said.

"Home where?"

"Home to the farm home."

"Home to Fresno?"

"Just home to Mom and Dad for a while."

"Darling, don't do that."

"I don't know where else to keep all this stuff, and these boxes of books."

"Ingrid, just come stay with us for a while."

"I am so stupid, stupid, stupid."

"Until you figure out what to do."

"I know what I want to do."

"Just stay with us."

"Will you drive me?" Even the car I drove belonged to Howard.

Charlie opened a bottle of Far Niente and an old bottle of Mondavi, from when Robert was alive and still owned it. He wasn't joking when he said we'd drink our way through his wine cellar. Until the wine got opened, Anne and Charlie didn't speak to each other much. Opening the wine meant the start of a dinner-long truce. Anne put corn on the grill and steamed tiny white potatoes the size of marbles. She sautéed sole in butter with toasted almonds, exactly the way our mother had done it when we were little.

"Annie says you're going back to the farm."

"Why don't you come with us?" I said.

"Someone has to work in this family."

"Someone has to buy the wine," Anne said from the kitchen.

"Someone's got to drink the wine," I said.

"Yes," said Anne. "That's our job."

"You're both very good at your job," said Charlie.

The sole had crispy little fins and a crispy tail. I let Anne eat my crispy tail. I enjoyed how much she enjoyed it. I enjoyed that she ate off my plate with her fingers.

"Charlie, can I eat your tail?" she said.

"Very funny, Anne."

"Don't you want to see me happy?" she said.

He ate the tail.

Anne said, "You're not eating, Ingrid." She put her hand on my shoulder blade and rubbed the knot out of it.

"I've got something stuck in my throat."

Charlie said, "Let's have bourbon, okay, Ingrid?"

"I'm sorry," I said. "The sole is beautiful, Anne."

"We all have beautiful soles," Anne said.

Charlie brought out tumblers and a small bottle of bourbon made in California. "Yankee bourbon," Charlie said.

"We need more ice," Anne said.

"One ice cube each," said Charlie. "You don't want to ruin the bourbon." He filled our glasses to the very top. "To the free world!" he said.

"Ha!" Anne laughed and grabbed his wrist. "Charlie," she said. He leaned over and bit her cheekbone, lightly.

"Charlie," she said, laughing, "you're funny." She bit him back on the side of his chin.

"To the free world," I agreed.

"For tomorrow, we shall return to the farm," he said.

2. Over the Grapevine down into the Central Valley, you travel through the dried-up hills of the Tejon Pass with the blond grass and parched landscape. You pass the water museum and Pyramid Lake and Smokey Bear Road and you pass through a little town called Gorman split by the highway with two fast-food restaurants and two gas stations and one vintage furniture store. There are signs advising drivers to turn off their air-conditioning to avoid overheating. An hour and a half north of Hollywood, you crest and descend toward a 23,000-square-mile quilted valley floor in varying shades of brown and green. More than twenty thousand acres of the best land in that valley belonged to Dad. He had assembled his ranch entirely on his own, beginning with one hundred acres his parents had bequeathed.

On the road from Bakersfield to Fresno, the farms on either side have small blue signs identifying what's grown there: table grapes, wine grapes, pomegranates. English walnuts, peaches, nectarines, almonds. Apricots, pistachios, plums. For years there were oranges, but the oranges were replaced by clementines and soon after the clementines were replaced by pistachios. Everyone grows pistachios these days, or almonds. Even the packing house that used to bundle small wooden boxes of tangerines now sorts and distributes nuts. I can tell the difference between the peaches and the nectarines before I see the sign: the leaves of the nectarine tree start to go brown earlier in the summer.

Anne can't even tell the almonds from apricots.

Before Gorman there was a sign advertising GUNS AND WINE: THIS EXIT. Farther on, a billboard with a rejoicing grandmother said BINGO! WHERE SHOUTING IS FUN! Other signs reminded us that JESUS IS LORD, ABORTION STOPS A BEATING HEART, and NO WATER = NO JOBS.

White grapes were getting picked: Thompsons, chardonnay, sauvignon. The chenin blanc and some of the early viognier. Picking started in the south and followed the weather north. From the Grapevine to Bakersfield, pickups and water tents and harvesting trucks lined up against the fences of the highway. When Bakersfield was done, Tulare would get started, and Visalia, and Selma, and then Fresno and the north.

Past the dairies in Hanford, you could smell the cows for twenty miles.

Fresno smelled like dust and the start of rotting fruit. It was afternoon when we arrived and the sun was high and hot. Once we got out of the center of town, off the 99 down Avenue 7 halfway to Firebaugh, through the vineyards on the one-lane road to the house, you could begin to smell the briny river and the algae that grows up the sides of canals. It had been the third bad year in a row for water; the canals were nearly empty. The smell of the river and the dust in the vineyards always made me homesick, homesick while I was standing right there at home.

"I think I'm developing a limp," I said.

"Okay," Anne said. She pulled my small suitcase out of the back. "Don't angle for attention when I'm already giving it to you."

"I can't move." I sat in the car with the door open. The heat hit you hard enough to make your ears ring, an open-handed smack. The air was sharp with dust.

"You're being pathetic." She dragged the suitcase through the carport to the kitchen. "You need to get something in you." Through the screen door I saw our mother playing solitaire at the table in her nightgown, the back of her hair pushed up flat into a pile from sleeping, her free hotel slippers worn through to the soles. Mother had a whole closet full of free hotel slippers still in their canvas bags, but she would keep washing the old ones until they entirely disintegrated. Free hotel slippers last longer than you think. Mother had been collecting them for thirty years.

"Let me finish this game," Mom said to Anne as she came through the door. "This does not look good!" she said to the cards, shaking her head. "This is not good," as if she blamed our arrival.

"It's sweltering in here," Anne said.

"We're conserving electricity," Mother said.

"It's a hundred degrees out there," Anne said. "Turn on the air, will you?"

"Have some ice water," Mother told her. "There she is!" Mother called out to the car. "Don't sit there, Inky. Come inside."

"It's cooler in the car," Anne said.

"If you would like to pay the electric bill, Anne, that's fine," Mother said.

"What's wrong with the screen door?" It didn't slam behind me the way it usually did. The spring was broken.

"I don't know," Mom said. "You step into this house and you start complaining. When I ask for your opinion, you don't give it. When I don't want it, you're yakkin' all over the place." One eyelash extension wobbled independently of the rest.

"This house is falling apart," Anne said. "Don't you fall apart, Mother."

"Me," Mother said, "I am entirely put together." She smoothed down the front of her wild hair. "I just got up." Tiny pieces of down were stuck in the dark curls around her face. "How was the drive?" She hugged me. She was damp with sweat and she smelled like sleep.

Anne said, "The rumors are true. There's not a tree full of fruit between here and Ventura."

"Now the nut guys are worried," Mother said. "Walter's almonds have started dropping their leaves, the hulls have begun to split too early. A thousand acres or so. Every farmer in town is thrilled."

"And scared," I said.

No matter how much love you feel for another farmer, no matter if he's your brother or your best friend, no farmer ever wants another to do well. Walter grew a strain of large, beautiful almonds and, during good years, got a premium from the specialty food people. While all the other nut guys might be delighted at Walter's misfortune (it would mean, after all, higher prices for their own crop), every one of them could be terrorized by the very possibility of early hull split on his own trees.

"Everyone's afraid," Mother said, and scraped a spot of breakfast from the front of her dressing gown. There was not supposed to be a lot of money this year, or demand, even for the large and lovely almonds. "No one knows if what killed the stone fruit is going to kill the nuts, too."

"Or all the drupe," I said.

"Yes," said Mother.

"We hear this every year," Anne said.

That June, the peaches didn't grow. The leaves of the peach trees wilted and curled and sprung pits with no flesh. There were no fruit flies, no infestations of worms. That year, the peaches had been stunted by water-stressed trees and a fungus nothing seemed to kill. "But we're fine, you don't want to hear about us," Mother said. "Or do you want to hear?"

"Yes, we do," I said.

"You know, those peaches they get from South America are grown in human shit," Mother said.

"We know about the South American peaches," I said. When I first moved to Los Angeles, the sewer in Howard's backyard had exploded. Months later, in that patch of grass to the side of the house where the toilet paper and feces and old tampons had come up, tomatoes appeared so plentiful, the vines so tall and abundant, I thought for a week the tomatoes were bougainvillea. Seeds must have made their way through the disposal. The vines grew up the side of the house and over the fence shared with the cranky neighbor. Those tomatoes were more delicious even than the ones my grandmother had grown. They were more delicious than any fruit I had eaten in years.

"Don't get me started on the peaches from Georgia."

Anne said, "We know the peaches from Georgia, Mom." The peaches grown in Georgia, like most of the peaches grown in California the years we could grow peaches, were grown for color and for cold-storage endurance. They tasted like nothing, like wood pulp. Dad's peaches were yellowy orange and didn't store very well, but they tasted the way a peach ought to taste, like sun and sugar, and Dad's peaches were so juicy you had to eat them over a sink.

"The Georgia peaches are just not fruit. They're barely drupe. You should see the commercials they're running on television. Have you seen the commercials?"

"Are there commercials?" I didn't mention that this year, and for three years running, the California peaches were barely drupe. I really hadn't seen the commercials.

"They're running commercials with worms coming out of our peaches. We don't even have worms this year."

Anne said, "You don't even have peaches."

"You can imagine your father. All those years with that bank, and now what they've done to him. You can imagine."

"Yes," Anne said.

"But you don't want to hear about us. What can I make you to eat?" Mother said.

Anne said, "She won't eat."

"Can't," I said.

"She might have to see the doctor," Anne said.

"No one sees a doctor over a breakup," my mother said. "Do you mean a shrink? Do you have a fever?"

"Ingrid, if you don't start eating, I'm going to take you to the hospital, but a bad hospital. With rats," Anne said.

"I want to go to the hospital."

"We can find you a shrink, Ingrid," Mother said. "I'm sure there must be some decent shrinks here in Fresno."

"I am not going to see some Fresno shrink," I said. "I'm going to stay here for a few days and sleep."

"Do you want to talk about what happened?"

"No, Mother."

The kitchen window looked out to the yard, terraced down to the river. Each of the terraces indicated a year that peaches and grapes had done well. The tennis court for the year I was in fourth grade and peaches were forty dollars a box. The swimming pool the year I was in seventh and Dad put in the packing plant. The landscaping and floodlights along the river one of the years no one else could grow cabernet. This year, the grass on the terraces had gone brown from neglect and the untended swimming pool was green like the river and canals.

"How about a fried egg?" my mother said. "A fried egg will make you feel better."

"I told you, she won't do it," Anne said. "But you should have a slice of nectarine or something, Ingrid."

"There are no nectarines," Mother said.

"No nectarines either?"

"You could have grapes," Mother said. "We have plenty of grapes."

Vines would save us. That's what the tree fruit people always say—when the tree fruit doesn't work, the vines save you. Years you can't sell your grapes or the rain comes before the raisins are dry, the peaches and nectarines and almonds keep you going.

"Give her a drink," Anne said to our mother.

"It's not even three."

"Give her a drink, it's got grain in it." Anne took a tumbler from the cabinet and piled it with frozen Thompson seedless, one of the earliest grapes to be harvested in the valley, grapes that Mother had probably picked herself from the vines near the house, individually washed and plucked from the rachis and placed in freezer bags to be used instead of ice. "And loads of nutritious fruit," Anne said, pouring five counts of vodka to the rim. "Eat," she said, handing me the glass.

Mother said, "I don't like that, Anne. I don't like it." She went back to her cards.

I drank the vodka and I ate the slushy, vodka-soaked grapes, and then I ate a piece of bread from a loaf open on the counter.

"One piece of bread at a time," Anne said.

It was easier to eat after I'd had a drink.

"If we have to drink vodka, we drink it with grapes," Mother said.

"She has to drink vodka," Anne said.

I ate the bread and went upstairs. The house continued to vibrate with the sound of voices from the kitchen.

Mom and Dad built the house on the river when Anne and I were tiny. It had long 1970s ranch-type lines, open Frank Lloyd Wright spaces finished with red Mexican tiles and dark wood. There was an enormous fireplace in the living room—twelve feet wide and six feet high—large enough so that the huge trunks of felled walnut trees could be brought in to burn. Mr. Ellison next door grew almonds and walnuts, and kept Mom and Dad in giant-sized firewood. Sometimes, in December or January, with the flue left open, the wind would come down that chimney like thunder, like an earthquake, and the white walls of the living room would turn black with ash.

Mother considered building the house on the river the great achievement of her life. On the coffee table in the living room, she kept a thirty-year-old copy of *Sunset* magazine, the cover faded into beige, featuring a six-page spread of the house just after it was finished. Inside, Mother and Dad were thin and glamorous, glossy and coifed in their riverside vineyard.

My old bedroom had framed pictures of me as Helen Keller in the fifth grade and packs of girls at Friday-night football games. (Stella was dead now, killed on the back of her boyfriend's motorcycle; Eileen had developed a cocaine habit to accompany her eating disorders and married the son of a developer in town; I'd heard that Bootsie had returned to Fresno well after our falling out in New York—Bootsie, I missed her the most.) My slouchy high school silhouette, carved by George Sweet from the side of a Kleenex box, still wedged into the windowpane, exactly where he had put it fifteen years ago. Sweet George Sweet.

I liked the heat. You could feel it in your chest, like an emotion. The heat was something you could count on. I took off my clothes and fell asleep, the kind of sleep so heavy you don't know how long you've been under by the time you get up.

3. Uncle Felix drank wine with every meal, including two tablespoons in his coffee at breakfast. He was round and red and always happy. Uncle Felix was Dad's oldest friend. Their parents' and grandparents' vineyards had been side by side. Uncle Felix's big fat stomach was full of muscle, the way it is with some men who spend their lives digging up the stumps of old vines and planting new ones. He wore blue cashmere V-necks, even in the summer. His shoes were all work boots. Recently he had started dating his manicurist, much younger than he was, and from Visalia. Mother didn't like her. Mother said, "All the sluts come from Visalia." Mother missed Aunt Jane, who just after her fifty-fifth birthday bled to death in her bed from the last stages of bone cancer. Everyone's always got cancer in Fresno.

It was dark out; my room was a box of stale heat. There was the echo of laughter from the kitchen. Uncle Felix and Dad and Anne were having a bottle of wine.

"There she is," Anne said.

"How do you feel?"

"I feel all right."

"Would you like me to kill him?" Uncle Felix asked.

"What time is it?"

"I mean have him killed."

"No, but thank you, Uncle Felix." Uncle Felix had walked the two miles to our house in the hot evening. He liked to walk.

"Past dinner," Dad said. "But no one's eaten dinner."

"I've eaten," said Uncle Felix.

I opened and closed the pantry door: five-gallon jars of raisins and dried mint and bay leaves and walnuts. I opened and closed the refrigerator.

"This always happens to Ingrid," Anne said.

"It doesn't always happen to me."

"Five years ago, Fourth of July, at Newton's parents' house in Cornwall."

Five years ago, on the Fourth of July, essentially the same thing had happened: I had moved from New York to London to live with Newton Greene, a floppy-haired English political consultant I'd met at a dinner party in New York, and shortly after I'd moved, during a weekend at his parents' house in the country, he told me he thought we'd made a mistake. "That was one other time," I said.

"I'll make it look like a car accident," Uncle Felix said.

Dad was quiet. He patted my arm. "You want a vodka?" he said. He got up to pour me a vodka.

"Why don't you come back to Fresno and marry Wilson?" Uncle Felix said. Wilson was Uncle Felix's nephew. He did the accounting for Uncle Felix and my parents and a couple of other growers in the valley.

"Wilson needs to find a nice Fresno girl," Anne said.

"Ingrid's a nice Fresno girl," Uncle Felix said.

"Let's leave Ingrid alone," Dad said, handing me the vodka. He'd poured it over grapes from the freezer.

"Is this how you guys are drinking vodka now?" I said.

"Be happy we're drinking vodka at all," Anne said. Among farmers in the valley, it's a complicated thing to drink anything but wine. The back of my parents' deep bar cabinet still had a bottle of cognac given to them the year they got married, and bottles of Canadian Club and Beefeater they'd bought, naively, for parties they'd given twenty-five years ago.

"It's a conspiracy to use the grapes," said Uncle Felix. "Those are my grapes you're eating."

"You don't buy the Thompsons," I said.

"I do," said Uncle Felix.

"He does," said Dad. "Uncle Felix is making wine you'd be embarrassed to drink."

"I'm not embarrassed to drink anything," Anne said.

"I remember," said Dad.

"What kind of wine, Uncle Felix?"

"The Australians, the Chileans, the Italians are beating us at low-priced wine. With grapes we can grow here. Grapes your father grows."

"You're going to make cheap wine?" I said. "Cheaper than before?" Uncle Felix's wine went for eight or nine dollars a bottle. He had a huge operation, in vineyards and in wine. The wine part of the business had grown so much in the past twenty years that his vineyards couldn't produce enough, and he bought juice from farmers all over the valley.

"Nice wine," he said. "But inexpensive."

"They make nice wine in Napa," Anne said. "You make plonk."

"Just because they charge more doesn't mean it's nice, fancy pants." Uncle Felix liked to say that no bottle of wine was worth more than ten dollars. The Napa guys hated Uncle Felix.

"How low is low?" I asked.

"Four dollars. Five dollars. We'll see."

"Two dollars," I said.

"We'll see."

"A drinkable wine for a dollar fifty a bottle would make you a billionaire," I said.

"Well," he said. "We'll see how those Thompsons turn out."

The sun had gone down to the west end of the river. The real beauty of Fresno always pained me. The vibrant sunsets, the magenta and lucid orange only a sky of pesticides and exhaust can make: there is nothing quite like a sunset on fire over a vineyard in July, before the grapes have been picked and the vines are thick, abundant. The orange light reflected off the fruit. I tried to ignore this real beauty. I preferred to think of the stretch of used-car lots in the middle of town and the expensive new homes built side by side around the shallow veneer of a man-made lake.

Uncle Felix poured the last of the bottle into Dad's glass. Anne opened another. "Where's my mother?" Anne said.

"Let's have toast," Dad said, and he put four slices of bread in the toaster for us. It was exactly what I'd had in mind for dinner.

Uncle Felix asked, "What are you working on now, Ingrid?"

"Nothing I want to talk about, Uncle Felix." After I'd quit my job and moved to Los Angeles, I got a grant from a human rights organization to finish a screenplay I'd been writing for a while: a comedy about genocide, loosely based on the true story of my father's grandparents. Although I had a good idea of how to write a grant application (I'd had a couple of those jobs, too), I had no idea how to write a screenplay, and I each day learned a little more that I didn't care. I sat at my desk, and had every day for six months, and while I told people who asked that I was at work on my project, in fact I had written nothing, I had been depressed by all the screenwriting books with their embarrassing sentences, and I'd spent nearly the entire grant. It's amazing how fast you can run through $25,000.

When the toast popped up, Dad said, "I cooked you dinner."

"Thank you, Dad." Anne can be wonderful, and she can be an asshole, but for the most part she is always sincere. It's when she's being most sincere that she's most an asshole. "You're excellent at making toast."

"How long are you staying?" Uncle Felix said.

"Just a little bit," I said. "I don't know." I opened the kitchen window, so we could smell the ripening fruit of the summer night.

"Let's go hit a few balls."

"You'll be frustrated golfing with me, Uncle Felix."

"I'll fix your backswing."

"Dad, tell him."

"She's a good golfer," Dad said. Except that I wasn't.

"Stay for a while," Uncle Felix said. "Your dad misses you."

I looked at Dad. "Hi, Dad."

"Hi, Inky."

Later, Anne came into my room as I was getting ready for bed, opening the door wide without knocking.

"I'm naked," I said. The heat seemed to get bigger at night, like a terror. It would come and get you. You had to let it roll over you; you had to sleep underneath a thin sheet with no clothes on. "Could you wait?" I was standing in the middle of my bedroom, in front of the mirror on the closet door, flossing my teeth, admiring my muscular stomach after six days of not eating. "Just a minute."

She came in anyway. "Do you always use that much dental floss?" she said. "That's, like, a really long string of dental floss."

"Dental floss: an affordable luxury."

"Listen, Ingrid. Don't stay here too long, okay?"

"Anne," I said.

"This place always gives me a sore throat," she said. It was the air, the fires, the sprays used on fruit. "Don't be one of those people who comes back home to Fresno, Ingrid."

"Who are those people?"

"Bootsie, for one." Anne and I had felt gratifyingly superior when we'd heard that Bootsie Calhoun had moved back home. Bootsie had called me in New York a little over a year ago, after she had moved back to Fresno, right after her father died, just before I moved to LA. I didn't return the call. You know how these things go—you don't call right away and then all manner of other distractions impose themselves and then it becomes increasingly impossible to make what could have been a relatively easy phone call. Simple avoidance can shift the burden of guilt. Now I felt so bad for ignoring her grief and despair because the timing was wrong, and because we hadn't spoken since our petty fight, I was too embarrassed to do anything about it.

"Anne," I said. "Are you trying to rescue me?" I went to brush my teeth.

"If you want money, ask me for it," she said. "You might need a tiny bit of rescuing."

"Okay."

"I mean, about the peaches and everything. It's not good. What do you think?"

"It'll be fine."

"And Mother's eyelashes. What is going on with Mother's eyelashes? Something is wrong. I mean, with the whole thing, this whole farm, this whole town. Mom looks like a crazy person."

I didn't answer her. Anne could be thoroughly exhausting.

She said, "Anyway, you can come live with me if you need to."

"Yes, Anne," I said. "I have money, Anne."

"What a rotten sort he is."

"He is rotten," I said.

"Rotten."

"Breaking up with me is very unattractive." I had to remind myself of Howard's character flaws. I had to forget about his stupid flat stomach, the idiot way he brought me coffee in bed.

"I want you to be okay."

"Thank you, Annie. I'm okay."

"Don't stay here too long. I mean, it's comfortable and cozy and everything, but in a *Who's Afraid of Virginia Woolf?* sort of way, you know?" She shook out her hair like a whip. It fell in delicate wavy pieces over her white polo. Anne's plain beauty got on my nerves.

"Okay, Anne, all right. I'm naked." I was done with my teeth and found a San Joaquin Memorial High School T-shirt to wear in bed and slipped underneath the sheet. It occurred to me, anyway, that Anne's house was a little more *Who's Afraid of Virginia Woolf?* than the house here with Mom and Dad, who never had cruel words for each other. I wondered all the time how I could repeatedly find myself in mean relationships when my parents were so kind together.

"Your stomach muscles look great," Anne said. "You should buy a bikini."

"Anorexia divorsa."

She smoothed my hair over the pillow. It felt good to have her touch my hair. "You're adorable," she said. "You're an adorable girl."

"Will you draw on my back?"

She pulled down the sheet and drew a treasure map on my back, with *X marks the spot*. When we were younger, she would pound her fist really hard when X marked the *spot*. "Four big boulders, one teeny dot," she said, pounding and pinching, but lightly.

"Annie?"

"Inky."

"Could you stay here until I fall asleep?"

She crawled onto the sheets and spooned me, Anne who liked everything to be perfect and nice and crisp and clean before bedtime, who scrubbed her face vigorously with ground-up apricot pits every night. She rubbed her nose on the base of my neck. "Soon you will forget you were ever in pain in the first place," she said. "People forget pain. It's proven." Anne is like a mother dog: growling most of the time, but then warm when she needs to be.

"It's not that kind of pain," I said.

"Sure it is. It's physical, isn't it?"

"I can't tell what's physical yet."

We were quiet for a while and then she started going *tick, tick, tick*, a sound she makes with her tongue right before she falls asleep, and I heard her light snoring.

I had a tiny bit of a headache from drinking without food and in the dark I started to worry a little about the peaches, about the farm, about how bad Anne thought things were. Everything seems worse in the dark.

"Annie," I whispered, and she made that light grunty noise she makes that tells me she's really asleep.

I chewed on my knuckle until I went under.

Anne drove back to Los Angeles early the next morning. Her body was set to an internal alarm. Since college she'd had a successful career as an actress, and working actresses don't sleep past 5:00 a.m. For the past four years she'd done the voice of Annie the Cow in a popular children's cartoon. Charlie said the producers had been forced to call the cow Annie so she'd answer to her character's name. This was Charlie's subtle way of suggesting Anne's consuming self-centeredness. She woke at 4:00 to drive to the studio.

In the kitchen sink there were two coffee cups.

"Did you talk to Anne?" I said to Dad, later, home for lunch. I had opened a bag of raw almonds and set them out in one of my grandmother's cut-glass bowls. Dad and I picked at the nuts.

"Annie seems happy, don't you think?" He coughed, and then kept coughing.

"Dad, I can feel that cough in my knees."

"What cough?" he said.

I said, "I think Annie's almost suspiciously happy. You can never tell with Anne."

"You don't seem suspiciously happy," he said.

The first conversations I have with my father after a breakup are always sort of harrowing. I fear he'll see my failure as his own. My father is much too generous and faithful to see a breakup as any failure of mine. "I don't mean she's suspiciously happy. I just mean you can never tell with Anne. She's always got that Annie veneer." The steadier and more solid Anne's veneer, the more I worried about her. That weekend I came back from Aspen, Annie's veneer had seemed particularly steady.

"It's not suspicious. Your mother and I were that happy for a long time."

"You're still happy," I said.

"Yes," he said. "Happiness changes all the time," he said. "You think, What are the other options? You think you're going to be happier somewhere else, with someone else? You're wrong."

"I like Charlie," I said. "He's always nice to me." I didn't want to discuss my parents' happiness, or their options, or Anne's, or my options, for sure.

"You never know what goes on in someone else's marriage," Dad said. "Don't reprimand me for using a cliché." Dad started a fit of coughing on the word *cliché*. He had a sharp, wet cough, and he spit his phlegm into the garbage beneath the sink.

I said, "He understands us, our family. Or at least he understands that he doesn't understand us. And he's been with us a long time."

"That matters," Dad said, unwinding a package of soft white bread to make himself a ham-and-Swiss sandwich. "What else matters?" He dunked a butter knife into the jar of mayonnaise. He stifled another cough, or tried to stifle it.

"To me?"

"What's important to you?"

"You and Mom and Anne and Charlie."

He laid wispy pieces of ham on the bread. He waited for more.

"This house a little. Wine and peaches a little. I guess I would like to finish this project I'm trying to work on." I looked at him. He seemed to be waiting for even more. "I think that's all, Daddy." It occurred to me I didn't have an awfully long list of things that matter.

"You don't care about how people use words? Art doesn't matter to you at all? You don't care if someone shakes your Manhattan? What about really offensive words?"

"You matter, Daddy, so I care if you use offensive words. I do care a little bit if you shake my Manhattan. Try not to." He ate some almonds. I said, "As for art, you know. Growing grapes is art. Did I say I cared about grapes?"

"You said wine."

"Wine and grapes and those things."

"Listen, Ingrid. I'm glad things are important to you. That's who I hoped you would be. I want you to be happy. But I don't want you to be a Communist."

"I'm not a Communist, Dad."

"Let's not talk about politics."

"No, Daddy. I don't know why anyone talks about politics."

"I want you to be a happy woman, Ingrid."

Sometimes my love for my father could cause a little pain in my chest. "I'm happy, Dad. One or two or three breakups, you know, doesn't make a person miserable."

"No," he said, "I think you just skipped a couple of really bad divorces."

"You have orange shoes."

"The dust." The dust was everywhere: on shoes, on cars, blown into little dunes against the porch steps. It was worse this year, without any water.

"The dust didn't used to be orange."

"You girls have this idea about how things used to be. And things were always the same."

"Dad, your shoes are orange." The dust used to be a sort of gold.

"It's orange now, then," he said. Farmers work on the present and on the future. They don't truck with the past.

"Shall you and I play some golf this week?"

"Are you saving your money, Inky?"

"I don't have any money."

"No money. There's no money."

"We could hit some balls, while you can still afford the club."

"I don't know, Inky. I don't know if I'm up to golf anymore."

"What are you talking about? Don't act like you're old, Dad."

"I was thinking, golf has ruined my life for twenty years and I'm done with it." He unwound the rubber band from the *LA Times* on the table, put the sports section in his beaten-raw leather portfolio, and tossed the rest on the kitchen counter. He kept nothing in that portfolio but the sports news and *California Vintner*. Until recently, Dad didn't have a computer in his office— he did everything on paper and by telephone.

"You could just read that online," I said.

"I'm old, Inky. I like newsprint."

"Are you having sugar?" I stirred the grounds in the French press.

"No sugar," he said. "Sugar beets," he said, and shook his head. "No one's paying anything for those, either." It was better, sometimes, to let Dad talk to himself.

Many of the farmers in the valley that year had bet on rain, but the rain didn't come. When it did, it came too light and too late. The peaches turned yellowy orange and red, but when a scarcity of water left the fruit vulnerable to that fungus, they stayed small like nuts. Then, toward the end of August, the small red nutlike peaches fell between the rows, so that from the golf course and from Lake Millerton and from certain houses along the river, you could see bright orange-red stripes between the spotty green rows of trees.

4. "Why would I want to go to Carmel and see all the people I hate in Fresno?" Summers, my mother preferred to stay in her house on the river with all the windows open. She would play solitaire at the kitchen table for six hours straight, without getting up to eat. "I just stay here and don't go into town and pretend I'm in the Dordogne," she said. "It works. Try it."

"Are you depressed?" I said.

"Why would I be depressed?" she said.

"You're in your pajamas all day." Her long white nightgown had holes in it all over. She didn't bother to change when she went outside to prune roses, and the thorns had snagged holes in all of her house clothes. Often she pruned roses without wearing any underwear beneath her nightgown, and this was one of those days.

"Well," she said, as if it were a secret, "I went out to get the roses in the front, and then I was coming around to the back, but I saw the cards here on the table. So I thought I'd come in for a while and play. And then you came in."

"It's after three."

"I'm not going anywhere."

"It just seems like, I don't know."

"Dad is coming in for lunch."

"I know!" It was insulting when she talked about Dad like I didn't know who Dad was. Dad had been coming in for lunch every day since I was four. (As they say, grapes don't stop growing on Saturday.) "Don't you see anybody?"

"I see people."

"Who?"

"I see people who come to the house."

"Uncle Felix. That's all."

"Sometimes Miguel comes to the house." Miguel was my father's foreman. "Have you eaten?" she said. "Let's have eggs."

"Mom, when you run out of things to talk about, you talk about food."

"I don't like the way you're speaking to me."

"I'm not hungry. I've told you I'm not hungry."

"But they're Miguel's eggs," she said. They were a great luxury. "Or I made the grape pie. I made it with Leonard's Bakersfield grapes. We went down there to pick the ends of the rows." The mechanical harvesters can't get to the ends of the rows, so all these overripe, juicy, fragile grapes are left for Leonard's friends to forage—the sort of grapes that explode if you just slightly pinch them. The real delicacy, of course, is if you're in the field yourself and eat those end-grapes right off the vine. All that tension and sugar bursts with just the slightest pressure, a warm explosion of sweet and tart pulp. These are the secrets of the Central Valley that make us farm kids feel superior. No one who grew up in a city has eaten an after-harvest grape picked directly from the end of a vine during the last hot days of the season. This is a thing you can't know unless you knew it already. Also, you can't get a 100-degree grape in a market. There is nothing like a hot grape, too sweet even to pick, the bunch carefully broken off the vine and eaten directly from the spine.

"I'll try the grape pie."

"I just had to go get those grapes," she said. "First extra grapes of the summer."

Mother was so skinny you couldn't help but notice she must think of nothing but food. When you make concord grape pie, you must pick all the hundreds of tiny grapes off the stems, one by one, and concord grapes don't come off all that easily. Your fingernails are stained for days.

Years ago, more than thirty years ago, Mother had known a German woman who married a farmer in town, and this German woman would make the grape pie with the tender stems still in it. Mr. Coleman complained and complained about his wife's grape pie, and his wife refused, as if on principle, to take the time to pick the grapes from the stems. The stems do cook down and you can hardly tell they're there. But they're there, and they have a little bite.

When Mr. Coleman and his wife divorced, she failed to pay her electric bill, an attempt to demonstrate to the court how little money he was giving her. She'd come from Hamburg and wasn't used to the heat. The summer of their separation was particularly hot, even for Fresno, and temperatures outside rose past 120 degrees. Mrs. Coleman died at her kitchen table of heatstroke. She was very German, Mrs. Coleman, and had been keeping a log of her body temperature to show to her lawyer. When she last recorded, she wrote down 105 degrees. When the police found her, her body was at 120. Mr. Coleman married again soon after, and there aren't many people in the valley who remember his first wife.

Nearly every time Mother makes the grape pie, she reminds us about the German woman who had married Mr. Coleman and how she left the stems in, how the stems led to a heat-rotten body slumped at the kitchen table, and how no one remembers her. Mother recites this as if it were a morality tale.

That afternoon, Mother's fingernails were clean and white, because in thirty years she'd learned to wear surgical gloves when she removed the grapes from the stem.

"Who's not hungry for eggs? They're Miguel's eggs."

"I'd rather have a drink."

"I wish you wouldn't drink."

"I wish you wouldn't talk about food the whole time."

"It's bad for your skin," she said. "And you're still young."

Miguel's wife raised chickens in the back of their house, just up the road from ours, in a shed my father and Miguel built themselves one weekend when I was a child. I remember the weekend, because I remember the splinters I got trying to help, and that a few splinters stuck in my hands until my body got rid of them on its own. I wanted a chicken coop, too, very badly, and Miguel said I could share his. Even now, twenty-five years on, Miguel brought over weekly eggs, keeping his promise.

Mother said, then, "Eggs are so easy to eat." She focused on the cards in front of her. "Put on the water, Inky."

"Who do you see, Mom?" I filled the blue iron pot we used for boiled eggs.

"Don't forget to put in the toast." She tapped at an orphaned jack. "Not good, not good."

"Do you see Wilson? What does Wilson have to say about the bank and everything?"

"Wilson's an idiot. Uncle Felix is an idiot. I'm surrounded by idiots."

"You need to manage Wilson better."

"He's supposed to manage us."

"Maybe you should get a new accountant."

"Charlie says I should get a lawyer."

"Of course you need a lawyer."

"Wilson says a lawyer would just take our money and make no difference in the end."

"You just told me Wilson's an idiot."

The banks had started to call in the loans from everyone in town. This happened every few years, but Dad, in the past, had enough sway that the bank gave him time. This year the banks weren't listening to Dad's pleas and they weren't, apparently, willing to wait to see what next year's peaches did. It was an unusual scenario. Felix thought the banks were bluffing. Only small farmers ever lost their land.

Still, as they say, the grapes would save us.

The bougainvillea had taken over the arbor outside the kitchen and the drying pink leaves blanketed the tile, so the patio was all dust and crepelike leaves and dead bees disintegrating and the vague smell of rot. A small brown spider with a thick triangular belly sped in through a gap in the screen, through the open window by the sink. "Spiders," I said, "are good luck."

"Not in the house," Mother said. "Smash it, will you?"

"Not good, not good." I squashed the thing with a paper towel. "Bad luck," I said.

"Wilson says to wait until the grapes are picked and see what the situation looks like then." Mother got that crease between her eyebrows she gets when she's angry or tired or sad.

"I don't know why you listen to what Wilson says."

"Your father wants to listen to Wilson," Mother said. With her index finger, she tried to put her eyelashes back in order. They were all crisscrossed one over the other. "Your father is a wonderful farmer and a wonderful husband, but he can't spot an idiot."

"Felix listens to Wilson, I guess."

"Felix doesn't listen to anyone but Felix."

"You know, he talks a lot, but I've had wines that cost more than ten dollars at Uncle Felix's house."

She looked at me, and all I could see was that awful crease. "You really can't believe one word he says." When I was in high school, Uncle Felix had federal charges brought against him for trying to pass off cheap grapes as cabernet. He had tossed cabernet leaves over grapes from a less expensive varietal. He worked out a plea to avoid jail, but he is now, technically, a felon. "You know that, right?"

"Let's go to Zapato's," I said. Even the flicker of heat from the stove to boil the eggs was too much to bear in this house, in July, in Fresno. I don't know how Mother managed to bake the pie. "And then let's go get you new nightgowns."

"I don't like the food at Zapato's. You like Zapato's because you want a margarita."

"Or Bootsie's."

"Yes, you should go see Bootsie," Mother said. "Poor Bootsie." Bootsie Calhoun moved back from New York to look after the family's property (her brother was useless and smoked too much heroin) and had opened a small but popular restaurant in the Tower District. Her father was killed in a car accident on Avenue 22. He'd gone missing, and by the time they found him in his overturned car on the dry embankment of the Mendota Canal, his identification and sheepskin seat covers and the hubcaps from his old Mercedes had been stolen.

"You should come with me," I said.

"I don't want to go out of the house."

"Mother."

"I lost the keys to the silver drawer. I don't know where the keys are." She continued playing cards.

"They'll turn up."

"Do you think someone came into the house and took the keys?"

"No. I don't think that."

"Well, my heart is racing. I don't want to leave the house without knowing where those keys are. Don't tell your father."

"Do you want me to crack your eggs for you?"

"You always mess up the yolk." She tapped the egg delicately. "I'm afraid someone took those keys out of my purse."

"They'll turn up, Mom."

"Did you make toast?"

I sliced the toast into six little strips and placed them in front of her, next to the cards.

Mother dunked her toast soldiers deep into the egg so that yolk ran over the shell. "You made a nice egg," she said. "I want you to eat yours."

"I can't really eat."

She nodded. "You should call Bootsie Calhoun."

My throat filled. "You should call a lawyer."

There was a silence in which she flipped cards, gathered them up, and shuffled. "Maybe we should have a party. A party like we used to," she said.

"You hate parties."

"I hate other people's parties. My parties are fun."

"A party's a party."

"I don't like having to make conversation with people I didn't pick myself."

"People might steal your stuff."

"I'm not telling you anything from now on." Mother wiped her fingertips on a paper napkin printed with green grapes, taken from a pile in the center of the table. "We need something cheerful around here. A harvest party is what we need. Turkeys lined up down the length of the dining room table. Doesn't it sound fun?"

"It's too hot. Grandma's parties were in the fall."

"Oh, Ingrid, you're really a buzzkill."

"I thought you were poor."

"Not too poor for a harvest party." She swept her fingers again and again across the paper napkin. "With absolutely everyone. A party like your grandmother used to give."

"Are you going to roast a lamb on a spit?"

"Don't be sarcastic."

Every Easter, my father's parents really had roasted a lamb on a spit. They had learned it from the Greeks who owned the land next door. "There are going to be many more harvests, Mom. We don't need to have a party this summer."

"But why not this summer? Or we could wait until the fall. But by the fall you'll be busy, you'll be gone."

"All right, if you like, this summer."

"After I find the keys to the silver."

5. The heat did not slow down and the drought kept up and the grapes grew plump. Dad's grapes, fed largely by well water and protected by riparian rights and not wholly dependent on the water districts, grew especially plump. Vines love a little bit of stress. The grapes would get us through another year after all.

There had been earlier seasons when Dad grew a few thousand acres of Thompson grapes and sold them as fruit or laid them out to dry, but table grapes and raisins weren't as profitable as the cabernet, and many years ago he had ripped out half the Thompsons and put in wine grapes. He'd left a thousand acres of Thompsons in the vineyards surrounding the house, because big green grapes reflect more light on the vine. Thompsons were part of Mother and Dad's landscape.

Now, apparently, they were making wine from the table grapes.

It was the middle of July, and Dad liked to pick early, so the fruit would have a little less sugar than usual but there'd be no chance of the grapes being ruined by rain or late-season bugs or an unexpected spike in heat that could spoil them. Under Uncle

Felix's high-Brix plan, the Thompsons had at least another couple weeks to hang. They already tasted delicious to me, and those first few days and then weeks I was back home, neither working nor pretending to work, I liked to walk up and down the vines like I did when I was little and pick the ripest fruit direct from the sun-warm bunches.

I took Mother's little black Jaguar through the dusty squares of the ranch toward Madera and found Dad riding his tractor through the vines of cabernet, the grapes he would sell to Uncle Felix just before the fall set in. Cabernet doesn't thrive in the Central Valley except on a few thousand acres of Dad's land, land that originally had peaches, and then Thompson seedless, and then, in the past twenty years, cabernet. The climate throughout the valley is too dry and too hot for it. Syrah does well, and merlot does fine, and for a long time those varieties had been shipped to Napa and Sonoma, but cab is more of a challenge. The grapes need moisture and cooler temperatures. Forty years ago, after Dad had inherited his original hundred acres but while he was still scrubbing tanks at Mello to support the farm, he started buying small parcels of land along the river, cheap land no one else really wanted; the humidity and the slightly lower temperatures can be dangerous for peaches or citrus or nuts. Some of this cheap and useless land, Dad thought, might be an ideal microclimate for cabernet.

I saw the top of his red tractor deep in the vineyard before he saw me. He kept his father's original tractor out here in a shed by the river, so he could ride through his favorite vines. He would stop every few rows to check how the bunches were forming, with enough space but not too much, heavy but not too heavy early on. Grapes too heavy earlier in the season need less water as the summer goes on, but watering less in the middle of a central California summer introduces an extra set of risks.

Other farmers, growers far smaller than Dad, were in their pink stucco offices in the center of Fresno, making phone calls to their packing houses, to their buyers, to the chemical people for next season. Only Dad would be out now, checking his grapes.

Daddy doesn't even have e-mail.

From Paso Robles to Lodi and to Napa, people always told Dad his grapes were the nicest. They were: tight and big and deeply colored. Dad was no good at business, but he was good at land. He only bought ground next to good farmers, and he only bought land that came with its own water. When he bought the ten thousand acres of peaches in the early eighties, he knew by then to rip out the trees within view of the river and plant cabernet in the sandy loam. Dad felt something beyond affection for the grapes, something much closer to love.

I worried, then that summer but maybe always, that Daddy could be such a good farmer that he would get ruined. Dad thought farming was about ground and attention. He didn't think quite enough about cost and return. Poor Dad.

He climbed down from the tractor and rubbed dust and yeast from a cluster of young cabernet. I parked the car at the end of the row.

"They're beautiful, Daddy."

He looked up, surprised not so much that I found him in forty-five thousand acres of vines and trees, but perhaps that I was still here, in Fresno, at all. He didn't ask how I knew he'd be right here. Those few hundred acres were the first he'd bought; he saved checking them for the end of the day. He brushed dust off his pants, off his shirt. "They all wanted dry valley land. By the river you could flood," he said. This was one of the things he said all the time.

"I know it."

Dad loved to remind us how well he'd done by buying the land near the San Joaquin. We could hear the air move past the slow river from where we were standing. "So much for flooding."

Every year in California, the farmers got less and less water from the state. That year the state started talking about opening up the Friant Dam, saving the delta smelt, a tiny fish you can't eat, and the farmers were beside themselves about the loss of water. Farmers get upset when it rains and upset when it doesn't. Two years ago, a light rain fell in June and split all the cherries. Mother said every year, "They're always complaining about something."

"When do these get picked?"

"Why don't you move back here and work for me, Inky? The business isn't so hard to learn."

"I have a job, Dad. I don't want to scrub Uncle Felix's tanks." In fact, scrubbing Uncle Felix's tanks would likely have been more satisfying than the work I was not doing every day. There's something to be said for doing the kind of work you can see. But I wasn't qualified to scrub tanks. It's demanding physical labor, usually done by muscled twenty-two-year-old Davis graduates desperate to work in the wine industry, and I was pretty certainly not capable of it.

"We won't make you scrub tanks."

Girls I'd gone to school with had come back from their spells in San Francisco or Boulder or New York to work in sales or management for their family farms or shopping centers or packing companies. Maria Angelico, who'd gone to high school and college with me, had given up a career as a talent agent to come back to Fresno and run AngelCo, her father's box company. AngelCo was the only company in the valley still making boxes out of wood. In Los Angeles, representing writers at CAA, Maria had had a beautiful girlfriend, a model with a burgeoning career as an actress. She and Maria showed up in the gossip more than once. A particularly affectionate picture appeared in the *Daily Mail*, which we all thought surely no one in Fresno would ever see. Surely, though, everyone in Fresno did. Soon after, Mr. Angelico sent Maria a copy of his will, which stipulated that in order to inherit anything at all, Maria must be married, "to a white male." After resigning from the agency and moving back to Fresno to run the family business, Maria married a plain, pale-haired man—an accountant she met on a Christian dating website. She quickly got pregnant. At the wedding, all five of us who had known Maria during the days with her gorgeous girlfriend were seated at the same table in the far corner of St. Anthony's reception hall. To me, nothing could be more horrifying than what had become of Maria. "I'm not coming back, Dad."

"But it's tempting, isn't it?" He picked a tiny green-purple bulb from the top of a vine. "You can see and smell and feel and taste your work." This was another one of the things he said all the time.

"When do you pick?"

"Maybe October. You can see veraison's under way." He cupped a bunch in his hand, as if to weigh it. "Felix likes to let them hang." He wiped dust from a grape on the shoulder. "I guess we say that all the time, right? Felix lets them hang. That's Felix. He likes the grapes when they're practically dry."

"Is all the cabernet going to Uncle Felix?" Allowing Felix to buy the whole crop this year was an act of love and fidelity on Dad's part. Dad's best juice had always gone to Napa, Sonoma, or, locally, to Mello. Only a small portion had ever gone to Uncle Felix, and even then he usually bought the cheap stuff.

"He's trying some new things."

"But why let them hang?"

"That's how Felix likes them." There's a tense balance when you let the grapes hang—a very tiny window when the grapes stop growing and start concentrating. Uncle Felix had a reputation for buying cheap juice and then adding water to the wine. He'd buy from any producer—big growers with ill-tended vines in bad soil—the kind of hearty grapes used for color. You can mask any flavor by letting the grapes get a high concentration of sugar. But Dad's grapes were not cheap grapes. Even his common Thompsons were the largest and most flavorful in the valley. They were too valuable to let hang. It was nearly criminal to waste Dad's grapes by letting them get too brown and sweet. My hands started to hurt.

"These are your favorite, Dad, aren't they."

"You're my favorite."

"I know. Don't tell Anne."

"She's my favorite, too."

"But you love me the most." I kicked up dust just to see it puff through the air in tufts. "I'm the cab and Anne is the Thompsons."

Dad's smile went wide. "All right."

I said, "Too bad Charlie's last name isn't Thompson."

He patted my back. "Why don't you give me a ride home in that fast car?"

"Come on home," I said. "You'll never in a million years guess who we're meeting for dinner."

"Your mother doesn't like very many people," Dad said.

"She doesn't even care for the people she likes."

My mother's determination to dislike most of the people she met had a manic, devotional quality to it. Not liking people was her hobby. Anything could be cause for disapproval: speaking softly, for example, was a manipulative way of getting people to listen to you closely. Speaking too much meant you were boring, speaking too little was sneaky. People with allergies were control freaks, people with back problems were lazy, more than two drinks meant you were a drunk, but less than two meant you were a judgmental prick. If a wife attending Mother's dinner party didn't offer to help in the kitchen, she was an asshole; if she did offer, she filled the dishwasher wrong on purpose. If the air conditioner repair company sent one man out for the job, Mother was getting bad service; if they sent two, they were trying to overcharge her.

"She's difficult."

"At least she likes us."

"Most of the time," Dad said.

People she'd decided to like, usually because they were especially funny or good-looking or really knew farming, were excepted from her rules for human behavior. She didn't mind when Uncle Felix passed out at the kitchen table, because Felix, in spite of his faults, was truly brilliant. Bootsie's beauty meant her transgressions were probably my fault, and the Mondavis could be excused for being drunks because they were famous.

"You're in trouble if anything happens to Uncle Felix," I said.

"That's the end of my social life."

"You'd still have Wilson."

"Poor Wilson," Dad said. Nothing was interesting or beautiful or brilliant or famous about Wilson.

The San Joaquin Country Club overlooks the river and the hills and plains of farms on either side. The valley's mostly flat, but on Fresno's east side, at the base of the Sierras, many farms have a slight rise and fall, and the golf club has an excellent view of its members' trees and vines.

"There's Wilson," Mother said. And there was Wilson, with his fat pie face, returning his cart to the barn. "Go on out and say hello, Inky."

"I'll see him inside."

"Go and say hello," Mother said. "Wilson!" she called and waved. "Go on, Ingrid."

I wore a pink seersucker dress that tied around my neck and hung loose where just a week ago I'd had boobs. Mother was the first to notice this, of course. As we were leaving the house, she looked at the loose dress and declared without hesitation, "You can't wear that."

"I shrank," I said.

"In all the wrong places," she told me.

"What shall I do?"

"Wear something else. Do you have that white wraparound shirtdress?"

"There's nothing for it to wrap around," I said.

"Wrap it around your tiny little boobies."

I wore the loose pink dress. Now, through the car window, I waved to Wilson and smiled.

Mother said, "Get out of the car, Ingrid. Go."

"Inky P.!" He said, "Inky P. in a pink dress! Hello, friend." He grabbed me with his enormous hairy bear arms, rubbing all his fat and hair up against my naked back. He was damp and musky. He had the same stomach as Uncle Felix, only Wilson's wasn't tight with muscle. Wilson's stomach was flaccid with booze. I got smushed against it.

"Hi, Willy."

"Damn, you smell good." He held on to me too long.

"You got fat."

Wilson took a flask out of his golf bag. He drank straight from the flask. His face was pink and ugly; sweat rolled off his cheeks, his ill-defined chin, out from the thin remnants of his yellow-blond hair. "Booze weight."

"I thought alcoholics were skinny."

"Maybe city alcoholics. Country alcoholics, we just get fat."

"Something's got to soak it up."

"You mind if I don't change for dinner?"

"I don't mind."

"How you been, Inky?"

"I've been better."

"Uncle Felix says you demolished that guy."

"Right."

He gave his bag to Caesar, the caddy with the lazy eye. (For years I'd heard Caesar got extra-good tips by giving blow jobs to all the closeted husbands at the club. I'd decided, long ago, that those rumors were true. In Fresno, persistent rumors are more reliable than a wire service.) "Caesar, Ingrid came back to marry me," Wilson said. We sat down on the planter outside the cart barn so Wilson could change his shoes.

Caesar's good eye was brown, and the dead one blue. "No," he said. "Girls like that run off."

Wilson asked him, "Who am I going to marry, Caesar?"

Caesar shrugged and eyed me with the brown one. "Some younger girl who thinks you're king."

"Do you think I'm king, Ingrid?"

"Someone's going to think you're king," I said.

He said, then, "I would never drop you." Wilson didn't say these things with a wink. He had no cleverness or malice. He looked at me with the wide, sincere gaze of the idiot.

"Oh, Wilson, you know I'll always like you best."

"No you won't," he said. "You never did." He put his meaty arm around my shoulder. We walked up the hill toward the clubhouse. "Come here," he said, "look at this," and he turned me toward the putting green, with a wide view over the valley, lush green squares on either side of the river. "Isn't it funny how great everything looks when it's all just green?"

There is nothing more heartbreaking than thousands of acres of trees not producing anything.

Uncle Felix always sits at the head of the table, no matter who's paying. "Hello, Wilson. Too much trouble to ask you to change for dinner?"

The hem of Wilson's white polo still dripped with boozy perspiration. "Then I'd be late, Uncle Felix." He was looking around for the waitress.

"Ingrid, this is Debby." He'd brought the manicurist. She had tiny rhinestones glued to her nails, and her orange lipstick had already left a mark on her water glass. You could see halter-top tan lines above her strapless dress. My mother was doing her best not to look in Debby's direction.

"Welcome, Debby."

"I'd like a drink," said Wilson.

"They're bringing my wine," Uncle Felix said.

"I'd like a real drink." Wilson hailed one of the young girls carrying a tray. "Can you bring me two Plymouth martinis, both with olives and both with twists." Wilson's drink requests never ended with a question mark. Most everything Wilson said came followed by an exclamation point.

I had that feeling of emptiness so real that any slight movement or a deep breath might cause unbearable physical pain. I sat as still as possible. Sounds came at me as if through a tunnel. Outside the glass-walled dining room, the sky turned orange and red all around us, and the color reflected off the shallow river, a river so full in earlier years that one spring, recently, the water had flooded the entire fourth hole.

"Ingrid," Uncle Felix said, "you look like you're choking."

"I'm not choking."

He poured wine in my glass to the very top.

"Drink your dinner," he said. "It's good for you."

"That's what he says to me, too," said Debby. She smiled and laughed at her own funny joke. Her teeth were straight and overly, artificially white, what Mother would call socially aspirational middle-class teeth. I smiled back at her, but couldn't think of a response. No one said anything for a moment, so Debby laughed again.

My mother focused on the menu as if she had never seen it before.

"The fettuccini alfredo," Dad said. "It's the only thing that doesn't kill my stomach these days."

"It'll kill you in other ways," said Uncle Felix.

Wilson's martinis came and he handed one to me. He drank his quickly and ordered two more. "Country drunk," he whispered, nudging me. Poor Wilson. Despite his small gestures of defiance—not changing his shirt, not drinking the wine—he craved nothing more than for Uncle Felix to nod in approval, to give Wilson the Griffith wink.

The girl came over to take our orders, and I ordered the wedge salad all chopped up and tossed together, which is what I'd been eating at the club since I was eight. The San Joaquin Country Club made its wedge salad with romaine.

"Where's the roast turkey?" Mother said. "When did they stop serving the roast turkey?"

Dad pointed to the bottom of the menu, where the roast turkey had always been.

"Wilson," said Uncle Felix, "you drink like a slob."

"Oh, Felix, you're mad I don't want to drink your wine." Wilson sloshed his drink from one side of the glass to the other. "Some of us are sick of wine. Are you sick of wine, Debby?"

Mother started speaking before Debby could answer. "There's Hilda Sorensen," she said, nodding toward the other side of the dining room. "She's seeing Greg Kappas again, isn't she, Felix? She's after him to get married."

"Is she?" Dad said. "Seeing him, I mean." We didn't even bother to lower our voices. There are no acoustics in the dining room. The club has the same décor it had when it was built in 1961: wood paneling, shag carpet, one wall made entirely of local Oakhurst stone. In a more humid climate, this is the sort of building that would reek of mold.

"I'm not supposed to know that. Bootsie Calhoun told me. They go in there all the time." Mother gestured when she spoke, so that no one in the room would miss the oversized diamonds on her tennis bracelet.

"When did you speak to Bootsie?" I said.

"Bootsie misses you," Mother said. "You weren't so kind to her either, Ingrid. Also she makes this mojito with liquid nitrogen I think you'll like. It freezes into a sorbet."

"They can't get married," Uncle Felix said. "He can't get a divorce."

"Greg and Arlene?" Dad said.

"He's Greek Orthodox," Mother said. "He can get a divorce. They get divorced all the time."

"No, it's impossible," said Uncle Felix. "The riparian rights are in Arlene's name. They belong to her family."

"Arlene has the riparian rights!" my mother said, absolutely delighted, clapping her hands together. Mother didn't like the young, perky Hilda Sorensen, a rich cotton farmer's widow who'd turned much of her late husband's land into pink stucco malls and who Mother thought had a habitual liking for married men. Kurt Sorensen had been married when Hilda met him. It was true that, years ago, she had made an obvious and embarrassing play for Dad, for a period phoning him whenever Mother had left town and one time showing up with an arsenal of elaborately wrapped electrical tools for his birthday, with me and Anne and Mom all present. Now Hilda was seeing Greg Kappas, the late Kurt's married best friend. When my mother makes a judgment about someone, that person often lives up to her expectations. "Who told you that, Felix?"

"Wilson."

We all looked at Wilson, now on his third dinner martini. "Gossip is my business," he said. "The Mastersons are getting remarried. Your friend Bootsie is fucking her bartender. What else do you people want to know?"

Uncle Felix said, "Steady, Wilson."

"A lot of money in gossip," said Wilson.

"The Mastersons are getting remarried?" Mom said.

"Evelyn, voice down," said Dad.

"Arlene's riparian rights!" Mother said again, shaking her head and laughing. "Don't worry, Ingrid, you've got riparian rights."

"I'm not worried."

"You don't have to be," she said.

"Thanks, Mother."

Wilson started humming quietly. He'd done this since we were children, humming at dinner, in the middle of conversation. He turned to Debby and whispered, "Do you know Lionel Ritchie is the only musician who owns all the rights to his songs?" He looked at her, waiting for a response. No response came. "All of them," he said.

I said, "Uncle Felix, when do you pick the syrah?"

"Which syrah?"

"Dad's syrah."

"Dad's syrah's not ready yet. Do you think it's ready yet, Ned?"

"It's not quite ready," Dad said. "It's on the young side."

"It's on the young side," Uncle Felix said, nodding toward me. "I like my fruit ripe, Inks."

"It'll get too sugary," I said. "It's been so hot."

"Oh, Ingrid!" said Wilson. "Ingrid knows about wine now!" He was just on the edge of getting mean, I could tell. Soon he might say cruel things he'd pretend not to remember the next day.

Uncle Felix said, "When are you coming to work for me, Ingrid?"

"Not going to," Mother interrupted. Mother's worst nightmare was for either of her children to get stuck in Fresno. We ought to take our riparian rights and live comfortably in Los Angeles or Berlin. In case of financial emergency, we could take our knowledge of California grapes and move to France.

I said, "I've been fired from every job I've ever had. You don't want me to work for you, Uncle Felix."

"I do want you to come work for me, Inks. You can tell me what it is you want to do."

"You'll make me scrub tanks."

"Never would do that."

"You say that now," I said.

Mother said, looking at the menu, "Pick the grapes, Felix."

Wilson said, "Pick the grapes, Felix."

"What grapes?" said Felix.

"At least pick those Thompsons," I said.

Dad was quiet and drank long gulps of his wine.

Debby sat throughout the rest of dinner without speaking and kept sending hopeful unrequited glances at my mother.

After dinner, we went back to the house to eat baklava and to drink the cognac I'd brought from France and taken from Howard's house.

Cognac always winds everyone up. An hour after Dad and

I had gone to bed but were each lying awake in the hammering heat, while Mom was still up in the kitchen with the dessert plates soaking, playing solitaire, the doorbell rang.

"Get the guy with the tractor," Uncle Felix told Mother, his cashmere vest missing, shirt untucked, buttons off by two. "My car went into the ditch."

"Oh, God, Felix," Mother said casually, dialing the foreman. "Chappaquiddick." It was not the first time since Jane died that Mom had come to his rescue in one form or another, towing cars from canals or playing hostess for his business dinners or fetching dry clothes from his house after Felix's drunken swims in the river.

Miguel came with the tractor and pulled the car off the side of the canal. Mother took Debby back to town. When I made my way out to breakfast later that morning, I found Uncle Felix asleep at the kitchen table, his head on his arms. It wasn't altogether uncommon to find Uncle Felix sleeping at the kitchen table. I started coffee for two.

"Some night," he said, woken by the faucet and the clink of the kettle. His shirt was still done up the wrong way.

"I guess you'd better apologize to Miguel."

"I'll write him a check."

"And Mother."

"Oh, your mother," he said, half starting to laugh. "Your mother lives to save the day."

"You did tear her away from her cards."

"Your mother," he said, patting his chest, as if just now realizing his vest was missing, "is wonderful," he said.

"Debby seems nice."

He looked at me, skeptical. "She's up for fun," he said. Then, "Where did I leave my shoes?"

"Uncle Felix, I like to see you having fun."

"It's not fun," he said, lighting a cigarette. I handed him a dessert plate to use as an ashtray. "It's goddamn lonesome."

"You have us for when you get lonesome." I patted his shoulder, kissed his wet forehead.

"I do." Smoke came out of his nostrils, like a bull. He nodded down toward the table, kept nodding. "Yes, I do have you."

"And Wilson," I said.

"Wilson."

I sat across from him at the kitchen table. "Wilson's afraid girls like Debby will take advantage of you and break your heart."

He shook his head. He winked at me, the Griffith wink, so quick you couldn't be sure it had happened. "My heart's already broken." I looked at him and felt a flush of humiliation, which he surely must have seen. "You told me that story a long time ago," he said.

"Which one?"

"Your friend Gil, with the fungus underneath his nails that grew after he found his dead mother."

I plunged the French press. "I don't remember telling you that."

"The fungus of grief," he said. "I remember everything."

I stirred sugars into our coffee. I said, "How many broken hearts do you think a person can endure before the heart is just permanently broken?"

"Don't worry, Ingrid, you won't end up like me." He tapped ashes onto the plate. "You're far too pretty."

"That's not what I meant," I said.

He tapped salt out of the shaker and began to eat it off the table with the tip of his finger. "You should have married George Sweet. But your mother put a stop to that, didn't she?"

There had never been a boyfriend Mother had approved of.

When I pointed out to her that she had never liked anyone I dated, she said, "So far I've been right about every one."

Uncle Felix stood up. "I don't know what happened to my sweater."

"Do you want some grape pie?"

"Midsummer pies are the best." He sat down again. "We're acquiring more acres," he said.

"Do you want a big piece or a little piece?" Even our plates— my grandmother's plates—had grapes and vines painted on them. "How many more acres?" Uncle Felix already had more vines than anyone else in the valley.

"You already know everything you need to know to work in this business. I wouldn't have to teach you much."

"Why are you pushing this so hard?" I said. "I don't want to move back here, I don't want to make wine." I sliced the pie. "I'm giving you a big piece."

"It's a good living."

"If I want to come back, I'll work for Dad. And I'll make you give me a higher price for that juice, or I just won't sell to you."

He laughed a closed-mouth laugh. He tapped more salt on the table. "I'm too big not to sell to, sweetheart."

6. My mother had been coloring her hair herself.

In the past, there had been bad years for farming, years with no vacations, cars with bad radiators, a year Mom sold two paintings given to her by Francesco Clemente (he fell so in love with her the January they met in Rome that he followed her and Dad all around the middle regions of France; she'll tell you that story if you give her six minutes), and one season bricks fell from the disintegrating fireplace. There had never been a year that the pool had gone green, though. Never a year my parents couldn't afford to pay the cleaning lady. Never a year my mother colored her hair herself.

"Go gray, or go to the hairdresser," I said.

"Gray," my mother scoffed. She had black dye all over her face and her hands and the bathroom sink. She had no idea what she was doing. "You cannot imagine how gray I am. The whole head."

"If you'd been nicer to Debby, she might have done this for you."

"She's a manicurist," Mother said. "And a slut."

"It's too dark, that color."

"This is my natural color!"

I sat on the edge of the tub, far away from the sink and Mother's explosion of black hair dye. She was still very beautiful, in spite of the mess, in spite of the hair color. She had big, deep cartoon eyes. She and Anne had the same wide cheekbones. Skin never wrinkles on wide, high cheekbones. "You're so short with me," I said. "Why are you angry?"

"I'm not used to having anyone else in the bathroom."

As a child, I had been forbidden to come into this bathroom after once shattering a bottle of red nail polish on the white tile. Anne could enter the bathroom, but until I was thirteen, I had to stand outside the door. Then I went away to school, and when I stopped sleeping and returned for good, three years later, it was as if everyone had forgotten all the old rules. There were no forbidden rooms, no regulations on drinking or swearing or going to bed. When I came home from school, Mother and Dad didn't even bother with a curfew. George Sweet and I used to spend nights together in the studio apartment above his parents' garage, and no one ever questioned the lies I told as to where I'd been.

"What have you heard about George Sweet?" I said.

"George Sweet?"

"You know, what have you heard? What's the gossip?"

"Well, I think he got married."

"Did he."

"I think so. To the Prentiss girl. Prentiss Chevrolet."

"I know Ellie Prentiss."

"How do you know her?"

"We went to grade school together, Mother. She played soccer with me." Ellie Prentiss was tall and wispy and could score on every penalty kick she took. She had a slow, dull voice in which I'd never heard her say anything useful. She went on to play center forward at Stanford. Her family owned car dealerships. She was popular—the kind of unthreateningly pretty girl who made mouth-breathing look attractive. I considered her an aggressive bore.

"I had heard he married the Prentiss girl, but I don't know. You know how the Prentisses are—they'd never want you to know if their daughter married one of the Sweet boys." Mother tucked black-drenched cotton around her hair line, beneath the plastic coloring cap. "It depresses me when you ask about George Sweet, Inky."

"It sort of depresses me, too."

"George Sweet was not right for you. Just think of that family. That mother."

"Oh yes, and Howard's family would have been so much better."

"Well, at least his mother was dead." She scraped a bar of Ivory soap with her fingertips, trying to get the black dye out from underneath her nails. She knew to wear surgical gloves while removing grapes from the stem, but missed the plastic gloves included in the box with the hair dye.

The year after George and I broke up, I let him trounce me over and over and over, under the guise of friendship, while I listened to his travails with different girls. I listened to him pine for the cartoonist (he called her "the illustrator"), and then I sat with him while he dissected the sex-only affair he had with the waitress from his Sunday-morning brunch spot. I waited for him to want to go on the way we had before, thinking he might realize you ought to be in love with the person who knows you the best, but he never did. One evening, he stood me up for drinks. I waited for two hours outside the Sidewalk Café on Sixth and A before walking the eighty blocks home, which gave me an excellent excuse to stop being friends with him.

"What else did Bootsie have to say?" I asked.

"I went there just once, Inky," Mother said, as close as she would get to apologizing, for anything. "She has the only decent food in this whole damn town."

"I wasn't accusing you of anything."

"All you do is criticize me."

"It was just conversation."

"Tell me what's happening with you. We never talk."

"This is talking."

"I mean really talk. About anything that means anything to anyone. I feel like no one in this family talks and no one listens."

I thought for a moment of one true thing I could say that wouldn't be construed as an insult. Something honest and plain that Mother didn't already know. I felt that big dark vacuum in my stomach, and didn't know if I was hungry or sad. Maybe the feeling was dread. "I love the way Fresno smells in the summer." It was plain and true. "I love the way the heat haze makes the orchards look wavy. Even the asphalt is beautiful this time of year."

She nodded at herself in the mirror. "All right. I get the message. You think I'm boring."

The bathroom window was open wide, but the heat in the house only traded space with the heat outside. I wanted a drink but didn't want to be scolded for drinking.

Mother said, "I'm not boring. I could tell you things."

"I don't want to know things," I said. "Please."

She said, "Could you open that drawer and get me a new bar of soap? I've ruined this."

The bathroom drawer was full of hotel soaps in tiny boxes, lined up neatly like a grid. "The Fairmont," I said. "Smells just like the Marriott."

"Don't make fun," she said.

I said, "I wasn't making fun."

"Those soaps are a record of all my escape attempts." Mother took the soap and handed me the wrapper. "This is what will become of you if you stay here too long, Inky. You will collect soap."

The idea of staying in one place appealed to me. Mother had sent me across the country for school twenty years previously because she feared that if I stayed in Fresno any longer, I might never leave. I hadn't stopped leaving places since. "It sounds like Bootsie's been happy here," I said.

"Don't start," Mother said. "Poor Bootsie."

"Not poor Bootsie. Why?"

"All she's got now is that awful brother. What was his name?"

"Fionn."

"Fionn. Terrible what's become of Fionn. You know, I think they put him in prison last year? Remember how nice and darling he was, Inky?"

I threw out the Fairmont soap wrapper and noticed, in the trash, dry clumps of Mother's hair. "Do you say things like that to make me feel bad?"

"I'm on your side, I'm on your side. It's a boring topic of conversation." She rubbed the soap across her cuticles, across her knuckles. "I'm boring," she said. "I didn't used to be boring, but I am now." We listened to the low hum of the house, and then the approaching sound of a tractor somewhere close by. "You know," she said, "if you don't want to get your heart broken, you have to break up with them first."

"Thanks for the tip," I said. There were at least a dozen small black nests in the trash, twisted into circles.

"You and Annie, you think I'm so ignorant. But I'm older than you, I have more experience."

"I don't think you're ignorant."

Mother met Dad when she was eight and married him ten years later. Her father was the John Deere distributor in Madera, where my father's father bought the machines for the farm. Everyone had chased the tractor dealer's pretty daughter. Uncle Felix had chased her hardest of all. As far as I knew, Mother's experience in love had been limited to the boys who chased her at her father's shop, and Uncle Felix had been the first.

Uncle Felix was still in love with Mother. Even Aunt Jane used to say so. When I was little, he'd come to dinner with his hair fresh and combed back, still wet from the shower. He'd tell twice as many jokes with Mother in the room. When he felt particularly affectionate or lonely or drunk, he'd call her Muffin. He still sometimes called her Muffin.

Scrubbing her hands, she said, "Why haven't any of your friends phoned you?"

Every question had a way of being a jibe.

"Anne is my friend," I said. Anne had been calling up to six times a day, with never anything to ask or report. I'd answer the phone and she thought it was very funny, when I said hello, to say, "Who is this?!"

"I mean aside from Anne."

"What am I going to say to people?"

A tiny river of black dye made its way beside the vein in my mother's temple and emptied into her eyebrow. "I'm getting this everywhere," she said. She rubbed at her eyebrow with a newly ruined bath towel, removed the drenched black cotton, and replaced it with a fresh piece, which got immediately soaked. "Oh, God," she said, looking at the cotton and looking at herself. In the mirror I could see her breasts sag beneath her worn white nightgown, now spotted with black. Somehow, inexplicably, she'd got little pieces of old Scotch tape all over the back. She said, looking at herself, her face an undone knot, "Do you think if

I had made something of my life that my children would be more successful?"

"I think Dad needs to see a doctor," I said.

She looked at me in the mirror. "You're a very nice young lady, Ingrid."

"Thanks, Mother."

"Except you're not young anymore."

I stood to leave. "He doesn't look well and the cough is worse and worse."

"Daddy's fine."

"He's not fine. He needs to see a doctor."

"All right, Ingrid. You know everything."

I went to my room and sat for a while in the closet. I had forgotten the clothes still there: a long black velvet Christmas formal, a tiered violet dress from an Easter fifteen years ago, the deteriorated mink coat Anne had appropriated from our grandmother and abandoned. A fire escape ladder still sealed in the box. I checked the toes of old ballet slippers and sneakers in case I had hidden money or pain pills. In a pink Oilily high-top, barely worn, I found three hundred-dollar bills, rolled together as tightly as a cigarette. Opportunities will present themselves.

The closet, I noticed, was the coolest place in the house, and big enough to lie down flat in, which I did. I fell asleep and had a dream that I had given birth to a soft, cottony, buttery-yellow chick that I left in a box and forgot so that it dried up like a leaf.

7. In the afternoons, those first couple of weeks I was back, I walked and walked. Exhaustion was a good cure for anxiety. I'd walk past the vines near the house (they went on for a half mile up Avenue 7), away from the river through Mr. Ellison's almonds, and past two canals through more grapes to Uncle Felix's house. Uncle Felix lived in the same small, flat clapboard ranch house his parents had given him when he married Aunt Jane forty years ago. It had been a foreman's house before the Griffiths' ranch absorbed the property. Many kids of farming families lived in houses like this, houses originally built to house workers, managers, helpers to sustain the farm. But most people, when parents passed on the operating duties or else died and fortunes were inherited, bought 1920s Spanish mansions commissioned by the lumber barons of Old Fig Garden or built themselves obnoxious palaces on the north side of town, houses with twenty-foot front doors and entire tile floors imported piece by piece from monasteries in France. The small, disintegrating ranch houses got rented to farmworkers and then, eventually, were razed. Uncle Felix didn't go in for that sort of competition. "I prefer my real estate to generate income," he said. The types of people who built houses on the north side, he thought, were the types of people who turn their family's land into pink stucco shopping centers. "The best reason not to have children," Uncle Felix said.

The first few times I walked up to Uncle Felix's house, I used the driveway as a destination and then turned around to come home. I liked to walk by myself. But lately I had started ringing the bell, and Uncle Felix would walk me back to the river.

It was nice to walk next to someone.

I said, "You think Wilson's not going to turn a big swath of your land into a housing development?" We took a route along the canal, with vines on one side and trees on the other. Often on these walks, the conversation came back to what would become of the land: Dad's land, Felix's land, the land in general. Pavement can't be reversed.

"I'm working on Wilson," he said. "He'll need the vineyards to make the wine. If he wants to sell the company, well. Then."

"Maybe you should sell the company before Wilson gets to it."

"I'd rather be dead. I wish you'd stay here. I'll teach you everything you need to know about the business. You already know most of it."

"Please, Uncle Felix."

"I don't understand you girls. You're going to barely scrape out some meager living for yourself down south, jump from one job to another, using your brains to make money for strangers, when you could come back here and be with your family and work in an honest industry and get rich." It was evening, late July, and the temperature hadn't yet fallen below 100.

"I hardly see Dad getting rich." It was a stupid, spoiled thing to say.

"Farming's been very good to your dad. And you. There were a lot of rich years. Your father would have a hell of a lot more money if he'd get rid of Phillip."

"Phillip has no loyalty."

"Loyalty isn't Phillip's problem. Embezzling is Phillip's problem." Phillip was the orchard manager. Everyone in town knew he'd been buying the chemicals for his own two hundred acres on Dad's account, putting the orders in on Dad's peaches. Twenty years of chemicals for two hundred acres of vines and trees costs in the range of $2 million. The only person in town who didn't consider this sort of pilfering embezzlement was my father. My beleaguered, kind, dear father, who never suspected a sinister motive from anyone.

"He won't listen to anyone about that. He thinks everyone is as honest as he is."

"He's lousy at business, your father."

"What Dad wants most of all is to be liked."

"There's no money made in being liked," Uncle Felix said.

"You'd know."

"Still. You wouldn't have the luxury to hop around doing nothing without farming."

"I'm not doing nothing."

"That's right," he said, meaning *yes you are*. "If you came back here and worked with me, I'd be sure you got rich."

"I don't care about money."

"That's bull. Everyone cares about money."

"I don't."

"You'd care if you had to, but you don't know what it's like to be poor."

"I'm poor now."

He looked at me, disgusted. "That's the stupidest thing I've ever heard you say."

Part of what we all loved about Uncle Felix was his opinions, but it stung when he turned them against you. Somehow we wanted Felix's approval above all others.

He knew I was angry, or that he'd hurt my feelings. Sometimes I can't tell the difference myself. "Forget the money," he said. "Why don't you just come back here to be close to your family?"

"I am close to my family."

"You're stubborn. You're set on the idea that anyplace is better than here. Your mother did that to you." He stopped walking. "Look," he said, gesturing to the trees on one side of us, abundant with nuts, and the canal just beginning to reflect the orange light. "No place is better than right here."

I continued walking. It was too distressing to admit that certain patches of that mean little town were, in fact, more beautiful than anyplace else in the world. And I'd looked, believe me, hoping to find someplace. I'd seen all sorts of rural agricultural valleys and hills I wouldn't go back to. I'd looked and looked for someplace that felt more like home than right there. Leave it to Uncle Felix to find the exact spot that was most beautiful of all, at exactly the moment he needed it.

"What would I do here for fun? Who would my friends be?"

"I'm not talking about fun," he said. We walked on a little. The trees were dense with fuzzy green almonds. "You have Wilson. And that Bootsie. You need more than two friends in this world? You think you've got more than two friends, you're fooling yourself."

"What would I do on Saturday afternoons, for example?" I asked myself this question as much as I asked Uncle Felix. "My mother has spent her whole life playing cards by herself."

"That's your mother. You want to be your mother?"

"No, I don't."

"I've asked you to play golf, but you won't play golf."

"The club reminds me of how people were mean to me when I was little," I said.

"You think too much about other people."

"The older kids used to play ditch 'em and I was always the one they were trying to ditch."

He laughed. He liked that. "Me, too," he said. He patted the taut drum of his stomach. "They still try to ditch me."

"That is just not true."

"You see anyone else walking with us?"

"You're not understanding what I'm telling you."

"I understand exactly." It was true, Uncle Felix had friends at fund-raisers and wine events and at the Vineyard for lunch, but tonight, and every night, he was alone. Even Mother didn't much care to see him anymore.

I said, "No one tries to ditch me in New York, or LA. Or London. Or Paris or Berlin or anywhere else but right here in this sad little town. If I stay here I'll be alone all the time."

"You have no idea, Inks."

"Of what."

He stopped and plucked an almond off Mr. Ellison's tree, as if the almonds were his. We grew up understanding that you never, ever, ever took anyone else's crop. My whole childhood I never took an almond or apricot from Mr. Ellison's trees. That evening, Uncle Felix plucked the green almond and then threw it down the middle of the row, to see how far he could throw. "Of what people are like," he said.

I had read in *The Fresno Bee* that day about two neighbors, Bill and Emory, with a long-standing dispute about Bill's dog— it kept getting into Emory's yard and digging up the bulbs. It turns out Emory was a florist, and yesterday, having had enough, he kicked the dog (a cocker spaniel called Tutu, the paper said), wounding its hind leg. The two neighbors then engaged in a fistfight, and Emory, ten years younger, got the better of Bill. Minutes later, Bill returned to Emory's house with a handgun to put eight bullets into his neighbor's knees, chest, and head. Bill then drove to the Chevy's at the Riverbend Shops and shot himself in his car. What astonished me the most was that while Bill was firing, Emory never turned his back. And why did Emory open his front door in the first place? Reading *The Fresno Bee* could give you a pretty good idea of what people were like.

8.

"You know what Charlie and I talk about most of the time?" Anne said. "Other couples."

"What about other couples?"

"You know, we judge them. Assess how miserable they are."

"Are they miserable?"

"They're just bored, most of them. Bored bored bored."

"Are you bored?"

"I don't think *bored* is the word," she said.

I waited for the word. "What's the word?" I said, finally.

"I don't know," she said. "*Lonely?*"

She had driven up for the weekend. Charlie didn't come. I tried not to wonder too much about Anne's relationship with Charlie.

"I'll ask you something," she said that night.

"Yes."

"Doesn't lots of casual sex make you lonesome?" We were sitting in the kitchen, in the dark, waiting for the night to cool the house down.

"Who's having casual sex?"

"Sex between friends. It makes you feel loved for a second, but it really just puts an exclamation point on your loneliness."

"I'm not having sex with any friends."

"Not everything is about you, Ingrid."

I went away to school to get away from Anne. Not just to avoid her popularity or her success or her criticisms, not just to avoid being compared with her, but to avoid hearing her voice or seeing her face. There are times when that feeling seems juvenile and distant, and times when that feeling is immediate. Visceral. It's no coincidence that I came back from Massachusetts just as Anne left for college.

"I don't see any sex as casual."

"But when you're with someone for a long time, like me and Charlie, the sex feels very casual then, too."

"Please, Annie, I don't want to talk about your sex life."

"Don't be such a puritan. Let's have drinks."

She arrived around eight in the evening, having missed the mean heat of the day. She'd come directly from voice-over. (Anne never called the show "the show"; she only ever called it "voice-over.") "Why don't they have the air-conditioning on in here?" she said.

"It's only me. I don't want to run the air when it's only me here in the kitchen."

"Well, now it's you and me. Jesus, Ingrid, run the air."

"Wilson didn't tell me not to worry, you know."

"Wilson, God. Felix is loving this, I'll bet."

"He's been kind," I said. "Sometimes I think you say things just to be ornery."

"I'm telling you, Felix only cares about Felix. He's probably encouraging the bank to take the land back so he can gobble it up."

"He's doing what he can. He's buying the juice."

"He gets a great price, Inky, and it's the best juice in the valley. He's lucky he gets that juice."

"Well, you know everything."

"I'm just telling you. You never trust my instincts, and my instincts are always right. What's all this Ararat brandy?" she said, checking in Dad's liquor cabinet, seeing the twelve bottles Mom had had delivered to the house. Emilio at Fiesta Market on Avenue 7 let Mom buy things on credit. I imagined she'd probably have to order the turkeys from him, too.

"Mom has this idea that we're going to have a party. Like Grandma's."

"And invite whom? She hates everyone."

"Felix's friends, probably." Mother didn't mind Felix's friends too much, because they were all a little famous in a farming sort of way, wine people from Livermore and Lodi and all the way up to Napa. "Ask her."

"Does she know she's going to have to turn on the air-conditioning?"

Mother and Dad had gone to bed early, Mother with a stack of fashion magazines and Dad with his exhausting cough, which we could hear from the kitchen.

Anne said, "I think I might get a dog. Do you think I should get a dog?"

"I'm lonely, too," I said.

"Well," she said, still facing the cabinet, "I didn't say that."

"You said *lonely* was the word."

"I asked if I should get a dog."

"People get dogs when they're lonely."

"Or, no. People get dogs when they want something to distract them from themselves."

"That's lonely. That's like the definition of lonely."

"Lonely and selfish are not the same thing." She started taking bottles from the cabinet: American vodka, French vodka, nice gin and rough gin. She lined them up.

"Is Charlie lonely?" I said.

"He doesn't tell me," she said. "Look at this Gordon's gin. How old do you think this is?"

"Does Charlie want a dog?"

"Charlie's allergic. Didn't you know that Charlie's allergic?"

"That gin's older than you, I think." It hadn't even been opened.

"God, it's hot." She twisted her hair and clipped it all up with her barrette. "How long do you intend to stay here?"

"Did you come to ask me that?"

"No," Anne said. "Not really."

"Did you come to wrap me up while I'm sleeping and secret me back to Los Angeles?" I leaned over and pinched her waist.

"Don't, it hurts."

"You came to steal me."

"I came because it's cold in LA and all the peaches in Hollywood come from Georgia."

"Maybe I'll go back with you."

"I miss you," she said. "But it turns out it's not a good time for you to come stay with us."

"Why?"

"Just not right now. I know it's all bad timing."

"Is Charlie fed up with me?" While it was Anne's duty to come to my rescue, I could understand how for Charlie my breakups could become a tiresome burden.

"Things are stressful for Charlie at work." She stood at the bar off the kitchen, with the cupboard open, her back to me.

"I'll find someplace to go," I said. "Or I'll stay here."

"Also, I guess I am not going to have a baby."

I stood and joined her. I put ice in two rocks glasses. "What does that mean?"

"I can't have a baby. I guess." She waved her hand casually, as if shooing away a wasp. Anne doesn't cry or wince or move with emotion. "Anyway, it's funny how you bring everything back to you all the time. And you think I'm the one who's selfish."

"Who told you this? How do you know?"

"My doctor."

"How long have you been trying to have a baby?"

She put a piece of ice in her mouth. "Charlie doesn't really like me." She stroked my wrist. She put her arm through mine. "Do you like me?" she said.

I hugged her, but then didn't want my hug to seem like pity. "Anniekins," I said.

She crunched ice right in my ear. "He hates when I crunch ice," she said.

"I like you the best in the world."

She blew my hair out of her face and pushed me away. "Don't tell Mom and Dad." She stacked ice on top of her drink in a little pyramid. "I hate brandy. I hate sidecars. I've always thought your coffee is terrible, too, Ingrid, by the way. While I'm being frank. I'm sorry I have to tell you."

"All right," I said.

"It's always bitter."

"It's strong, I like it strong."

"Great women don't have children. Katharine Hepburn, for example. Or Virginia Woolf. I can't think of any great women who had children. Margaret Thatcher, maybe, but she probably had a barn full of nannies. Alice Neel had children but she totally abused them." She went on talking, as if to fill the space with something else besides the two of us. "Did Marie Curie have children?"

"I don't know anything about Marie Curie."

"Or George Eliot."

"Have you been thinking about George Eliot lately? I've been thinking about George Eliot, too."

"Because you're lonely," she said. There was a pause where she looked like she couldn't breathe. "Don't tell them about what the doctor said." Anne rarely drank anything but red wine. Tonight she drank the vodka so fast it splashed around her upper lip. She crunched and crunched the ice. "They think the whole point of life is to have children."

"Do you want to have a baby?" I said.

"I don't know. I want to have a puppy."

"I know how you feel."

"I've started flirting with Elroy." Elroy was her childhood toy. "He thinks I am very funny."

"Stuffed dogs are good to flirt with."

"They're not threatening and they won't kiss you when you're not expecting it. Elroy is better than a real dog or a husband."

"Have you eaten?"

"I had sliced turkey and string cheese earlier. Soon I will eat some spinach." Like me, Anne couldn't eat when upset. She tipped empty the second glass of vodka.

"You want to go into town and get some pasta?"

"Yes," she said, unwinding herself from the bar. "And let's get drunk, too."

Fresno is less than ten stories tall. When one outdoor mall gets old, Fresno builds another; for example, the Riverbend Shops, where Mr. Delucci's cantaloupe ranch used to be. Mr. Delucci now grows mushrooms on the ten acres he kept, behind the Office Depot and California Pizza Kitchen. His children have moved to New York and Hong Kong. The McAdamses have an egg farm next to the five hundred acres of cattle ranch they sold to the

Prentisses for the new auto mall. The McAdamses' daughter Laura fell in love with a newspaper editor during a trip to England ten years ago and never came home. The Prentisses' younger son has made a career of renovating apartments in farther and farther reaches of Brooklyn.

Anne and I love to hate Fresno. We take great pleasure in the insubstantial bookstores, the striking resemblance of everyone in line at the Starbucks with their identical suburban haircuts (Anne calls it the "Fresno Crop"), the treeless boulevards and pink shopping mall after pink shopping mall. There is beauty there, too, but the real beauty of the place causes us anxiety and irreconcilable conflict.

As a teenager, I drove Mother's old red Mustang up and down Blackstone, the city's main thoroughfare and a boulevard of broken car lots, going nowhere. My friends piled blonde after blonde in the passenger seat and nearly stacked on top of each other in the back. I never let them smoke pot or even cigarettes in the back. They would complain, but I was firm. I was a sixteen-year-old dictator. Our screaming streak of hair whipped along Blackstone Avenue, from Herndon past Shaw, past Ashlan to McKinley, and back again up Blackstone. My parents would answer phone calls from their friends, "First I saw the red car, and then I noticed it was full of young blond girls, and then I saw Ingrid driving." I was bad at driving but excellent at talking my way out of tickets. I loved to go fast.

That night, Anne and I stopped at Lorenzo's in the Tower District, across from the dinner theater, next to the Salvation Army and not far from Bootsie's Quality Food and Beverage.

A man dressed as a wolf smoked a cigarette outside the back door of the dinner theater. He had a real beard, a long, rough beard. He looked like a wolf that hadn't showered in some time.

He threw the cigarette down and crushed it with his back paw, and then he stood there watching Anne and me as we walked through the parking lot to Lorenzo's.

"That wolf is watching you," I said to Anne.

"In a past life, he would have been just my type."

"He was never your type."

"I loved wolves."

Lorenzo's was crowded with actors from the dinner theater's rehearsal space next door—married accountants and young house-wives and pimply city college students with loud voices all eating and drinking and carrying on, engaging in assignations of one sort or another. As everyone in Fresno knows, doing plays at the dinner theater is a sure sign that your marriage is over.

Soon the place would be packed entrance to emergency exit with dinner theater actors, once the wolf and his friends finished their show and got out of costume.

Anne and I sat at the bar and ordered vodka gimlets that came in teeny-tiny glasses.

"It's depressing when drinks come in small glasses," Anne said, "because then you have to drink so many more of them."

"I like small drinks," I said. "This way you don't feel bad when you have four gimlets."

There were red-and-white checked tablecloths in the dining room and elk heads on the rafters above the bar. The walls were plastered with advertisements for every show at Roger Rocka's Music Hall from 1978 through the present day: *Pajama Game*! *Godspell*! *Merrily We Roll Along*!

I took off my glasses so as not to see any grade school friends or friends' parents, parents' friends, or boys I'd kissed who were now paunchy men.

Anne spun her tennis bracelet around and around her wrist.

Our mother's old tennis bracelet. She must have just taken it. Anne appropriates any valuables she's afraid I might get to first. "The Matheuses are sitting in the corner."

"I'm not wearing my glasses."

"Put on your glasses, for chrissake, Ingrid."

"I prefer not to wear them."

The Matheus brothers used to have thirty thousand acres of row crops—primarily melon. But the wives didn't get along and this led to the predictable strife and so, years ago, the ranch was split in half, the greatest of all misfortunes that can befall an agricultural family. As it turned out, one brother was good at numbers and the other was good at land, and separately they each lost everything. Jim Matheus had taken loans from the company selling him chemicals, and now his part of the ranch belonged to the Chemtech Corporation, based in Connecticut. The Matheus brothers now sell real estate, separately.

"Do you think we should say hello?"

"I don't have to say hello because I can't see them."

Everything, everything, everything about Fresno depressed me.

Anne said, "Why don't you come back to LA with me and we'll find you an apartment?"

"I don't have first month's and last month's and a deposit," I said. Then, to release us both from that alarming truth, as if that were not really the reason I was lingering in Fresno, I said, "I'm not sure I want to live in Los Angeles."

"Of course you do. Where else will you go?"

"I could go back to New York."

"And do what, darling? You can't be a journalist anymore. Journalism is an anachronism."

"Anne, stick to your drink."

"Being a journalist is like being a phrenologist."

"Anne."

"We can get you a job writing at voice-over. Or you could get a job on any show, Ingrid."

"I don't want to work in Hollywood."

"Yes you do. What else are you going to do?"

"What?"

"Where else are you going to go?" Anne had a special talent for making me feel awful. Only sisters know how to make you feel so loved and understood and then, moments later, make you want to hang yourself.

"Here comes Broadway," Anne said.

A group thrust through the door, laughing and exclaiming and speaking in voices far too loud for any dining room. The wolf was there, with his beard. Without his paws and fur, the wolf looked quite nice. He looked like a gentle professor of Italian, or a poet living in Williamsburg. I'd always enjoyed the companionship of the bearded poets of Williamsburg.

I looked at the elk on the wall. Poor elk, stuck in this place forever, nailed here, frozen.

There was a lot of noise, made of voices and feet and clattering plates. Lorenzo's is always cozy. We ordered a spicy penne alla vodka and spaghetti carbonara with thin, melty slivers of dissolving pancetta.

"When will you start eating again?" Anne said. Her blond hair fell over her shoulders in feathered pieces. I could smell her soapiness from where I was sitting.

"When will you start eating?" I said.

"I never eat. Please don't bring up what I told you. Please forget I told you. I'm miserable that I told you."

"Why?"

"Stop talking. Start eating." Anne wasn't eating, either. When we were little, Mother had these cross-stitched cocktail napkins embroidered with *Dinner is poured*. We always thought that was very funny. We still think it's very funny.

"I'm eating. I'm practically over this."

"You're still on the mend."

"I'm practically over it," I said. No one likes to see grief go on for longer than two weeks. Forty days, possibly, but only if your mother has died—that's what the Armenians say. It wasn't like I hadn't been through this before, and continuing to mourn over Howard seemed plain indulgent. I would do it in secret. "I'm not even hurt, really. I'm just upset that I failed. The worst thing about a breakup is this feeling of humiliation."

"Humiliation is ninety percent of sadness."

For a moment I believed that to be true, because I believed most everything Anne said, even then. "That's strange, that you think that."

Anne casually raised her finger to the bartender. Bartenders love Anne and respond to her smallest gestures. "I'm strange," she said. "I'm glad it's taken you this long to realize it. But I must tell you, other people catch on much quicker." The food was for show. We drank our gimlets and drank small thimbles of grappa for dessert. Despite the dinner theater people and despite our general discomfort with anything in Fresno resembling familiarity, I liked it here because Lorenzo's was the kind of place that could make you nostalgic. We'd been coming to Lorenzo's as a family since before the house on the river was built, when we lived two blocks away, on the corner of Palm, in a 1927 Craftsman with a tire swing hung from the front yard's magnolia.

There were only a few places in Fresno that felt safe: Lorenzo's, the club, the house on the river.

Afterward, we were good and drunk, so Anne and I walked up the street, back past the dinner theater and past the Chicken Pie

Shop and across Olive Avenue to Bootsie's Quality Food and Beverage, a former dry cleaner's right next to Roger's Theatre in the Round.

"I don't think we should get in the car," Anne said.

Bootsie's was still throbbing with people after midnight, the sidewalk crowded with smokers. Inside, there were orange booths and heavy wood tables, wide planks on the floor and naked bulbs hanging from the ceiling. There were several women with the Fresno Crop. The kitchen opened onto the bar and onto the restaurant, so you could see the sweat-soaked chef in his white smock at the stove. The backsplash behind the bar was made of tiny orange and yellow glass tiles, and the tiles spelled BOOTSIE'S.

And then there was Bootsie, a bomb of blond curls, like a beacon in the center of everything, laughing a girlish horse laugh with a customer seated in a booth at the edge of the room. Her tank top showed off her sharp shoulders and long clavicles and no cleavage. Her tank top made her look like a boy, but then there was her face: peachy, apple-like, all girlishness. Her smile took up the whole thing.

"Let's sit," Anne said. The place was very small and very crowded but cool even so, a relief from the hot night and the short walk from Lorenzo's. A girl in a yellow dress came up to take our order. "Two frozen mojitos," Anne said. "Each."

"Not each," I said. "Just one for me."

"All right, just one each."

Without making eye contact, the girl in the yellow dress took our place settings away. She had a great volume of hair held back in a messy knot with an elastic. She was probably here temporarily, working for Bootsie on her way from one place to another and didn't look very Fresno at all. Bootsie had this effect on people: she could keep you places you didn't belong.

Bootsie laughed her explosive laugh and across the room we could hear her say, "Embrace your bed head, Sheila, embrace it!" She made her way around the restaurant, enjoying herself.

She was the usual Bootsie, the Bootsie I could never be sure whether I could trust. You never knew with Bootsie if that smile was for real, if she was being sincere or putting you on. We had played soccer together from the time we were six. Bootsie was her soccer name, because she could boot that ball from one end of the field to the other, and would occasionally boot people, too. I was always glad to be on Bootsie's team, because if you were not on her team, she would invariably knock her knee into your ribs or stick her elbow in your jaw when the officials were not looking. Bootsie was the best at that.

We hadn't spoken in years: Three years? Four?

She put her hand on the back of our booth and turned around to greet us as a proprietor greets her guests. She hardly even took a beat when she realized who we were. "Well, hello! It's you." As if she had been waiting and waiting for us, expecting us. "Oh, I missed you," she said, sliding into the seat next to Anne.

"We missed you," Anne said. "That's why we're here."

"Is it really, or are you just saying?" Bootsie's big huge mouthy smile made you happy and exhilarated just to be near her.

"It's why we're here," I said.

"You two." Her voice got as quiet as it could. "I have missed you. I mean, like, really missed you. Especially you." She looked at me. "I'm sorry," she said.

"I'm sorry," I said.

"Why didn't you call me back?" The restaurant was busy and Bootsie did always get right to the point of things.

"Because I'm here now," I said.

"You knew I had moved back, so you knew things were bad,

very bad," she said. She smiled her spacious smile as she said these things, so that nothing she said seemed confrontational.

"I know."

"I wouldn't have ever called you again if I hadn't really needed you. Really needed to speak to you."

"If you had needed to speak to me, you might have called me twice."

"But I know you," she said. "If you're not going to call, you're not going to call." She did know me. "Why didn't you call me, then, Inky?"

"I don't know. Eventually I didn't call you because I was so embarrassed that I hadn't called you back."

She reached across the table and took my wrist, gently, as if she were taking my pulse. "But you're here now," she said. Her hand was cool and dry.

"We're here!" Anne exclaimed, in her cartoon voice, the fake high pitch she uses for protection. My mother did that, too. They were alike in more ways than either would admit.

"What happened between us was awful and stupid and my fault," Bootsie said.

"I was stupid, too."

"You were only stupid when you didn't call me back."

"Yes."

"But that was my fault also."

Four years previous, after I'd left Newton Greene and come back to New York, directionless, jobless, the way I sometimes am, Bootsie suggested I come live with her until I sorted myself out. She was living on Laight Street then, in an unfinished loft her father had purchased for her when she got her first graphics position at the *Times*. He hadn't been so impressed by the job—in the Central Valley, it's much more respectable to be employed by *The Fresno Bee* than *The New York Times*—but she'd been hired just after the terrorist attacks downtown, and for two or three months in the fall of 2001, property in TriBeCa was very cheap. Mr. Calhoun couldn't pass up an excellent deal.

"Can we be friends now?" Bootsie said. "Or do we have to rehash everything that went on between us?"

"I don't think that's the best idea I've ever heard," Anne said.

"Did so much go on between us?" I said. "What went on was between you and Hasso."

"Hasso!" Bootsie said. "That was his name."

Just after moving in with Bootsie, I'd started seeing an old friend of mine from Berlin, a cotton broker's dilettante son who'd pursued me relentlessly, over two continents, but for whom I had no real feelings. Bootsie disapproved of my ambivalence. Hasso was kind to me and handsome in that brooding German wire-rimmed-glasses sort of way, and he passed the time and made me feel pretty, but he was lazy and dull and I saw no future with him. Still, he and I dated for several months while I recovered from the disaster with Newton.

When I did finally get up the nerve to break things off with Hasso, he said, "Are you upset about what went on with me and Bootsie?"

"You and Bootsie where?" I asked, stupidly.

When I confronted Bootsie, quite gently, maybe not believing what I'd been told, she blamed me for my cruelty to Hasso and leading him on and insisted she'd done it just to keep his spirits up. "You know how much sex means to me," she'd said at the time. This was true, I knew, but still I couldn't bear to look at her.

"Hasso says it was that week I had the flu," I had said.

"Yes," she'd said. Seeing I had been stunned quiet, she added, "What, do you think now I'm going to lie about it?"

I packed my little suitcase and spent an expensive week in a cheap hotel before finding an illegal sublet on the Upper East

Side, someplace I was certain to never, ever run into Bootsie, who didn't travel north of Bergdorf's.

Immediately I'd begun to miss her. It was no fun to eat french fries alone at the McDonald's on Union Square, or go looking by myself for a cart or market that served its coffee in those old blue paper cups with the Acropolis drawings on the side, or do any of the other things no one but Bootsie appreciated as much as I did.

Now Bootsie said, "I was depressed, on the verge of a breakdown, and what I didn't tell you was that I'd been pregnant when you came back from London. I was a mess. But you were a mess, too."

"You were pregnant," I said.

"And I apologize for that. Not for getting pregnant. For not telling you."

"We're done apologizing," Anne said.

"Is this too much?" Bootsie said to Anne.

"I missed you," I said.

"But, Ingrid, you were so caught up in yourself," Bootsie said. "You didn't even notice the day I went to the doctor. You didn't even notice I was in bed for two days."

"I don't remember," I said. "I remember so little about that whole period."

Anne nodded at me. "You know how you can get, Ingrid."

"How can I get?"

"Selfish."

I said, "I thought we weren't going to talk about this."

Bootsie went on, "I got angry that I couldn't tell you everything, but I felt bad for you, too, because Newton had really wrecked you." She looked around the room, as if to make sure everything was in order. "It's really hard to train good servers," she said. Bootsie could be forgiven anything, eventually, because of her cheekbones and her posture and her crazy hair and frankness. "Do you remember Linus? He was so sweet, Linus, and so handsome. The baby would have been beautiful." She paused a half second. "I should have married Linus, don't you think, Inky? I could have had a baby and sent her to Brearley and had one of those nice, safe New York lives."

I said, "I think that would have been worse than coming back here." I had adored Linus. He was very well and happily employed as an editor at *The New York Times*, and he was content. Bootsie feared a life with such a person might lack adventure. She had said at the time, "If I wanted a lack of adventure, I'd move back to Fresno." Now Linus was a stranger and her dad was dead and she was right there back in Fresno after all. "But I always thought you should have married Linus," I said.

"Well, I didn't," Bootsie said, then, "I just went to the doctor and had it taken care of."

I said, "Oh, Boots."

She said, "I don't see myself being in love for the rest of my life. I'll get married and all of that, but I can't see any relationship lasting for more than ten years."

I said, "Our relationship has lasted more than ten years."

She said, "Yes, but I'm not fucking you."

In New York, when she was in art school, Bootsie had had a yearlong affair with a girl in her class. Bootsie did these sorts of things just so she could say that she'd done them: affairs with women, affairs with married men, threesomes and foursomes and sex in the tiny, filthy bathroom of the Heathrow Express, fifteen minutes to Central London. She kept looking just in case she was missing something. "Nothing really turns me on," she told me once. "Except being choked. I like to be choked."

There was a pause during which Anne checked twice that her tennis bracelet was still there. Anne doesn't like scenes of rapprochement, she doesn't like nostalgia, she doesn't like displays of soft feeling. She's very un-actressy in that way. But Bootsie had her boxed into the booth and she couldn't escape.

"It's funny," Bootsie said, "for a long time I thought you were the bad friend." Our drinks came, and one for Bootsie. "Then my dad died. Cheers," she said, and we all clinked glasses.

"We don't really have to talk about this," I said.

"I like it," Bootsie said. "Don't you like it? Don't you think it's a relief?"

"Maybe we should have some food," Anne said.

"We keep trying to order food," I said. "And then it comes and it's not what we thought we wanted."

"A lot of things are like that." Bootsie hailed one of the waitresses. "Fritters," she said. "I like to talk about the past. It's as if you can fix it."

"That sounds nice," I said.

"It's true. Here's what I should have done: not quit the *Times*. Apologized to my father before he was dead. Taken a semester abroad. Actually learned calculus instead of stealing the exams." When she talked, her curls bobbed all around. "Not sold my place on Laight. What should you have done, Annie?"

Anne looked up toward the busy restaurant, as if for an idea or quick getaway. "I don't know," she said. "I'm very happy."

I said, "Come on, Anne."

"You lie," said Bootsie. "What do you wish you had done, Inks?"

"Not got fired so much," I said. "Stayed in one place. Berlin, maybe." Berlin was the one place I had moved for myself instead of a boyfriend. I'd moved there to practice my high school German and to manage an American café that served crabs and chowder. I missed Berlin all the time. "Bought an apartment in New York while I was employed and while my parents had money." I couldn't think of anything else.

"Berlin," Anne said. "You were miserable in Berlin. It was so cold there, you barely went outdoors in the winter. Berlin," she said, shaking her head.

I said, "The point is to change the past. It's a game, Anne."

"You were so lonely in Berlin," she said.

"I'm lonely now," I told her.

There was the uncomfortable silence of truth at the table.

Bootsie said, "I always thought it was crazy you didn't stay with George Sweet. He was good for you. You'd probably still be in New York, running some international media company, living in a town house on West Sixty-ninth."

"I'd live on East Sixty-ninth," I said.

"Of course you would," said Bootsie. "But that's your mother talking."

You see what she could do: she could turn things around in twenty seconds so that once again you were in the position of weakness.

"People take marriage too seriously," Bootsie said. "If it doesn't work out, you just get a divorce."

"Then what's the point of getting married?" Anne said.

"Just to see what it feels like."

"It doesn't really feel like anything," Anne said.

The fritters came and I recognized them as my own, the fritters I make for myself and for everyone else for brunch or when there's no other food or when we're all too drunk to even get ourselves to a drive-through. My grandmother taught me how to make them when I was tiny. These things sometimes skip a generation. I had three deep scars on my left hand from cubing zucchini after drinking. "My fritters," I said.

"Surprised but not happy," Bootsie said. "Right? I grow the squash myself. You can't open a restaurant and not have Ingrid's fritters on the secret menu."

I was quite drunk, and only being quite drunk can make such a reconciliation possible. Of course, this must have been Anne's plan all along. To our table they brought three more sorbet dishes, filled with mojitos frozen with liquid nitrogen. It was a very dangerous way to drink a mojito.

"You think I brought up George Sweet because I'm an asshole," Bootsie said.

"No," I lied.

"But that's not why," she said. "I brought him up because he's sitting at the bar."

We all looked. My throat seized up a bit. There was his straight broad back with the sharp wing bones. His blond curls had gone dark; he'd cut them short. He was heftier, like his father. In high school and in his twenties, George was a skinny string, long and muscular and light. Now he'd gotten darker and heavier, like all of us.

"He's still so lovely," said Bootsie.

"I like George," Anne said. "I always liked George."

"Everyone loves George," said Bootsie. "He's like the town mascot. He's darling. And he comes in here all the time."

"I sort of wish he hadn't come in tonight," I said. I wanted to be more like Anne, more like Bootsie, more like the sort of person who doesn't feel anything, who doesn't sting and sear when seeing again someone she'd loved a long, long time ago. I really had loved him.

"He plays rugby, too. In some league. He's always all scratched up. It's very sexy."

Anne said, "Ingrid just got demolished two weeks ago."

"I'm just talking," Bootsie said.

"Tell me some gossip about someone else," I said. "Let's talk about someone else, can we?"

"Who?"

"Hilda Sorensen," I said.

"She's seeing Greg Kappas and she wants him to divorce Arlene and marry her, but Greg and Arlene can't get divorced."

"The land with the riparian rights belongs to Arlene's family."

"You already know all my gossip. How long have you been here?" I didn't tell her what I knew about her and her bartender. It was important to keep any small advantage with Bootsie.

Since that night at the club, and maybe because I'd been reading *Middlemarch*, I'd been thinking of the tragic and mercenary ways people are bound. Greg and Arlene had become this enormous mythical representation of everything I could have been, had I made even more bad decisions. I'd been thinking of the narrowness of small towns, Fresno in particular, and how it could be possible to have some significant life here, or even a happy one. Of course, completely happy people are tedious and stupid, but here was Bootsie: happy and bright and brilliant, as she had always seemed destined to be. I felt I must keep my distance from her, as if her comfort in our provincial hometown could somehow be catching.

The music had gone up and the place was loud now, so even though we were no more than fifteen feet from him, George was all the way across a crowded, noisy room.

Bootsie said, "You could have married George just to see what it was like."

"That's something else I should have done."

"There are reasons you and George broke up," Anne said.

"Yes," I said. "Remember that song 'Detachable Penis'?"

Anne said, "Ingrid, come on."

I continued, "I loved that song. Once we were driving and I

said to George, 'If you had a detachable penis and you were going away for a week, would you leave me your penis so I could use it?' He said no. I said, 'Do you mean you don't trust me with your penis?' It turned into a real fight. I said, 'If you don't trust me enough to leave your penis with me, do you even love me?' That was where the end started, and that was right at the beginning."

"You're drunk," Anne said.

"At least he was honest," said Bootsie.

Really the end had started after George and I had moved to New York, to the bright studio on West Eighty-fourth Street, and I told him we ought to think about living in separate apartments. It was my mother's idea; she had coached me through the conversation, providing a script that started with "Artists should know what it's like to live alone." George sat in the crook of our tiny sectional sofa and sobbed. "It's fine," he had said the next day. "Everything is fine. Give me a couple months."

Soon afterward, George fell for one of the tall, smart, silky-haired girls who worked with him at Marvel Comics. I knew but pretended not to know. Both he and this silky-haired cartoonist got jobs in DC, and he moved out of the apartment on Eighty-fourth Street with the floor-to-ceiling bookshelves and the built-in desk he had designed himself. We visited each other for a while, acting as if nothing was wrong, but eventually he told me he'd given up. I guess I'd given up, too. It didn't last long between George and the silky-haired cartoonist. A few years on, he wrote a thriller and came back to Fresno. The thriller made some money. He wrote another one, which made even more.

"Mom says he got married," I said.

"He's not married," said Bootsie. "I don't think it ended well." Bootsie started waving her long, wiry arm.

"Don't," I said.

"Don't," Anne said.

"He's coming over here," Bootsie said.

He took such a long time to extinguish his cigarette and make the fifteen-foot trip.

"What is this town going to do with a table of girls like this?" he said. His voice was the same: soft, deep, with rocks in it. I would never not be in love with George Sweet. "Hi," he said.

Seeing George was easier because I was drunk, and I tried to feel even drunker than I was so that his face and his posture and the cowlick at his temple wouldn't give me a deep pain in my sternum. He sat next to me and put his arm around me and said, "How long are you here?"

"Not long," Anne told him.

"You should come see my bees," as if nothing at all had passed between us, no time, no parts of me he owned, no relationship at all. "You should come see my bees," as if I were a reporter or a distant acquaintance. "I wish you would," he said.

"What bees?" I said.

Bootsie said, "We use George's honey in the honey vanilla ice cream."

"I thought you were writing trashy books," Anne said. "That's what Ingrid said."

"I didn't say trash."

"You did, too."

"I'm sure I would not have said that."

Bootsie said, "That's all right, girls. George hasn't opened his typewriter for years. Have you, George?"

George said, "I'll tell you, during bad years for pistachios, writing a thriller seems like pretty good money."

I said, "I didn't say trash, George. I never said that."

He smiled his bent smile at me. "But no, I haven't written anything for a while. Not even letters. Not even long e-mails."

"Well, of course, no one writes letters," Anne said.

"Ingrid used to write beautiful letters," he said.

"Yes. And then I stopped."

The girl with the yellow dress came over and took our empty glasses.

"You had the mojitos," George said. "How many?"

"Too late to catch up," I said. "Were going home soon."

It had been such a long night. A sensible part of me thought I should keep going on being angry with Bootsie and especially with George, but anger takes so much energy, and I was running low on energy then. I was so busy being angry with Howard, I didn't have room for the anger usually reserved for Bootsie or George. Anyway, Bootsie had that wild explosion of hair and that smile and George owned a small part of me I couldn't get back and it was impossible to stay angry with either of them.

George said, "Ingrid, do you remember the Post-its?"

I said, "I still have all those Post-its," scrawled with lines from the movies we watched ("Do you like a cold apple?") or reminders: "This coffee pot does not clean itself" or "laundry multiplies" or just "I love you." When we lived together, these pale yellow squares were everywhere, on the walls and floors, in drawers and on window ledges, like moths.

The place was emptying out, and George lit a cigarette from a pack in his breast pocket. He still smoked. "Isn't it funny to think that once you and I ate dinner together every night."

Even now, he knew exactly the things to say that could knock me over with regret.

"We could eat together now," I said.

"This establishment stopped serving food at eleven," said Bootsie.

"We could eat together tomorrow," said George.

"And the night after that," I said.

"George," Anne warned, "you leave my fragile sister alone."

George removed his arm from around my shoulder. Bootsie got up and locked the front door. "They're fining everyone around here for after-hours cigarettes." She lowered the blinds at the front window, took ashtrays from behind the bar, and passed them out. People smoking had been ashing and extinguishing on the plank floor.

Anne said, "We're waiting for our drinks to wear off and then we're going home. We have got to stop drinking and driving."

"They fine for that, too, I hear," said Bootsie.

George smoked and we all sat and suddenly there was nothing to say.

The girl in the yellow dress sat at the bar, dipping her finger into a rocks glass and speaking quietly to Bootsie's bartender. Two couples had been sitting at separate tables, lingering, smoking.

"Listen, you guys," Bootsie said then, behind her, to her customers, her voice itself an announcement. "I'm going to make you a deal. Elliot is going to give you all shots on the house. You're going to drink them, and then you're going to leave so we can go home."

The bartender lined ten glasses on the bar and began to pour shots.

"The end of the night always feels so sad," Anne said.

"Not for me," said Bootsie. "At the end of the night I get to count all the money."

"I liked seeing you," I said to George.

He said, "You just say that because it's the end of the night."

"And you feel sad," Anne said.

"Maybe. I'm drunk, too."

"Come see the bees," he said.

"Drunk?" said Anne. "Who is going to drive us home?"

"There are services for this," Bootsie said, dialing her phone.

Finally the two couples got up from their tables and began to shake the front door. "It's locked," Bootsie said to us, to herself, to the phone. "It's locked!" she said louder, to her customers. "To keep out the police."

9.

Of course, Howard wrote.

I didn't even want to hear from him. But then sometimes I did. I had been wondering when, or whether, I'd hear from him.

He wrote a letter, typed and printed on the white cotton paper he used at the office. He'd sent it to Anne's house, where it sat for two weeks in a stack of unopened bank statements and small residual checks before Charlie spotted it.

"Look at that handwriting," Anne said.

"I know, don't point it out."

"I have to point it out." Howard's handwriting leaned the wrong way and sloped at a downward angle along the envelope.

"He was neglected by his parents," I said.

"I have to point it out so you don't make the same mistake again," she said, running her finger along the diagonal line of my name. "He's practically illiterate."

I don't have too much of a birth order thing, but would an older child ever get a breakup letter sent to her little sister's house?

"I thought it better if I brought it to you in person," Anne said. "You don't want to open these things by yourself."

"Don't I?"

"Do you?"

Howard wanted to apologize for the way things ended on the airplane and for the uncomfortable trip to Aspen and for not helping me to pack my things, but he did not want to apologize for the things he should have, things like asking me to sell my grandmother's armoire before I moved to Los Angeles and for lying about loving me the way he said he did.

Anne counted the apologies. This is the sort of unforgivable thing an older sister will do for you. There were eight. He even apologized for one night he spent out doing coke with his brother, which didn't require an apology. He had padded his contrition. "He wrote this to make himself feel better," she said.

"Maybe he regrets things."

"Maybe," she said. And then, "No."

"I won't read any more letters from him."

"There won't be any more." We were sitting on her bed. Her bed was just next to the window, and looked onto the overgrown tennis court and the green pool, down to the river and across to the vines on the other bank. It was nighttime and the orange light of evening was just sinking under the blue and black. At the ranch, the real dark of night didn't come until a bit later than the dark came in town. Light reflected over the water and took a long time to get past the long, flat vineyards. We were lucky to be out here in the middle of ranches, and not in town, where most of the farmers now lived, in new houses as big as office buildings, lined up one right after the other, surrounded by lawns wet with night sprinklers and the air full of gasoline and the chlorine smells of swimming pools. Out here there was no sound but crickets and dust moving through the willow trees. The night air smelled of bursting fruit. We had slept all day and were still hungover from the night before. "I sort of wish the tennis court and the pool were still just a hill," she said.

"Less upkeep."

"Remember when it was just a hill?"

"Why do you always complain about everything?" I said.

"I'm not complaining. I'm talking."

"Dad likes his pool and his tennis court."

"It just looks so damaged."

"There's a difference between damaged and neglected, Annie." The clay on the tennis court hadn't been groomed for ten years or more. The net had been torn away by weather and ground into the dirt. "Felix will get them a loan."

"No one ever played on that tennis court anyway," she said.

"We played."

"Two seasons." Those were a couple good years, when Mother had hired a coach to come to the house. Nothing ever came of the competitive tennis hopes she had for us. One coach told me, "You could be really good at this game if you were just slightly more ambitious." I stopped playing in high school, discouraged by opponents who consistently called the in balls out.

"I'm glad you have a job," I said.

Anne would leave the next morning. Her sandals and sundresses were neatly stacked in a boat bag by the door. She taped the cartoon three days a week. "I want you to look after our mother," she said. "And Dad."

"Don't tell me what to do," I said. Then the coldness of Howard's letter hit me, or something hit me, it was my hangover probably, and I started to cry. I like to cry in front of Anne because she never asks me to stop. It's like she doesn't even register tears; she is completely resistant. "Of course I am going to look after them. I'm going to stay until Dad sees the doctor."

"Just make the appointment."

"He won't go. You know him. He won't go."

"Trick him."

"You're the one who's good at tricks, Anne."

"Maybe I'll do a play," she said then. "When voice-over is done. I'll go to New York and do a play so people know I can actually act. And you and I can get an apartment together. How's that?"

"We'll have to live in Brooklyn."

"There are nice parts of Brooklyn."

"Probably," I said.

There was nothing in Anne's old room to remind you of Anne—after college she had taken the books and photographs she wanted and had discarded everything else: ticket stubs to football games, teenage journals, old tennis rackets, middle school ceramics class mugs, all went into the dumpster. The room was blank, sterile as a hotel, which is how she preferred to use it. She rarely stayed for more than two nights. "I have to do something," she said. "I feel like everything is just still. Do you feel the stillness?"

So much about Anne seemed still to me. Every emotion, every scream or demonstration had been stilled into gauzy prettiness. "What will Charlie do?" I said.

"Charlie will miss me."

"What do you mean by that?"

"Charlie is fine." She waved her hand the way she did. "Charlie's always fine." Anne stopped taking naps as a toddler, so in the afternoons Mother had slept with a wooden spoon in her fist to swat Anne away. Anne learned early not to come too near. "Are you letting your hair go brown?" she said then.

"I can't afford to go to the colorist as often. Anyway, he's in Beverly Hills."

"Well, make an effort, sweet pea. Have it lightened up. I want you to look pretty."

"It's fine."

"You never listen to me, and later you always say you should have listened."

"Should I write him back?" I said.

"You should do what will make you feel better."

"I want to know what happened."

"He's a liar is what happened."

"It doesn't make sense."

"There's something else, Ingrid."

"Something else to what."

"Well, there's a girl. Charlie told me."

"Well," I said. "It's not like I was planning to go back."

"He saw them at dinner."

"When did this happen?"

"She's nothing like you, apparently. She was dressed in business casual."

"Did Charlie talk to them?"

"It doesn't matter. His letter doesn't matter. The nicest thing he ever did for you was break up with you."

"Everyone else can see that, right?"

"Yes."

For a while after Eighty-fourth Street I stayed with an unimportant but doting boyfriend called Quinn, and his apartment was across the street from the editorial offices of one of the food magazines I occasionally wrote for. Of all the apartments and all the windows in New York City, Quinn's looked directly onto my editor's office, so over at *Gourmet* they knew when I woke up at noon or that I was eating packaged doughnuts on the couch or that I was reading the *Post* and not the *Times*. I'd been over there, across the street, and you could see everything: You could see the cereal left on Quinn's countertop and which magazines were on his coffee table. You could see if he'd left his socks on the floor. The day I realized who sat in the offices across the way, I told Anne, "They've been watching me in my underwear all day. Now I can't go out of the bedroom until I'm completely dressed." She said, "Are you kidding me? Now you know to walk around in your underwear all the time. You'll get a lot more work that way." Anne took a sensible angle on most everything.

"He doesn't want a letter in return, then," I said.

"Do what's going to make you feel better," she repeated. "No need to think about him."

"Let's have gimlets," I said. "That will make me feel better."

"A little hair of the dog."

"Have you ever tried pickle juice?" It was Mother's cure.

"Let's have gin and tonics."

"Gin is very good for bad news," I said.

"Gin was invented for bad news." It's humiliating enough to get dumped, but it's much worse to find out you were among the last to know it was coming.

The kitchen was dark and hot. We opened the windows and squeezed limes into a pitcher of gin and we drank until we couldn't feel the heat anymore.

"This place isn't as comforting as I thought it would be," Anne said. "Why is it comforting for you but not for me?"

"You have someplace else that's home."

"Charlie has never watched the cartoon, you know."

I had seen only a couple episodes of Anne's cartoon. "It's not your life's work, Anne."

"It's my work right now. It pays half our mortgage. And he never watches my guest spots, either. He hardly knows what it is I do."

"Do you know what it is he does?"

"All he does is look at his phone." She dipped her finger into her drink, pushing the ice cubes below the surface. "We don't really get along, Inky. We just live together in that house with the shutters. I don't even think he likes the shutters."

You know that feeling when a deep hole opens up inside you and you feel like, physically, your whole body is being sucked into it? It can take all your energy not to disappear into that hole. "Maybe you should talk to another doctor," I said.

"There's a doctor in Sherman Oaks everyone goes to."

"Do you want a child or is that just what Charlie wants?"

"It's all so expensive," she said. "God, doesn't the heat tire you out?"

"I don't know yet."

"How can you not know in twenty seconds?"

"I'm not tired yet."

"You're depressing to talk to."

Mother appeared in the doorway. We hadn't heard her come out of her room. "What's this chitchat about?" she said.

"The heat," Anne said. "The weather. Isn't that what everyone talks about around here?"

"Around here, the weather is business," Mother said.

Anne poured herself another drink. The white tile on the kitchen counter had several sticky rings where we'd lifted and set the pitcher of gimlets.

"Stop drinking," she said to Anne. "You girls drink too much."

Anne did not respond.

"Well, don't stop speaking because I came in," Mother said.

"We were out of things to say," I said.

"We never have anything to say to one another," Mother said. "Other mothers and daughters speak to each other."

"Didn't you tell us when we were little that we were different from other people?" Anne said.

"Did I tell you that?"

"Very, very different. Special," Anne said. "Don't lower your expectations now."

"You are special," Mother said. "Of course I had high expectations. I still have high expectations." She held her slender hand up to the window screen, checking for a breeze.

"You can't have it all ways, Mother," Anne said, taking more than one gulp from her glass. "Do you want common daughters who tell you all their trashy, vulgar personal details, or do you want daughters who are exceptional? Make up your mind."

"I want you," Mother said. "You're exceptional."

"Oh, very exceptional. Very special," Anne said.

"Ingrid? What's she upset about?"

Anne gave me a gentle look I couldn't interpret. It could have meant *Tell Mother my news so I don't have to*, or it could have meant *Please keep your mouth shut*. I said, "I think Anne might feel a little bit of pressure to come up with things to tell you," which was the truest and least revealing thing I could think of.

"Oh," Mother said. "That's all right. We can sit in silence." She gently touched the side of her face, as if she were feeling for a hair growing in.

We did, for a few moments, sit in silence.

But Mother can't stand to sit in silence.

"I thought we were very happy out here at the house on the river," she said. She opened the backgammon board and began to set it up.

"When?" Anne said.

"Well, always. Still, now," said Mother. "But when you were growing up, when you're saying I wanted you to be exceptional. I didn't want you to be exceptional, you just were. That's not my fault." She waited for us to respond. She said, "Or anyone's fault." She rattled the dice in their cup.

"We've always been happy here," I said. "We were happy growing up."

"Well, not you," Mother said. "You weren't so happy."

She was referring to my teenage years, when first I left for Massachusetts because I hated school in Fresno, and then three years later when I came home from school in Massachusetts and the shrink told my parents to hospitalize me for depression. My parents decided I'd be more comfortable at home on the river than in the juvenile psychiatric hospital, which I was. "I was never that unhappy," I said. "It was other people who kept telling me I was unhappy."

"You stopped sleeping."

"That's anxiety. There's a difference between anxiety and unhappy."

"You should have told me this twenty years ago," Mother said.

"I did tell you," I said. Then we were quiet again, and I felt sorry for Mother. "I'm saying no one is unhappy. No one is angry."

"I'm a little bit angry," Anne said. Her cheeks were red from drink and from keeping everything from Mother and from herself.

"Don't be angry," Mother said.

"Oh, all right. Thank you. I'll not be angry."

"You have nothing to be angry about."

"Oh, I know," said Anne. "Think of the tennis lessons, and the horses, and the vacations. Think of the way we were treated in France. 'Think of the clothes you had.'" Anne imitated Mother's voice, which she did perfectly, like a song.

"Well, yes," Mother said.

"All right," Anne said. "This is why we can't have this conversation."

Mother said, "We never have any conversation."

I said, "We're having a conversation right now."

"Not really," Anne said.

"No, not really," Mother agreed. Even when they were arguing with each other, Anne and Mother could find a way to side against me.

I felt that deep hole opening up in me and all my insides got desperate, as if they were trying to crawl out for survival. Nothing resolved this feeling as well as a Tylenol PM. "I guess I'll go to bed," I said.

"Because I came in?" asked Mother.

"I'm tired," I said. "My head hurts a little." I put my glass in the sink. I took the old sponge and wiped sticky rings of gimlet from the tiles on the kitchen counter.

"Mom," Anne said, ignoring us both, "what in the world is going on with your hair?"

Mother touched her hair tenderly, as if she didn't want to muss it, but her hair, as usual these days, was lopsided from sleeping. "Is it too dark? Ingrid says it's too dark."

"Good night, you two," I said.

"You look like a vampire. Who is doing the color? What is it with hair color in this family?"

"Let's have cigarettes," Mother whispered to Anne. "Good night, Inky."

Anne went on, "I don't know why you don't come to LA and have my guy do it."

"Good night, Annie." I stood in the doorway.

"It's early yet," Anne said. "Stay with us."

"I'm still tired from last night," I said.

"I didn't know you were that drunk last night," she said. Right in front of Mother. She'd had more to drink than I had the night before, and had been twice as drunk.

"All right," I said, and turned to go.

I heard them as I walked through the living room and down the hall: "Why do you think I have cigarettes?"

"I know you have cigarettes. I saw them in your purse. I suspect you want me to see them."

"You always look in my purse," Anne said.

My sheets were crumpled and slightly smelly. I hadn't yet changed them since I got home almost two weeks ago. There is nothing worse than old sheets, especially when the temperatures at night are over 100 and you're sweating out booze. Tomorrow I would get new, crisp sheets. I would iron them, maybe, so they would be cool and flat for bedtime. I took the Tylenol PM and waited to feel drowsy. Tomorrow everything would be new, in fact. Tomorrow I would start to fix things, or think of a way to start to fix things.

I should have had another gimlet. Alcohol increases the speed of the Tylenol, even if the combination kills you quicker.

Mother and Anne thought they were so clever and furtive with their cigarettes, but the smoke came straight from the kitchen terrace up through my open window. I could hear the shoosh of their whispering. Being left out of their pretty-girl clique was a feeling so familiar I could almost nestle into it for comfort. They had the same low, delicate laugh. Had they swept the dead bees off the crisscross chairs before sitting down? Their laughs sounded like chiffon. I would have shouted to them to quiet down but I didn't want to wake Dad. Poor Dad, with his cough and worrying about the grapes and no booze tonight and no cigarettes. He'd been in bed all evening, long before dark. I did not hear his gentle, wavelike snoring. I heard only chiffon laughing and crickets.

I started to think about those nights George and I had spent in the garage apartment at his parents' house. George always made sure to have new sheets. There was a polyester quilt that a renter had left. The long closet had accordion doors and stored clothes no one in the family wore anymore, like worn-out work boots and boys' vinyl raincoats and old football jerseys George and his brothers had not returned to the high school.

I started to feel that heaviness in the forehead from the Tylenol PM. I took one more to make sure it worked.

George's mother had these plates with strawberries in the middle, and she always made sure when setting the table that the big strawberry pointed down. She liked pink things: sweaters and umbrellas and plates. This was something else my mother found unforgivable, the affinity for anything pink.

After George's dad died, his mother instructed him to sell the old shotguns in the attic. They turned out to be extremely valuable, much older and in much better condition than anyone had guessed. George sold them to one of the Wentes of Lodi and bought a black Alfa Romeo convertible with the money his mother allowed him to keep.

I started to feel the heaviness of that Tylenol PM in my nose and my throat.

The Sweets' apartment above the garage had unfinished pine planks on the walls and a wet bar as big as the tiny kitchen. And it had clean carpet.

Anne always left very early in the morning, so she didn't have to say goodbye to anyone. Still, it was always slightly a surprise to wake up and find her gone.

10.

Escape plans were my specialty. I had done this so many times, from so many places. I had escaped from Fresno twice before.

I set a routine. I had a plan and I wrote it down in a fresh college-ruled notebook. There is nothing more promising than a blank notebook. I would get up at seven and work on the screenplay. Two pages a day, I decided, and I could be done with the thing by October, whether or not it was any good. I had abandoned all ideas of it being any good. By October Mother and Dad would have the money from the grapes and could possibly loan me something to rent an apartment near Anne's house. I hoped that by then she and Charlie would have worked out the discomfort between them. I liked spending time with Anne and Charlie when they were happy with each other. It gave me the sense of being part of a couple.

"I read online that runny yolks are good for your brain," I said to Mother that morning as we tapped our eggs.

"Good how?"

"Good like they keep you energetic and sharp."

"Why?"

"Butter, too, it said. We can eat all the things we like."

"I always eat the things I like," Mother said, which was not true, of course. Mother ate nearly nothing. Her body was like skin poured over muscle, with realistic fake breasts, two pears hung from sinew.

"Eat your toast soldiers."

"I do like toast soldiers," she said.

"What did Anne have to say?"

"You always ask that," Mother said, "as if you haven't talked to her yourself. Didn't you talk to her the whole time she was here?"

"I mean when you were outside."

"Oh, Ingrid. You sound like a spy. You sound like an East German."

Mother knew nothing about East Germany apart from what she might have heard on reruns of *Murder She Wrote*. "I'm making conversation," I said. "I thought you liked making conversation."

"You didn't even notice that I invoked East Germany." She got that long-necked look that Anne gets, too, chin up, neck like a garden hose.

"I noticed," I said. At the house in Fresno, my feelings were hurt about 60 percent of the time.

"You think I am so dumb."

"No."

"You think I don't know the difference between Africa and South Africa."

"Where did you come up with that?"

"I do know about South Africa, though. I learned all about it in the eighties when we went to see their vines."

"What did you learn?"

"I learned about vines!" she said. "They can do red and white, but mostly white. And I learned they have these lovely batik tunics at stalls in the marketplace. I'll bet they don't have those anymore." She sucked the white from the lopped-off top of her egg. I always saved that part for last, but Mother ate it first thing.

"You must have learned a lot," I said.

Marianela's old red Toyota pulled into the carport.

"Oh, good," Mother said. "More eggs."

Marianela, still slender, always looked so glamorous in the printed cotton shirtwaist dresses she sewed herself. Her long black hair had gone wiry with veins of gray, but she fixed it as she always had, pinned up on the top of her head like a countess. She still wore the low-heeled pumps she insisted were the only type of shoe that didn't hurt her back. Marianela had four children and worked for the Madera school district and looked after the chickens and farmed twenty acres of vines almost entirely by herself, with little help from Miguel, who was busy enough with my father. And yet she never seemed as if she were in a hurry. She moved like a river, slowly, unbothered, deliberate. Marianela had an ease and a calmness about her that seemed almost spiritual. She had the kind of maternal beauty that felt soft, tactile.

She rang the kitchen bell with her elbow, a box of eggs in each hand.

"I heard you were here, little one," she said through the screen door.

"I would have come to you," I said. "I still will." I opened the door and hugged her before she had a chance to put her boxes on the counter. When I was little, Marianela provided all the hugs my mother couldn't.

"We have too many eggs to eat," she said. "You come home in time for harvest, Inky?"

"Marianela, this is too much for us. We haven't finished the last batch," I said.

Mother said, "We'll eat the eggs."

"I can't give them to the workers, I don't have enough for all," Marianela said. "You know, I have no one at home anymore. Just me and Miguel."

The last time I had gone to see Miguel and Marianela, only their oldest had gone away to college. That was six years ago, at least. Eight? Ten? "Where's Emily?"

"Emily is taller than her father," Mother said, balancing a tiny spoonful of egg on a toast soldier. "And so beautiful, Ingrid, with these wide cheekbones. Marianela, do you want a soft-boiled egg?" There was nothing to offer her but eggs and condiments and pie.

"No eggs," said Marianela. "She plays soccer, little one, like you. They gave her a scholarship to Stanford. But listen," she said.

"Why does no one tell me these things?" I said. "God, Marianela. Stanford. Emily must be brilliant."

"Like Ellie Prentiss," Mother said.

Marianela said, "Who's Ellie Prentiss?"

"Ingrid's old friend," Mother said. "Sit down. Do you want toast? Or I think we have cake."

"Nothing, nothing. You talk to Ned?" Marianela asked my mother.

"Talk to Ned when?"

"You know about Phillip?"

"What about Phillip?" said Mother.

"Phillip quit," Marianela said. She sat right down at the table, her circle skirt folded neatly beneath her, one red pump crossed over the other.

"Quit what?" said Mother.

"The job."

"Which job?"

Marianela looked at me, as if I should translate.

"What happened?" I said.

"You know, they're doing the equipment check," said Marianela. "I go down there to bring some doughnuts, but Miguel's not there. Where's Miguel? Some trouble at the office, the boys said. So I'm nervous, I call, but no answer from Miguel. So I drive to the office. They're there, you know. I see them through the glass door before they see me. Before the harvest, he leaves them like this."

Mother said, "He left them where?"

"Mom, he quit. He quit his job."

Mother looked dazed, as if she'd been slapped. "Why?"

"I didn't stay," Marianela said. "I thought maybe you spoke to Ned."

"Ned hasn't called," Mother said. "He comes home for lunch."

"Lunch, yes, I remember," said Marianela.

"No, Ned didn't call. I didn't speak to him."

"No," Marianela said.

"Was Phillip there?" I said.

"No, Phillip, no. Miguel and Jefe. And they were quiet, so quiet. Call him, Evelyn. Call now."

"No, no," Mother said. "He'll call me. He'll tell me when he gets home for lunch."

"Okay, no no," Marianela said. She took the eggs from the counter and put them in the refrigerator. "He leaves them now. For what? For another job? He has no other job, he told them so. He told them he's going to farm himself now, farm his own ground."

I laughed. "He can't do that without Dad's accounts."

Marianela shrugged. "Maybe he's stolen enough," she said quietly, carefully, as if stating the obvious might inflict pain.

"He thinks it's enough now, but wait," I said, dipping my spoon into the lukewarm egg. "It's not enough. He needs too much water. He's got bad ground. The math doesn't work."

"Low water table," Mother said, getting up to fetch her cards from the drawer in the kitchen. "And rocks! And an impossible slope. He bought that land after he started working for Dad. After!" she said, pointing her finger at no one, at God.

"We all knew then what we know now," Marianela said. "*Víbora*."

"What else did he say?" I asked.

"I said too much. I wanted to come by because I thought you would know already, and you might know more," she said. "You look beautiful, little one. Lovely like a string. Like a dancer." She held my fingers as if in a waltz.

"Too skinny, no boobs," Mother said.

"No," Marianela said, bringing me in, hugging me. "Just right."

"Thank you." I meant thank you for the hug, not the compliment. Mother hadn't hugged me since I arrived two weeks ago.

Marianela turned to the screen door. "I hope I didn't bring in bad news."

"No, no," Mother said. "Someone has to bring in the news."

"Come see me, Ingrid."

"I can't believe Emily's left," I said to her. "You're too young."

She laughed. She squeezed my hand with those strong, bony, vine-pruning fingers of hers. "Come see me and say that some more." Her pumps kicked up dust on the concrete between the doorstep and her old red car.

Mother flipped cards onto the breakfast table.

"Do you want another egg?" I said.

She pulled up the cards and shuffled again.

I said, "I think you should have another egg." I filled the pot with water.

"She loved that," Mother said, flipping the cards with velocity.

"She loves knowing more than we do, and she loves telling us so."

"I think she just likes to gossip," I said, in defense.

"That, too."

"Marianela's not against you, Mom."

"I didn't say she was against me. I'm just saying she's a bitch."

"All right." It was useless to defend Marianela. Any kind words about Marianela would be perceived by Mother as taking the wrong side. Marianela's affectionate nature outweighed her pettiness, in my opinion, but Mother had no use for affection.

"Do you want to call Daddy?" Mom said.

"Let's wait for lunch."

"Yes," she said, and looked for the right card to place on top of another. "But why wait for lunch?"

"Because he's distracted and he'll call you."

"Yes," she said. She slid cards around the table, one on top of the other, with fighter pilot attention.

I put fresh eggs in the pot. They were warm; Marianela must have taken them right from the coop. "I think you should have one of these, Mother. It's good for the brain."

"Does my brain seem deficient to you?"

I could hear the gas from the stove, the buzz of the refrigerator, the menacing conversation of crows from up and down the river. "Phillip has something lined up," I said. "Thick people like Phillip don't just quit to be entrepreneurial. They don't get inspired like that."

"I'm glad he's quit."

"But not right before the grape harvest, Mother. And not without giving notice. There's no point. It's the easiest time of year for him."

"Look at that," she said, tapping one of the royals, and quickly stacking one card on top of another. "Everything is working out."

The industry predicted a grape glut, so many farmers were culling their vines, leaving fruit on the ground. On certain days that summer, the air would catch the stink of rotten, fermenting fruit, and that smell would go on all day, from one end of the county to the other. This was one of those days.

Dad had the pale look of the office. "You know they're planning to push Wabnig for the Heisman," he said, pulling a chair from the table, the screen door hanging open behind him.

"Wabnig?" Mother said. She stood at the counter, layering papery slices of ham on bread in fanlike folds.

"Our quarterback, Sherman Wabnig. Wilson says the coaches think he's something this year."

"You talked to Wilson?" she said.

"It's a little early to think about the Heisman," I said.

"What else did he say?" Mother asked.

"Oh, I don't know. I saw Miguel. He says we're looking at high yields, even higher than we thought. Some of the smaller guys are culling the shoulders and wings."

"You don't cull anymore?" I said.

"Too expensive. The labor's too expensive, it's not worth it." Dad leaned back in the chair, hands on his thighs, more defeated than relaxed. "Harder and harder to find labor, Inky. You have to pay up."

There was a silence. Mother wouldn't look at either of us. Dad wasn't going to tell us about Phillip.

The heat was all mixed up with dust and the smell of ripening fruit. There are no cool parts to a Fresno summer. The heat doesn't dissipate the way it would in a desert. In a way, the heat felt familiar, like a relief. The windows were open but nothing moved.

"Marianela came by," I said.

"Ah," he said, leaning forward, unbuttoning his cuffs, rolling up the sleeves of that smart white shirt. "I thought she might." He nodded. We all listened to the kitchen for a moment: the refrigerator, the ice maker dropping a clank of ice into the bin. What was there to say about Phillip, really? "It doesn't make much sense. I guess he figured we'd get rid of him at some point anyway."

"At some point," said Mother.

"There's just a lot to catch up on now." The timing seemed cruel—to leave Dad, after twenty years of employment, right before harvest, when Phillip knew Dad wouldn't have the time or the focus to catch up on all Phillip was leaving behind: managing the vehicles, monitoring the chemicals, wrapping up the post-harvest duties.

"Did you ask him to stay through October?" I said.

"He insisted he had to leave now. He'd packed up his desk already. He must have done it late last night."

"It's a relief," Mother said.

"It will be," said Dad. "It's just one more thing, you know." His boots were clean. His scalp had started to sweat in the hot kitchen. "Can I get some water?"

I filled a glass from the bottle on the counter. Fresno tap water causes cancer, which the city denies but everybody knows. Mother handed him his sandwich, and Dad picked out the arugula.

"You don't want the arugula?" said Mother.

"My stomach's weak," he said.

"Would you like an egg?" she said.

"I'd like this sandwich," he said.

I ate the arugula from the side of his plate with my fingers, piece by piece. "I love you, Dad."

"You want a job?" Dad said. "I have one that just opened up."

"Maybe," I said.

"Do you?'

"No," I laughed. "I wouldn't know where to start."

He took very small bites of the sandwich. "I don't know where to start most of the time, either," he said.

"Don't torment your father," Mother said. "Leave him alone, you'll get his hopes up." She brought a paper towel to the table, folded it into a triangle, and dabbed the sweat from Dad's hairline. "You wouldn't have told us at all if Marianela hadn't intervened, would you?" she asked him.

"I don't know," he said. "But I knew when I saw her that she'd come straight over here. Did she bring eggs?"

"Two dozen eggs," Mother said.

Dad laughed a little. "I knew she'd bring eggs."

"Why keep a secret like that, Ned?" She sat next to him at the table.

"It's not a secret. I want to protect you." He rubbed the orange dust further into his forehead.

"I'm already protected. I can protect myself." She touched his shoulder and found his neck. "This shirt is wearing a bit on the collar, Neddy."

"I don't want any new shirts."

"I don't want people to think I don't take care of you," she said. "When people see that shirt, they'll think I don't care."

"I like a shirt that's worn in," I said. I could see the orange ring on Dad's collar from where I was sitting. When I was tiny, television had me believing that ring-around-the-collar was the worst tragedy that could befall a person or family. Worse than any illness or car crash or war, ring-around-the-collar was something so awful, it could only be alluded to on TV. Later, the danger of ring-around-the-collar would be replaced by terror of something called acid rain. Even now, I don't know what acid rain means.

"Ingrid likes it," Dad said.

"You think I'm so fragile you can't tell me Phillip quit?" She sat gracefully at the table, deliberately as if to demonstrate she had a plain happiness inside.

"I know you're not fragile. I'm tired. I'm just tired."

"Don't torment my father," I said.

"Ingrid, would you go to Daddy's closet and find him a new shirt?"

"This shirt is fine."

"Please, Ned, change your shirt for me."

"Daddy can find his own shirt," I said.

She forced herself to be calm, I could see. The line appeared in the center of her forehead. She folded and unfolded her hands, as if waiting for cards to shuffle. She said to Dad, "How was your sandwich?"

"A little heavy on the mustard," he said.

"It's the same amount as always."

Dad said, "Inky, when was the last time you came to the office?"

"Christmas sometime," I said. "You let me store Anne's bicycle there." That was ten years ago, when I had the job in London, the last time I'd had enough income to buy elaborate Christmas presents: Loro Piana sweaters for Dad and Charlie and a copper stock pot for Mother and a pale blue beachcomber for Annie, who kept the bicycle in storage in anticipation of the Malibu summer cottage she intended to purchase, someday. Anne's storage unit was like a hope chest.

"You should come see the office."

"I will. We can go to the Vineyard for lunch."

"You could use Phillip's office while you're here," he said. "Keep me company."

"Who's going to keep me company?" Mother said.

"You warriors don't need company," Dad said, taking her hand, kissing her knuckles.

"I'm not a warrior," Mother said. "I'm just not as fragile as you think."

"Or as you look," I said.

"Do I look fragile?" she said. "I think I look quite tough."

"You do look tough," Dad said, smiling at her. "Tough and beautiful." They held hands on the table. He looked at me. "Your mother was the most gorgeous girl in the whole valley. And I got her."

"I'm still the most gorgeous girl," she said.

"Yes," said Dad, quite sincerely. "I thought that was too obvious to say."

When Mother remodeled the kitchen more than twenty years ago, she had done the counters and backsplashes in these white-and-blue hand-painted Portuguese tiles. They looked slightly dated now—Portuguese tile had been very popular for a while—but she'd been right about the white tiles. White tiles made everything cooler, fresher, easier to touch in the Central Valley heat, even at night. And hers had pretty little boats and fishermen drawn on them with a slender brush.

Dad stood to put his plate in the sink. He coughed and spit into the disposal. Mother winced and tried to hide her wince.

"I'm going to change this filthy shirt," he said.

"I didn't say it was filthy," Mother told him.

"I think it's filthy," he said. He spoke to us as he walked through the living room. "Farming is dirty."

11.

Clever Bootsie sent an e-mail with two photographs attached. "Here is a picture of an olive branch," she wrote beneath the first. "And see also attached, the image of a broken fence, next to a nice mended fence! Could you accept them?"

"That's a solid fence," I wrote back. We know our fences in the valley.

She wrote: "I have fritters."

It was afternoon. The orange light had started to come over the vineyards. I'd been lying in bed all day reading *Middlemarch*. *Middlemarch* is an excellent book for a hard time. It has all sorts of interesting things to say about love and change and small failures of character. It has this clever younger sister who gives excellent advice when the older sister's marriage starts to go wrong. There is so much to learn from *Middlemarch*.

The strong smell of rot came through the windows. Dad had gone back to the office, abandoning his rounds through the vineyards, something he rarely did in the afternoons. Mother retreated to her bedroom, where she closed the windows and the shades and put a free Lufthansa eye mask over her face, one of dozens she had purloined from stewardesses on international flights more than fifteen years ago.

I missed Bootsie, but with friendships as with cities, it's important to remember what caused you to flee. She had been a good friend to me for a long time, until she wasn't.

In New York, if Bootsie started wearing something (knee-high athletic socks, fur-trimmed collars, the color orange), the following year everyone would be wearing it. She knew the best restaurants before it became impossible to get reservations. To me and Anne and to George and to Hasso and to my heartbroken friend Gil, Bootsie was the most sophisticated and important person in the whole of the city, and we looked to her for guidance on how to exist in the world. The large, spiky personalities that go over well in New York don't always go over very well in a place like Fresno, a place that has very little patience for anything beyond the hills outside the valley. But Bootsie seemed to go over well everywhere. That summer, the tables at Bootsie's Quality Food and Beverage were frequently full, and there were always attractive people in expensive shoes standing outside smoking.

I phoned the restaurant.

"Come on in," she said. "No one's here yet and we're all lonesome."

"Lonesome?!" A restaurant staff is never lonesome. Restaurant work is a team sport.

"You should meet my little family here. Also I'm serving whole trout with roast potatoes done just like the English do them."

"In duck fat?"

"Duck fat is nearly impossible to find. I'm using a local chicken fat."

"Poor little chickens."

"People get crazy about ducks and geese, but not about chickens."

"Remember all those chickens in the river?" When we were in high school, the Masterson chicken plant, facing an unannounced inspection, had dumped thousands of sick birds into the San Joaquin. This was the same chicken plant that just a couple of years earlier had displaced twenty or thirty homes using eminent domain. Never had there been a clear argument that the Mastersons could make any money raising chickens.

"My brother was lifeguarding in Merced, remember? He had to pull them out of the lake with a rake." Bootsie stretched her curly curls straight out from her forehead.

"That was the vomit summer," I said.

"Yes! God, you remember everything." It was the summer I decided not to go back east to school, and awful things kept happening, especially to Fionn Calhoun. After the Masterson chickens incident, a drunk bather waded too far into the lake. He went under and didn't come up, and then vomited into Fionn's mouth as Fionn performed CPR.

"Will you really make fritters?"

"Fritters are always on the menu for you."

That year, everyone was in trouble with the banks, but plenty of people had the money to be eating at Bootsie's. It was her thorough Bootsieness, I decided: people wanted to be near her, hoped part of her charm and beauty and easy glamour might rub off on them, and eating in her restaurant was money invested in their cultural and culinary education.

"Are you going to move here?" Bootsie asked.

I sat at the bar with a copy of *The Paris Review*. I never read *The Paris Review* anywhere but California. In California, reading *The Paris Review* was a very good way to keep people from talking to you.

"I'm just here until I can bear going back to LA."

"Why not stay here, then?"

"I can't bear here, either."

"I used to think that."

"And what happened."

"It's easier to run Dad's businesses from here." She stood at the bar next to me but kept her eye on the door. Bootsie always kept her eye on the door.

"I thought you ran your own business."

"No, really Elliot does most of this."

The bartender was called Elliot and he wasn't bad to talk to. During the day he taught German at the city college.

"I mean, he does the ordering and the books," Bootsie said. "Right, Elliot?"

He said, "My parents had a restaurant." He polished water glasses behind the bar. Elliot was always busying himself with something: polishing glasses, refilling ice, wiping bottles. He had the rawboned physique of a person in constant motion.

Elliot always refilled my drink before I was nearly done. He'd pour wonderful things I'd never have known to ask for, like the Springbank whisky I learned to like too much or an 1899 Madeira Bootsie had found two cases of in her father's basement.

"This really should be opened with a blowtorch," he said, decanting the port into my glass through a kitchen strainer. The name and the year 1899 had been stenciled on the bottle in white paint. "The cork just disintegrates."

It was lovely, like a hard syrup, rich and sweet and slightly tangy.

I said, "Elliot, is that true? Do you run this place?"

"She tells me what to do and I do it," he said. One half of his face smiled. He wiped bottles even though he had poured hardly any drinks yet and the bottles were clean.

"You see," said Bootsie, "he's perfect."

"We shouldn't be drinking this," I said. "How much is this per glass?"

"This is not on the menu," said Bootsie. She got herself a rocks glass from behind the bar and Elliot poured her some. She swirled it like brandy. "Elliot, have one."

"Later."

"I wish I'd known he had this stuff, just so I could have asked him what he planned to do with it."

"He planned to drink it," I said.

"He planned to auction it," said Elliot. "He planned to auction a lot of things, including the land, including the paintings."

"What paintings?" I said, inelegantly.

"He had all these paintings," Bootsie said. "That idiot who wasn't impressed when I got the job at the *Times*."

"What paintings?" I said again.

"Minor American artists," Bootsie said.

Elliot said, "And minor works by major artists."

I said, "Where did you find them?"

"There was a Joseph Cornell ink-blot drawing," said Bootsie.

"There was a Joan Mitchell painting," Elliot said.

"There was a small Copley."

"Bootsie, there was a Hopper sketch. It wasn't minor."

"Anyway, there were all these pieces that told me basically nothing," Bootsie said.

"Where did he keep them?" I said.

"He must have had someone telling him what to buy, but I have no idea who that could have been, because he never spoke to me like a person. He never told me anything, apparently."

"You froze him out, too," Elliot said.

"Elliot," she said, raising her pointy hand as a shield, "you have no idea, so please be quiet now."

Elliot crossed the bar and began to polish the wineglasses.

Bootsie said, "In the basement, behind the cases of emergency water."

"The paintings?"

"Oh, the paintings," she said. "In the map drawer in his office. It never crossed my mind there might be more than just maps in that drawer." She poured more of the Madeira into her glass and mine. "Can you imagine, I study art my whole life, and he doesn't even tell me he's buying this stuff."

"Maybe it was a surprise," I said.

She smiled her wide, clear smile. "I love you. You are so generous." She shook her head. Wild curly wisps were escaping her rubber band. "Elliot's right, he intended to auction it. That's why he never told me about it."

"What did Fionn say?"

"Oh, poor Fionn. Fionn had no chance at not failing for my Dad. Fionn just lived up to my father's expectations."

"Fionn will be okay."

"No, I don't think he will be." She tapped a pencil on the bar as if tamping down a cigarette. "If I had been anyone else's daughter, if I had been you, he would have been really proud of me." The door swooshed and customers came in. "Hey!" she said, as if they had been friends a long time, the way she said "Hey!" to me.

I had my little Spring-issue *Paris Review* on the bar.

"You know, we make excellent ports in Madera," Elliot said.

"I know, I know." I had heard all my life about the excellent ports from Madera.

"It's the right climate. Same as the Portuguese climate."

Another group came in, and another group right behind them. Elliot seemed to become smaller the more people he had to serve. This was the opposite of what I had observed of bartenders in large cities, who thrived on the show.

"Yes." Suddenly the room seemed full, and all the seats at the bar were taken by three couples waiting for a fourth. Bootsie had set up a long table at the front. "I guess this is the busy hour," I said.

"After work. This is our after-work crowd. In a little while we'll get the fancy crowd, and they wear too much cologne, and then later we get the after-dinner crowd, and they're okay."

"This crowd?"

"This crowd I don't think knows about cologne." He laughed a little, a cold laugh that said there's no reason for laughing.

Bootsie's waitresses seemed to appear from nowhere. Bootsie leaned against a booth, languid, as if she'd been waiting all day for those people to come talk to her. "My father grows grapes," I said to Elliot.

"Oh," he said, in the polite way of gentle men. "What kind of grapes?"

"All kinds." Dad was, then, still one of the two or three largest growers in the valley. It was embarrassing to be such a failure when your father was such a success. "I mean in the context of port, that's why I know about the port in Madera."

"Right. Of course." He half smiled, kindly, his eyes behind me. "George," he said, extending his hand over the bar.

Bootsie had told me George wouldn't come in until later. "George," I said, turning toward him, no way to get out of it.

"Here we all are," said George, taking the stool next to me. George took up more space than he used to.

I said, "We have a George and we have an Elliot, and I've been reading *Middlemarch*."

Elliot poured George a glass of Famous Grouse, neat. When I'd known George previously, in high school and then college and then those painful couple of years after school was done, neither of us drank much. Now he'd become a more substantial man with a drink so well established he didn't have to ask for it. Even his hands were larger than they had been. Everything about George seemed expanded and grown up.

"I'm happy you're here," he said.

Although I wasn't drunk enough to say it, I said, "You broke my heart so badly that no one else can break it the same."

"I know," he said, inspecting his drink casually, as if this were what he had expected me to say. "Elliot," he called, "may I have a water back?"

"Mom tells me you got married," I said.

"I did."

Elliot filled the tall water glass. The soda gun was right in front of us. It takes surprisingly long to fill a water glass.

I said, "Bootsie says that you're not married anymore." Where had Bootsie gone? She was off on the other side of the room, thirty feet away, practicing her laugh and cheekbones on a chiropractor and his wife.

"I'm not."

"How was that?"

"It was okay. I did love Ellie." He drank the whole glass of water in one go. "Also, I did what my mother wanted me to do."

"I mean what happened?"

"If I start at the beginning," he said, then stopped. "If I start at the beginning, I won't know where to start."

"Start at the end." I knew him so well, I knew exactly where he wanted to start this story of his marriage. I knew he would start with a very specific detail of a morning she was cruel, how her cruelty stunned him like a slap, and how that morning was the beginning of the end, as they say, as I say. No one changes. George is always the last to know something is wrong. Unless he's with me; then I'm the last to know.

"In San Francisco, her mother started introducing me as just George, instead of Ellie's husband, George. And her father was suddenly real nice to me, but he'd never been real nice to me before." He clicked the top of his lighter open and closed, open and closed. "And then one day we had this fight, this little fight about shampoo. I would always use her shampoo as soap. I don't know, it drove her crazy but I liked the smell. I didn't realize how expensive the shampoo was. The last fight is always a stupid fight, right?"

"It's the only fight we remember."

He liked that. He gave me his lippy grin. "You remember what you remember."

"I remember it all."

"No."

"Oh, yes."

"It was harvest so I had been out almost all night long, and she hadn't gone to tennis, she'd waited for me to come back. I hadn't been to sleep yet and the whole thing felt like a nightmare, and for two days after she left I thought maybe I'd had a nightmare." He stopped for a while. We watched Elliot whisk the frozen mojitos in a large steel mixing bowl. The happy noise of the restaurant started to feel like a party. "She waited for harvest, I think, because she knew I'd be too tired to fight it." Then he thought and said, "Not two days. For months I woke up thinking maybe I'd had a nightmare."

"It's harvest now," I said.

"Harvest of what? It's always harvest."

"How many years ago was this?"

He looked at me a little surprised that I didn't already know. "Last year," he said. "Last fall. Like five minutes ago."

It seemed so soon. It seemed almost as recent as my own

breakup. "Did you really love her?" I couldn't imagine someone as delicious and intuitive and hilarious and kind as George actually loving that normal, dumb Ellie Prentiss.

He tapped his empty glass on the bar. "I wasn't just faking."

I put my hand over his, of course. I knew how stupid it made you feel to be so surprised by an ending. And then I had to bite his shoulder, so I bit his shoulder. That beautiful shoulder, it felt just exactly the same, but with more meat on it.

12. Inevitably, August came, and the grapes continued to hang. They were spectacularly beautiful, full to bursting, as if with just the slightest tap they could explode. The Fiestas were past ready, the sugar was high, too high for table grapes, but apparently they were using anything to make wine these days. Bunches at the top of the vines had started to shrivel. They'd get picked any day, Dad said. When to pick grapes is not a choice the farmer makes. The buyer decides when to pick, and then the buyer buys by weight. This is why people hate selling to Mello, and why they hated selling to Uncle Felix. Mello and Uncle Felix paid in full upon delivery, while smaller producers paid on highly variable and often unreliable payment schedules. But both Felix and Mello had reputations for letting grapes hang until the juice was overly sweet and the fruit weighed slightly less. Or they would find rot where there had been no rot and pay less than what they'd contracted to pay. Sometimes, last minute, they wouldn't buy the fruit at all.

Table grapes in wine. I hadn't decided yet whether I thought this brilliant or disgraceful. It gives the grower more options for sale, at any rate. A grower wants options, like anyone.

"Felix leaves the call to his field guy," Dad said repeatedly that season.

The longer those grapes stayed on the vine, the worse Dad's cough got.

"Please see someone about the cough," I said. The cough couldn't be contained by covering his mouth with his hand. With his napkin he wiped little specks of spittle from his place at the breakfast table.

"It always gets worse later in the summer," he said. "The air gets drier and there's more dust."

Mother said, "None of that is true. Do you make this up as you go along?"

"There is more dust," Dad said.

This was true about the dust, but not about his cough and not about the field guy. Dad's cough was usually worse in the fall, when the rain came and the dirt got wet. Felix never left the call to his field guy. No one ever left the call to his field guy. The real guys made the call and stayed in the office; the field guys were just there to get yelled at by the farmers. We all knew this. I had known this since I was seven.

I knew a lot when I was seven. By the time I was seven, I could prune a vine better than anyone else on the ranch. I knew when the sap started to drip from pruned branches that the buds were about to break, and I could time just about down to ten days when we'd be harvesting that fall. Pretty much everything I knew about farming I had learned by the second grade.

Over the phone Anne said, "Get in the car and take him by force to have a chest X-ray. You have to stop giving him choices." Anne could say these things from Los Angeles. "This is what we call, in the industry, denial." Anne thought everything in life happened as it did in her life in cartoons: we'd just have a friendly argument and someone would make an idiotic joke and Dad would get in the car for the drive into town for a chest X-ray with a laugh track. In real life, she must have known, there was no possibility of Dad seeing the doctor until Dad decided on his own to see the doctor. Farmers choose farming because they don't like being told what to do.

I said, "Okay, Annie. We'll see."

She said, "Your name should be Willsee."

"Okay."

"Do I have to do absolutely everything in this family?"

Now Dad sat at the breakfast table with his lightly browned toast and butter, eating little bites between large coughs. "I will go," he said. "Once the harvest is complete."

"That's October," Mother said. "You can't wait until October. You can barely eat toast."

"I like toast," Dad said.

"What will you be eating by October?" Mother said.

"Toast," said Dad. "More and more toast."

"You think you're being very funny," Mother said. "When I try to be serious, you joke."

"Don't be serious," Dad told her. "It doesn't do us any good."

The beginning of August means not only certain harvests (late stone fruit, green grapes, early almonds), but, equally as important in the valley, the start of Fresno State football. Wilson had been a middle linebacker at San Joaquin Memorial High School and his greatest pleasure, outside of the golf club, was Fresno State football. Every Tuesday and Thursday afternoon of the fall, Wilson took his flask to the Fresno State practice field, surrounded on two sides by the Fresno State vineyards, to sit on the metal bleachers he called the happiest place on earth.

It kind of was. Fresh and open and empty with athletes smashing.

"Next time I'm going to bring a flask for you, too," he said.

"Make sure mine has a little lemonade in it."

He held out a bag of sunflower seeds, which I waved away. He said, "I have pistachios. Do you want pistachios?"

"Pistachios are too much work."

"That's your problem, Ingrid."

"I don't have a problem."

"Uninterested in getting the nut meat."

"You're a nut meat," I said.

I joined him for a few practices that season, because in an effort to distract myself from my various failures, I had begun to develop a sort of academic interest in college football. I told myself it was intellectual and not just a form of procrastination. I told myself I might even use this interest somehow, find a way to shoehorn it into the genocide screenplay. Wilson wasn't bad company. He knew a lot about the game and the players. It felt good, at the end of that unhappy summer, to sit on bleachers watching practice next to someone I knew would never not be waiting for me.

"I don't know why you keep asking," he said, cracking sunflower seeds and letting the shells fly with spit and a whistle. "There's nothing to tell you. Everything will be fine when the money from the grapes comes in." Wilson knew more about my parents' personal and professional finances than probably even my parents did.

"But what if the money from the grapes doesn't come in?"

"They're contracted to Felix, Inky. Don't worry about it."

"But say they don't weigh as much as we thought."

"Have you seen the cab? They're beautiful. And there's a lot of fruit. It's why it's taking the sugar so long to develop."

"Don't speak to me like an idiot." I had seen the cabernet. I couldn't remember a year the vines were so full. In the Central Valley, unlike Napa and Sonoma, farmers don't traditionally prune bunches to make room for sunlight. They just let every bunch grow and grow. The weight of the grapes is more valuable than the flavor.

"Look at that running back. He's shorter than you, Inky, but he'll be one of the best in the nation this year."

"Which one."

"The short one."

"But why are the banks so relentless right now?"

"Things are bad."

"Things are bad every year."

"It's bad this year, Ingrid. A grape glut after that thing with the peaches. The peach thing was the problem. A lot of people are going to lose their farms."

"But not Dad."

"I told you. How many times do you want me to repeat myself?"

"All right. I know."

"Look at that run! He's so good because he can keep so low to the ground. You can't tackle him."

He was good, Fresno's little running back. But the season hadn't started yet and you had to wonder how good he would look against a better defense. "I mean, why would Phillip leave like that, so suddenly?"

"Ingrid, your dad knows what he's doing."

"Not always," I said.

"Most of the time."

The quarterback was good, too. He was the skinny younger brother of Norbert Wabnig, a Fresno State legend and former number one draft pick, now sidelined somewhere in Dallas or Houston, or maybe Denver. I am always a sucker for the quarterback. It's adult compensation for being too much of a misfit in high school.

"You think he should get a lawyer?"

Wilson shrugged. "A lawyer can't do him any good. Just wait until the juice gets sold. Why are you worrying about this?"

"I'm not worried."

"Worry about yourself," he said, which was not an idiotic thing to say.

"Don't tell me what to do."

I have always liked the uniquely American crash and smack sound of helmets and pads after the staccato of the quarterback shouting to his team. College football was another glamorous part of regular suburban life I could study but knew nothing about, and now enjoyed being close to: all those beautiful young men suffering the destruction of their minds and bodies to do what it is they love the most. We all do that in our way, suffer if we can find something to love.

Little brother Wabnig wore number 2, which I couldn't help but feel, then, was just too painful a cliché to even digest.

"Will you shell me a pistachio?" I said.

"My goodness. What do you want from me?"

"Nothing."

"I know," Wilson said. "Which is kind of funny, because I want a lot from you." He pried open a pistachio and put the meat in my hand.

And then, just beyond the noise of the practice field, was the silence of the vineyards, with all that promise, food and booze and livelihood grown on plants, inescapable even for Norbert Wabnig's little brother or for a short running back, best in the nation.

"When did Dad get so overleveraged?" I said.

"When everybody did. When did he buy all those ranches by the river?"

I hadn't been certain until right then that Dad was over-leveraged at all. I knew he'd borrowed against his harvest, as all farmers do, but I didn't realize until that afternoon at the football practice, until Wilson let it slip, that Dad hadn't bought his land outright, or that his debt had lasted longer than a couple of seasons. "I guessed that he paid for all that land with his own money," I said.

"It is his own money," Wilson said. "What are you talking about?"

"I mean I didn't know he'd borrowed anything."

"God, you're out of touch," he said, and looked at me with his fat pink face, his moist, close-cropped hair all pale and spiky as if he'd been electrified. "I don't even grasp what you're saying."

Dad must have got overleveraged twenty years before, when he started buying all the cheap land that no one else knew was any good. As the land got more valuable, he could buy more on the cheap side, still soil worth more than anyone knew at the time. I had known all this for a long while. But Anne and I had always assumed Dad bought this land with the Napa money, the money from his cabernet.

At some point last year with the water restrictions and then a Malaysian strain of fruit flies and then a light but destructive late summer rain and then this year's unprecedented peach fungus and now a bit of a glut for common grapes, the banks began to call in the loans.

"Is all the land in debt?"

"Land in debt? Inky, make sense."

"How much does Dad owe?"

"Oh yeah," Wilson said, "all of it." He spat sunflower shells and then looked at me with his stupid, plain look. "I guess if you don't know that already I'm not supposed to tell you."

"I did know," I fabricated a little. "I'm just making conversation."

"Uncle Ned doesn't have to worry. What would the bank do with all that land? There's no one to buy it."

"But seriously," I said, "do you just tell anyone who asks whatever they want to know?"

Wilson cracked a seed and spit the shell. He didn't answer me. Crack, spit. Crack, spit. The crash of pads and helmets, the far-off yelling of the coaches down the field on the opposite sideline.

"I know you're the town cryer," I said.

The banks only ever called in loans from the small farmers. Then they gave that land for cheap to the big players: Uncle Felix, Mello, Paramount. Dad would have been one of those big players, too, but he didn't need a bank to tell him which land was undervalued. Dad didn't have time for things like being on the board, endowments, trusteeships for Fresno State or Davis or USC. He never went to the society wine auctions in Napa. He knew nothing about "marketing to the consumer." The things he should have been bothering with, Dad paid no attention. All his attention was on the land.

Wilson said, "I'd be so good to you, Inky. I'd take care of you."

"You've said that before." I accepted a swig from his flask. "It's getting tiresome."

13. The Palamede Farms offices were constructed, loft-like, on the upper half of the lot and warehouse that stored the trucks and harvesters. Through large windows you could, through a film of dust, look out from your desk to see tractors coming and going. Part of Dad's business for the past several years had been renting equipment to smaller farmers. This was something Phillip had taken care of.

"Where's Miguel's office?" I said.

"Miguel?"

"Where does Miguel work?"

"Miguel doesn't have an office," Dad said.

"Phillip needs an office but Miguel doesn't?"

"Miguel likes to do his work in the field."

"How does he keep track of everything?"

"How do you? Paper, your head."

"No," I said. "I don't keep track of anything on paper."

Phillip's office was cold and dark and empty, and I wrote perfectly there. Too perfectly. In ten days I finished my screenplay—it was a very silly screenplay—and used Dad's FedEx account to send it off to the foundation that had given me the money.

"Didn't Phillip have a computer?"

"He kept records on paper, too." He nodded toward a stack of binders on an extra chair against the wall.

"What is all that?"

"Invoices, work orders, contracts. I haven't gone through it entirely." Dad scraped dry skin off his lower lip with his thumb.

"This is a mess."

"It's fine, Inky. We'll get to it after the harvest."

"Let me create a database for you."

He nodded toward the chair. "You go ahead. Make something of those records, will you?"

Databases I could do. I knew databases from every assistant job I ever had.

Phillip's records were a catastrophe, scattered and incomplete, probably deliberately kept to confuse. There was no way to tell, for example, whether an invoice had been paid and when, how long farmers had had equipment, or which farmers had which trucks at the moment. There was no record of when Palamede had used vehicles and equipment and when trucks were used by other operations. This was information Phillip kept in his head, I suppose. I opened a simple series of spreadsheets and began entering information as I found it. Possibly an order would emerge. I didn't have much hope. Stupid people could be so clever. Phillip had been more of a disaster than I knew.

The cool of the air-conditioning had been set on high, too high, so that condensation blew from the vents in the floors and ceilings, and these sad laminate-wood-paneled rooms with the big dirty windows were quite chilly, almost to the point of discomfort.

The discomfort of the air-conditioning made me feel at home, sort of like the forced heat inside German buildings at the nadir of winter had made me feel at home. Maybe it's just the discomfort itself that seemed so familiar.

Here in Dad's ordinary office with the California Ag Grower of the Year award yellowing in the frame on the wall, the California Grape Growers tear-off desk calendar ready to be torn on every day of the week, the stapler made to look like a bunch of grapes, and those stacks and stacks of completely miscalculated and discombobulated and sneakily manipulated files, for the first time in a long time I had something to do. Inside that icebox of a loft-office, I was necessary. I was useful.

The raisin guys were cutting canes, so those machines were all rented out. We hadn't produced raisins for many years, so I started by trying to document that equipment: who had the harvesters and who had the cane cutters, which machines were going where in just the next two weeks. Phillip had scribbled records and reservations on the backs of receipts, on invoices for fertilizer, and occasionally on a more cohesive list he kept at the front of the newest binder. Phillip's system, if he'd had a system, made no sense.

"You want a job?" Dad asked from the doorway.

"Please don't ask me that again."

"I've got to pay someone to do this, and you're doing it." Dad ruffled his hair all over his head, like a happy dog, like a human being unable to contain his excitement that his dreams could possibly, with love and willingness, come true. There wasn't so much hair to ruffle—it came up in these lovely generous wisps of dry curls along the sides. Daddy is so handsome, but his hair disappeared anytime things got stressful. Hair is so unfaithful! (So is health.)

From the Formica wood-grain desk I could see the machines used for picking up the trays parked at the edge of the warehouse. Those vehicles wouldn't go out for another two or three weeks. Eleven pickup machines. "Do you have the same number of harvesters and cane cutters as you do pickup machines?"

"We bought those in clean sets as we needed them. I think we might have an extra pickup tractor."

"You might?" Pickup tractors retrieved the dried raisins from the ground.

"For the years the weather looked like changing and we needed to pick up quick." Dad loved to talk about the machines almost as much as he loved to talk about the fruit itself. He'd grown up pruning and caning and harvesting by hand; now there were trucks to do all of that, in a tenth the time. "Those machines shred the paper after drying, so the farmer doesn't have to burn anything. They just disk the trays back into the ground." As with the land, Dad had been one of the earliest to realize which technologies would work. Some people would call him an early adopter, but I'd call him a visionary. There was no doubting Dad's genius.

"I don't know how to find records of which equipment you have. Do you have in your head all the machines you own?"

"Let's get some lunch." He tapped his knuckles against the door frame. "Let's go see the boys at the Vineyard."

We walked down through the warehouse. The old dust made me sneeze and sneeze, the kind of sneezes that make you momentarily blind: full blow-out sneezes in shades of white and yellow. The first sneeze made my hand completely wet. Dad always carried tissues in his pocket. He handed me a fresh one without remarking.

"You want me to come work with you, but you can't answer half my questions," I said. I wiped my hand with Dad's tissue.

"You have a lot of questions." The seats in the pickup were sticky-hot to the touch. "We'll find the records we need, Ingrid. Right now I need to get through the harvest. If we can't rent out the trucks this year, we won't rent the trucks. Why don't we just give 'em to people when they call?"

"Is that how you run this operation?"

My father's face was soft and stuffed pink with wine, but it was exactly the kind of face I knew a person could trust. He had a gentle, round face, a high-cheekboned and open-eyed face, which I have read is scientifically trustworthy.

"A lot of guys are going to make raisins last minute. Mello's coming in with an offer of two fifty a ton for juice. That's a hundred less than last year."

"What about you, why don't you make some raisins?" I said.

"I've got a contract with Felix."

"Felix is going to get all the Thompsons he needs. He doesn't need your Thompsons."

"I've got a contract. We honor our contracts." He wiped dust from the dashboard with a handkerchief from his pocket. With the drought, there was more dust everywhere, constantly. "Some guys are delivering their crop to the wineries without a firm price. We have a firm price."

"A firm price on small grapes with not enough acid, if he keeps letting them hang."

"The grapes are fine, Inky."

"Annie doesn't trust Uncle Felix."

"Annie's spent too much time in Hollywood."

I did love lunch at the Vineyard in Madera, where all the farmers eat. When I was little, during school breaks, Dad would take us there on days he let us ride with him in the truck. I had a pair of embroidered pink cowboy boots we'd bought at the Golden Stallion on Blackstone, and I thought all you needed to really care for the land was an eye for broken irrigation lines and a pair of good boots.

Even now, the Vineyard felt like entering a special adult world understood only by the gruff men who inhabited the place, a secret society of farmers and the structure around them. The parking lot was full of clean white pickups.

Jack McGourty sat at the bar, with no one next to him. All the men in here had known Jack as long as they'd known anyone, but Jack was an insurance adjuster and a Democrat and so he sat by himself.

Jim Demerjian, the state assemblyman, and Gale Macpherson, former Kingsburg High quarterback and scion of three thousand acres of pistachios, sat at a circular table in the middle of the bar room. Nick Angelico was there too, the box manufacturer who had extorted his daughter to dump her girlfriend and return home, and Harry Cline, who grew a couple thousand acres of grapes and ran Cline Packing.

"You want to eat in the restaurant or the bar?" Dad said.

When I was a little girl, we always ate in the restaurant, with its white tablecloths and red leather armchairs. "I want to eat with the boys."

The bar was dark wood with no tablecloths and it smelled slightly of the cigars that had been smoked just outside.

The boys all raised their hands to Dad. Gale tipped his cowboy hat and stood to pull out my chair. "Living proof that farming's getting younger," Jim said.

"I'm just visiting," I said.

Harry Cline laughed that deep, rough farmer laugh, a laugh with dust in it. "They all come back," he said. "Right, Nick?"

"All you kids come back."

"If labor stays twelve dollars an hour, you'll all come back to build shopping malls," Gale said. Gale, still tall and broad, still held his team together like a quarterback.

Dad said, "Not this one."

"I'm not the shopping mall type," I said. "I'd rather see crops."

Nick said, "Have the salmon, Ned. I caught it myself last week." Other men, men with far less money than Nick Angelico, came back from fishing trips to Alaska and made gifts to their friends of long salmon filets. Nick Angelico was so cheap that he traded salmon he caught fishing in Alaska to the Vineyard for a dining credit.

"Jim was giving us a finance lesson," said Harry.

"Oh good," said Dad. "Politicians have such a firm grasp of money." He gave Jim's shoulder a pat. These guys depended on Jim for water from the state.

"He says we all ought to be drying our grapes," Harry said.

"Turkey had more than three hundred tons of raisins last year," Jim said. "They've got just under half that this year, and that's a huge opportunity for us in Europe."

"Us," said Dad. "You growing grapes, Jimmy?" The Demerjians had always been lawyers, not farmers.

"Doesn't make a lot of sense to harvest green," Jim said.

"You have something against wine?" said Dad.

"I have an interest in you boys making money," Jim said.

"Ingrid, what do you think?" Harry said.

"I think you guys should lay out half your crop."

"Ah, Ingrid likes to diversify," said Gale, leaning far back in his chair and crossing his big arms over that huge football chest.

"Higher risk, lower reward," Harry said, shaking his head, waving me away. "Two labor crews, two sets of machines. You don't diversify one crop."

"I would," I said. "Mello's tanks are still full from last year. Isn't that right, Dad?"

"And juice from overseas," Dad said.

"Still, Griffith is buying your juice. So why lay out to dry?" Harry said.

"Just in case," I said.

Harry laughed his rough laugh again. "You'll learn," he said.

"All right," I said. "Wait until the wineries start cutting off your deliveries."

Gale said, "How do you know so much, city girl?" Gale had that trace of a southern accent some have in the Central Valley, even when their families have been here four generations.

"I'm not all city," I said, patting Dad's hand. Dad had that subtle grin on his face I know is actually a huge, wide smile. He squeezed the tips of my fingers.

Then Nick said, "Griffith take that farm manager off your hands, Ned?"

The waitress set a plate of poached salmon in front of Dad. "Take what?" he said.

"Your farm manager. Felix says that guy was destroying you."

"Felix says that?" Dad picked up his fork but didn't eat.

"Says he brought him over to the winery so he couldn't do you any more damage."

"You believe everything Felix tells you?" Dad said.

Harry said, "You believe anything that guy tells you?"

Nick said, "I'm just repeating what I heard."

"Felix has a lot to say," Dad said. "Not all of it is worth repeating."

Every memory has a flavor, and that moment tastes like cold poached Alaskan salmon. That memory smells like cigars and grease.

"Can I eat your salmon?" I said.

Dad pushed the plate toward me. "Looks like Wabnig's filled out this year," he said toward Gale, toward Jim.

Nick continued, "Any way you like, it didn't take long for that guy to get a position with Griffith."

"Strong receivers, a strong running back," said Gale. "We might do something this year."

"You're right about the raisins," Dad said later, in the car on the way back home. "But we won't work that way. We stick to our contracts."

We had gone back to the office to get Phillip's records, which Dad now wanted to see. "I know, Daddy. I understand you. I was just talking."

"Integrity does count, especially on the land. You can't have integrity on the land if you haven't got it in your life."

"Yes, Dad."

"We'll rent those machines this year."

"Sure you will."

"Will you help me out with that?"

"I can help you."

He had his hands centered on the steering wheel. His mobile rang in the console, and he let it ring. "Do you think Felix really hired Phillip?" he said.

The question made me queasy. Dad never asked me questions about business, about instinct. He had been ignoring my opinions about Phillip for years. "I don't think it matters."

"He knows he's not doing me a favor," Dad said.

"He did know," I said, stumbling over whether I believed this myself, "he did know Phillip was stealing from you. Everyone knew that."

He nodded a half nod, a nod that says maybe. "I'm tired," he said. We turned left off Avenue 7, up the gravel road that led to the house. We drove over the canal and through the always-open iron gates. The red stone of the house looked an electrified orange in the evening light, just as the architect had planned thirty years ago. Light doesn't change as a landscape can, as landscapes do.

As we approached the carport, we could see Mother in the kitchen, washing lettuce. Dad coughed and spat into the handkerchief he kept in his pocket. "All right." He wiped his mouth. "There's a lot more dust, but this weather is good for the grapes." His face was sweating.

Mother came to the door. "Hello, little family." She had an honest smile, a real smile, the kind of smile we didn't see from Mother too often. She stepped toward the car and kissed Dad. "Hello, love." She put her hand on his face. "Are you warm?"

"I'm happy," he said. He held her, right there in the dust of the carport. The screen door swayed open.

"I've washed lettuce and sliced apples," she said, her face tucked into his shoulder. "And we have the first of Walter's almonds. Won't that make a nice salad? Would you like a salad, Neddy?"

His cough started before he spoke. He unwound himself from her wiry body, kissed the pointy shoulders beneath her white sundress, and stepped up into the house. He coughed into the sink.

"It's the pollen," Mother said. "Come inside." She put her arm on my waist as I came around the car. "It makes me so happy to see you here, in this truck with your father."

"I'm glad, Mom."

She lowered her voice. "It makes him happy, too, Inky. Has he told you that?"

"Sure."

"It's good to see him happy, isn't it?"

I said to her then, on the step, before we went inside, "It was Uncle Felix who hired Phillip away from Dad."

She looked at me as if I had insulted her. "Why would you say that?"

"We were at the Vineyard and Nick Angelico couldn't wait to tell us," I said. "He was just seething with gossip. He's a stereotypical small-town troublemaker."

"Is it true?"

The air across the vineyards was hazy with dust. Nothing moved. "I can imagine it being true. Why not?"

She went completely still. "What is he doing?" she said. "Why is he doing this?"

"Who, Felix?"

"Felix knows Daddy needs Phillip after the harvest. He knows he needs Phillip to rent out the trucks." Mother whispered now.

"The rentals aren't complicated. I can do that."

"He's coming over in a bit. Isn't he? Felix?"

"I don't know," I said. "Dad's tired."

"Neddy?" Mother called into the kitchen. Dad had walked right through and gone to his room. "Neddy?" The dust floated around us, unsettled. The dust coated Mother's hotel slippers brown-orange. "Come in," she said, holding the door wide for me. "It's too hot." She latched the screen so it would stay put.

Dad lay on his bed, watching the ceiling, the back of his hand on his forehead. "Could you close the windows and turn on the air?" he said.

"One night of air-conditioning is a good idea," Mother said.

"The pollen's heavy," Dad said.

"Should we tell Uncle Felix not to come?"

"I just need a rest before dinner," Dad said.

Mother said, "Call him, Inky, will you?"

"No," said Dad. "I want to see Felix."

Felix came at seven, the hour he usually did, and rang the kitchen bell. "You've got the house all closed up," he said when I answered the door. "I thought we were conserving energy around here. Open those windows and turn off the air."

"Nothing moves this time of year," I said. "The air won't move through the windows."

"Feels nice with the air on, though, doesn't it?" He handed me a bottle of wine, holding it by the neck. "This one's not cheap," he said.

"Shall I open it now?"

"Ask your dad. What's he got planned to drink?"

"Daddy doesn't feel well."

"I'm all right," Dad said, coming through the dining room, taking a seat at the kitchen table. "I'm just tired of being hot at night." He had changed his wet work shirt and put on clean boots.

Felix said, "Neddy, you owe me money."

"How's that?" Dad said.

"The change machine at the car wash ate my five dollars."

Dad owned a coin-operated car wash between Fresno and Madera. It had been his father's idea of diversifying. He took five dollars out of his pocket and handed it to Felix. "They keep telling me they've fixed that."

Felix fit the bill into his money clip carefully between the tens and the ones. "You want to open that?" Felix said.

"Do you want me to?" I asked him.

"What kind of question is that?"

"What kind of question is open that?" I said. "It's a demand, not a question."

He gave me a long, mean look, a surprised look. "What kind of conversation is this?"

I said, "It's just a bottle of wine, Felix. It doesn't even matter if we drink it or not."

He nodded his head at me, slowly. "Yes, I'd like you to open it," he said. "If you would like to open it."

I took tumblers out of the cabinet. There was now just the sound of cabinet doors and the squeaky twist of the wine key into the cork. I poured the wine and brought the filled glasses to the table. "Water?" I said. No one answered, so I put a bottle of water on the table. We rarely used separate glasses for water. When we wanted water, we'd finish the wine and use the same glass.

"Neddy," Felix said, "I guess you know now Phillip came to work for me."

"I guess I do," Dad said.

"He came to me looking. He was going to go somewhere, and this way I could get him away from your operation sooner than later."

"It would have been nice to have him at my operation through the harvest," Dad said.

"Who knows all the ways that kid is stealing from you?"

"He's not done with the finances from the peach season."

"Ned, I'm going to say something to you." Felix folded his hands on the table and leaned forward, looking Dad hard in the eye. "I'm going to be frank now. You can't afford to have anyone stealing from you this year. I know that, and you know that." Now he was pointing. He folded his hands again, to keep them from seeming aggressive. "I did what you weren't doing, what you needed to do."

"Don't tell me what I need to do, Felix."

Mother had pinned her hair into a twist and worn a bit of makeup: dark shadow in the creases of her eyelids, fresh false eyelashes, a swipe of blue-red on her lips. She wore that pretty white sundress and flitted into the kitchen, looking like an angel. "Felix," she said, "I have the first almonds of the season. Would you like a bit of salad? We're having salad. It's too hot for anything but salad." She kissed Dad on his crown, put her hand on his neck.

"Sure, yes," Felix said.

"I'm so glad!" Mother said. "You hardly ever eat with us, Felix."

I finished my wine and poured water.

"It's business," Dad said, softening. "I know. It's just business."

"And friendship, too," Felix said. "I know this is rough. It's a rough year for everyone, and looks like it's getting rougher."

"Right," Dad said.

Felix said, "You can't have a thief like that in charge of anything in a rough year, Ned. He's been pocketing half of whatever you think you've made from those trucks and pickers. What has he told you you've made?"

"I don't know," Dad said.

"What's the general idea?"

"I don't have a general idea. It's the beginning of the harvest."

Felix looked at me, at Mom, to see if Dad was joking. "You trust Phillip to keep all those numbers straight, not to skim? Just tell you what you've made?"

"It's fine, Felix," said Dad. "Everything is fine."

"I did you a bigger favor than I thought," Felix said, drinking half the tumbler of wine in one swig. He left sweaty fat fingerprints all over the glass.

"We allow you every license, Felix." Mother's hand rested on Felix's thick shoulder, thin and delicate as a sparrow. It was evening and still 110 degrees outside. Inside the air was on and the house was as cool as that house could get. He looked up at her, as if waiting for something else. There was nothing else.

It was always coolest in the kitchen, because of the trellis outside the window and because of the cold, hard Portuguese ceramic tile.

14. Bootsie bit into an apricot. It was so perfectly ripe, she had to slurp. A dollop of pink nectar slopped down her chin. "Such a mess," she said, leaning over the bar sink, running water, wiping off her face. "Eat one," she said. A bowl of them had been set out on the bar.

"I've been eating them hot off the tree," I said.

In the kitchen, a very short sous chef sliced apricots carefully in half and layered them into ramekins. He worked with his face close to what he was doing. He wore a red bandana, and I worried slightly if this might be a bad idea for a cook with an open kitchen in a small town nationally famous for its gang activity.

There were peppers roasting and a tray of garlic baking. It was early, 5:00 p.m., before Bootsie had unlocked the front door and two hours before the first reservation. She slurped the second half of the apricot and threw the pit in the sink. Bootsie said, "I don't know how the apricots survived whatever killed all the peaches."

"Good news for the almonds, though," I said.

"Thank God. The almond guys are thanking God."

"And olives, too, I guess."

This is the restaurant-bar chitchat of central California.

I'd come right from Dad's office, where I'd spent the day with Phillip's papers, trying to work out what money we'd made from the machines, if we'd made any money at all, and sorting chemical and fertilizer records from the business with the rentals. Phillip's papers were so exhausting, it was impossible to look at them for longer than eight hours. I took an apricot so ripe it had to be held very gently.

"I guess," she said. She rinsed her hands and wiped her mouth with a new bar towel. "Olive is a nice name for a girl."

"My back is strong," I sang. "My name is Peeaaches!" In New York, Bootsie and I had listened almost exclusively to Nina Simone's greatest hits, over and over on repeat for months.

"If I have a little girl, I'm going to call her Peaches. For you," she said.

"If I have a little girl, I'm going to call her Bootsie Calhoun," I said.

"Funny." She filled a wineglass with club soda and poured several dashes of bitters on top. "You want a drink?"

I watched her punch the bitters down into the soda with a straw, and the whole drink dissolved into brown-red. "Oh my," I said, realizing.

She looked at me, sipping from the cocktail straw, and then she took the straw out to chew it. "I know," she said, chewing the straw with her front teeth, shaking her head. "I know. You're the first, but everyone's going to figure it out if I stop drinking completely."

"I can't believe that."

"What's not to believe?"

"Is it Elliot?"

"Of course. Don't be an asshole." There was the clank of trays in the kitchen, the scrape of a spatula. The small chef had finished with apricots and begun to peel roasted garlic.

"This is the best thing that could have happened," I said. "Everyone but you can see you're in love with him."

"I don't know about love," she said. "I'm not in love."

She would not put on her wide smile. I tugged, gently, one of her blond spirals. "You," I said.

"I don't know how I'm going to begin to explain this to people."

"Who do you have to explain to?"

"My brother," she said, her mouth wobbling into a grimace. Bootsie rarely mentioned her brother. "Plus all my customers who think they know me."

"Everyone in town knows you guys are sleeping together."

"Fucking," she said. "Everyone in town knows we are fucking."

"There's no such thing as a secret in this town."

"Why, what happened to you?"

"You're infatuated, then. That can lead to love, you know."

"I'm not infatuated," she said. "He's just really great in bed. He smells good and he's into stuff I'm into."

"Well, this is good news," I said.

"It's really good news," said Bootsie. "I've met someone who doesn't make me reflexively want to get an abortion."

"Where is he?"

She laughed. "I think it makes him feel funny to have knocked up the boss." At the bar, she lit up a cigarette and sprayed water into a rocks glass for the ashes. "He said he has to stay in tonight and grade papers. Suddenly there are a lot of papers to grade." She shook her head. Bootsie took almost nothing very seriously.

"Don't smoke," I said.

"Don't be so bossy," she said. "You were always bossy, Ingrid Palamede."

"But come on."

"All our mothers smoked an occasional cigarette," she said, voice down, as if the kitchen staff might hear her. "You were born with all your limbs, weren't you?"

It was never any use arguing with Bootsie, or even making observations. Suggesting Bootsie might do one thing would ensure she did the other. "I did have childhood scoliosis," I told her. "And allergies." My mother's smoking had been limited to Aunt Jane's party-time extras.

"Correlation is not cause," she said. "You should read up a bit on Hitler and his position on smoking. Then talk to me about having a couple of cigarettes."

"What did he say?"

"Hitler?"

"What did Elliot say when you told him?"

"Maybe he went numb." She squinted at me a little. "Get yourself a drink. I hate when people sit at my bar and don't drink."

"A baby." I went behind the counter and poured myself a glass of wine from an open bottle in the refrigerator. "It's almost like you're an adult."

"I know!" she said, inhaling. "Good thing my father died before he could lose all his money."

"Or have any other children."

"God, really, we're all so fertile," she said, exhaling a straight stream of smoke toward the tile that spelled BOOTSIE's. She dropped the cigarette into the glass. "There," she said. "Half."

"Have you told anyone? Does George Sweet know this yet? Does your staff? Don't tell anyone you're pregnant until you quit smoking."

She pinched my arm and came close. "Did you come here to

see George Sweet?" she whispered. Her breath smelled like apricots and fresh cigarettes.

"I came to see you."

She gave me a long left-eyed wink. Bootsie could wink slowly or quickly without moving any other part of her face, like a cartoon. "I'm not telling anyone," she said. "Everyone can find out on their own. Obviously."

I said, "Who tends the bar when Elliot isn't here?"

"I do," she said. "I had another girl but she was stealing. Everyone steals in this business, Ingrid."

"Any business," I said.

"Sure." She rested her elbows on the bar. "When I opened this place, all I wanted was a diner where the farmers would come. Then I got the liquor license. And then I got ambitious. I wanted to use things like almonds and persimmons in all the dishes."

"Apricots."

"Yes. I wanted to use apricots." She smiled. She tapped her index finger on the bar. "All the years I spent resisting this place, when Fresno was home the whole time."

"You wouldn't know that if you hadn't left."

She nodded. "We had a good time, didn't we."

"For a while we did," I said.

"I mean we had a good time here. Playing soccer. Hanging out at the river."

"Sure."

The cook brought her a bruschetta piled high with fragrant tomatoes and ribbons of basil. "I could have opened a hot dog stand out of a cart on a corner and I'd be happy to be back here," she said. She bit into the toast. "Oh, my God, Arturo, brilliant."

"The valley smells like home, especially this time of year," I said.

"Do you want one of these?"

"All we eat at home is toast."

"Is that no? Arturo, bring one more, will you? Not toast like this," she said.

"I mean I like toast. Yes."

"You know, all those girls still live here," she said. She meant the girls we hung out with in high school: Muffy Levin, Kitty Urbano, Phyllis Tainter. "They're all married to accountants. They're all very Junior Leaguey. Grosgrain headbands, fundraisers in the backyard. You know."

I did know. "You could have opened one of those hot dog carts like they have at the football games in LA, with the peppers and onions grilling on the side and the bacon wrapped around the dogs."

"No," she said. "One like in New York, with the hot dogs sitting in steamy water all day and big vats of mustard. I would have made it fabulous. I would have had all sorts of smoked relishes and things, and I'd sell bottles of soju." She licked her fingertips. "Your idea of the world is larger than mine," she said. "When I think of the world away from here, all I think of is New York."

I laughed. I felt so much smaller than Bootsie. Since I'd come back from boarding school when I was sixteen, all I had wanted was to be a bit more antagonistic, a bit more contrarian, a bit more like Bootsie. "New York is all there is, anyway," I said.

"I want another one of these," she whispered. "Arturo, will you bring me one, too?"

Arturo oiled the bread with a brush and put another slice on the grill.

"Listen to this," I said, pulling out the bar chair next to me.

"I'm not going to sit. I can't sit."

"Okay, so listen to what happened."

"Oh, I heard. Your guy went to work for Griffith."

"How did you hear that? How did you know I was going to say that?"

She opened her mouth wide, as if she were coming in to bite my face. "I hear everything," she growled right next to my ear.

I moved away. "Really, where did you hear that?"

"Customers," she said. "Like you say, nothing is private in this town."

"Nothing is a secret, I said."

"Oh, boy. *Nothing is a secret*," she recited. "Does this mean you're going to stick around for a little while?"

"Why would I stick around?"

"To help out. I know how these things work, princess."

"I was going to anyway."

"Ha. I knew he would get you. I knew it when I saw you in here with Anne, before we even spoke. I could see it in your vulnerable demeanor." She lit another cigarette. "Where is my staff?"

"He didn't get me. He needs my help."

"They always need our help." She wrapped her bomb of hair tightly into a rubber band, took keys from under the counter, and unlocked the front door. "Alicia!" she shouted toward the kitchen. "Is Alicia here yet?"

"I don't think she's here," Arturo said.

"God," Bootsie said to me, "is it hard to show up at a certain time? Is it hard to just be in the place you're supposed to be?"

"This is an existential question."

"You may have to help out here, too," Bootsie said.

"I don't wait tables." All the awful jobs I ever had, I managed to never have to wait tables. I would have been terrible at waiting tables. I have no patience and I don't care if people are happy or not.

"It's better that you can help your dad now instead of when

he's dead. I'm not being funny. I wish I hadn't waited until my dad was dead to come home and look after things. I mean, what was the difference?"

"I know."

"Have I said that before?"

"I don't think so."

"It's in my head all the time," she said. "I'm never not thinking that. He was such a jerk, you know, but I was kind of a jerk, too."

"Like what happened with us," I said.

She knocked the tip of a freshly lit cigarette against the glass, tapping and tapping until there was ash. The air-conditioning kicked in, high, and made its low chugging motor sound. "Maybe."

"If he were around, you wouldn't have come back at all. He would have sold the land or figured something out so that you could go on living your life where you were. It's the surprise element, that's how they end up needing us."

"I wasn't happy, anyway," Bootsie said then. "I thought I was happy, but I was always just one bad step away from a nervous breakdown."

"I think that's where I am now," I said.

"Well, then, welcome home," she said, smiling. She put a cocktail glass in front of me and moved behind the bar to mix liquor. "Try not to get pregnant."

15. "Maybe you need a gin and tonic," I said the first morning Dad didn't get out of bed. I had read online that gin and tonics cured stomach ailments. I had been spending a lot of time awake at night, online, looking up cures for pain. I discovered, for example, that the symptoms for a broken heart are almost identical to the symptoms for pancreatic cancer: nausea, weight loss, an abdominal pain that radiates through to your back. If you make the mistake of looking up "physical effects of a broken heart" online, you'll learn that the searing feeling you get in your chest is actually a breaking down of the lining of the heart due to the stress of sadness that, in extreme cases, causes death.

"Or vodka with grapes," I said.

Dad never got so sick he didn't get out of bed. Dad could have had bronchitis in the middle of October, and he often did, but he'd still go to work. No hangover, no grief, no broken ankles or chest pains could keep Dad from work, which, as far as he could see, cured everything.

"No booze," he said.

"I'm kidding." I was not really kidding.

"You should go to the doctor," Mother said. She lay next to him in one of her gauzy white nightgowns with the thorn holes all over it. "Why do you never go to the doctor?"

"Which doctor?" Dad said. Dad didn't think there were any reliable doctors but orthopedists, because they patched up your broken bones. "Some quack?"

"The tummy doctor. Some normal doctor who tells you what to do."

"Doctors. I feel fine today anyway." He couldn't lift his head from the pillow.

"You don't look like you feel fine," I said.

"It's an ulcer, probably," Dad said. "I have this seaweed potion your mother told me to drink."

"What seaweed potion?" I said.

"It restores the nervous system," Mother said.

"Have you had a test? Did you drink barium and all that?" I asked.

"Drink barium. God, no," said Dad.

I said, "I have never heard of seaweed for an ulcer."

Mother said, "It's easily digestible vitamin B."

"I think you should eat an egg," I said.

Dad said, "Everything goes away eventually. You either die or you get better."

"Daddy."

I sat at the edge of the bed. Dad hurt too much to be propped up. When you've spent a good part of your life scrubbing tanks and digging up tree stumps and bent over trimming vines, a little pain between your shoulder blades can go on for a long time before it makes you pay any attention.

I said, "I'm going to call Dr. Epstein and see if he can take X-rays of your chest." Dad sent farmworkers with shingles and head colds and pregnancies to see Dr. Epstein, the team doctor for the Fresno State Bulldogs.

"It's the same cough Felix has got and Masterson has got, and half my men have got it," Dad said.

"Miguel and his wife have both got it," Mom said.

"It's not just a cough," I said. "It's your stomach, too. That's how bone cancer starts."

"It's how bone cancer ends," Mother said.

"If you haven't got a cough, you're not working hard enough," Dad said.

Mother agreed. It didn't help when she agreed.

"A cough and a stomachache have never kept you in bed, Dad."

"Don't get old," he said.

I said, as I was supposed to, "You're not old."

Mother said, with her fingers softly on his face, "You have no lines." Then she turned to me. "I take good care of him."

Dad said, "This is what forty years of marriage to your mother looks like." He grinned his small grin.

Both of them had loose skin and spots on their hands. There were times, like right now, that evidence of their age frightened me.

"Let me call Dr. Epstein."

"I'll call him myself," Dad said.

I said, "I'm not leaving the house until you call, and those phones are going to ring all day with men trying to rent your machines."

"I see," Dad said. "I see how you operate."

The midday air smelled of drying Thompsons. The house on the river was, literally, the center of a dehydrator. All over the valley, farmers had decided on raisins rather than harvesting green. I worried with something close to grief that we had made a mistake in leaving all our fruit on the vine. Felix should have started picking by now, at least with the grapes to the south.

That afternoon, sitting in Phillip's little office above the warehouse, I rented out all four caning machines, all four harvesters, and two of the pickup machines. I fielded phone calls from at least six other farmers looking for equipment. By the end of the day I had every machine we owned rented for the next two weeks. I charged what I could see Phillip had charged the previous season, and the farmers and farm managers seemed happy, too happy, at the price. A Mr. Singh came to fetch the harvester eight minutes after we'd hung up the phone, smiling with what I thought might be disbelief.

It hadn't occurred to me that rental prices might vary from season to season, depending on the volume of the crop and how many people were drying their grapes. It hadn't occurred to me until I met the delighted Mr. Singh. "You are very kind!" he said, and waved to me as he drove the machine down Avenue 7. I knew I had done something terrible.

I phoned Bootsie and she laughed at my prices. "Do you know how hard it is to find machines right now? Just about every farmer in the valley has decided to do raisins. The math says lay down your grapes. Lay down thy grapes!" She laughed some more. "I don't mean to laugh," she said. "Charge double the next time round. At least double."

"I already made deals for the next two weeks." In two weeks the raisin season would be nearly over. That year, grapes had to be picked by September 15, the deadline to collect crop insurance.

"Renege."

"No, I can't do that."

"Yes, of course you can."

"No, it's not how Dad wants to do things. He says an agreement is an agreement."

She took a big, long, daunting breath. "That is why your father is in trouble," she said. "He is the only person in the whole farming industry who feels that way."

"Any industry," I said.

"Yes," she said. "Any industry."

I phoned Wilson.

"It doesn't matter," he said.

"You don't think this is a huge disaster?"

"No, the money from the rentals is never a big deal. It's, like, a pittance. If you really want to make some money, sell the machines."

"Sell the machines?"

"Sure, sell the machines, sell the vines, sell those useless peach trees. Sell the warehouse and that packing shed. Sell everything."

"Dad sold the packing shed ten years ago."

"Oh, yeah. He did? We had some parties in that shed, remember?"

"Where are you?" I said. He sounded drunk.

"Football practice," he said.

"Listen to me. Uncle Felix made it sound like the truck rentals were especially important this year."

"I guess so," he said. "I don't think it's going to make that much of a difference. At this point you just have to wait for the money from the grapes to come in."

"Then Felix has to pick them."

"Talk to Felix."

"Can you talk to Felix, too?"

"You think Uncle Felix listens to me? He thinks I'm as dumb as my dad," Wilson said. "If you're worried, just call up the guys you made the deals with and tell them you have a different price."

"No, Dad would not be happy. Dad says that's not how we do business."

"I'm trying to watch some football, Ingrid. In a minute I'm going to start charging you for this conversation."

"Thank you, Wilson. Okay."

"Ingrid," he said.

I waited.

"Ingrid?"

"Yes. I'm here." He really was drunk.

"If you married me, none of this would matter at all, you know. Your dad could just retire."

"Thank you for the offer, Wilson. Dad doesn't want to retire." Through the skin of dust on the office windows I could see heat shimmer from the street and above the vines. The air was too thick to see the hills to the west. Windy days and days after rain, you could see the hills to the west.

"Ingrid," he said.

"Yes, Wilson."

"Who else are you going to marry?"

That evening I heard them come in, the echo of the heavy front door through the rest of the house. I had been in bed watching my room go from bright to bent evening light. I'd been itching and my calves and ankles were raw and bleeding slightly; somehow I'd been bitten by something, fleas maybe, or mosquitoes. I took *Middlemarch* from the bedside table and pretended to be reading. There was the clank of my mother's silver-trimmed handbag on the entry table. My parents rarely used the front entrance.

Mother said, "See how beautiful we made it?"

Dad said something softly, something I couldn't hear.

"We did it all ourselves," she said.

Across the living room, the light click of my mother's steps and the soft thud of my father's.

She appeared at my bedroom door. "How are you?"

"What happened?"

"Dad had spots on his lung," which is in fact exactly what I expected to hear her say. I'd imagined it already.

"What's that mean?"

"Little spots."

"Spots of what?"

"Dr. Epstein is sending him to a specialist."

"What kind of specialist?"

"I don't know, Ingrid, I don't ask questions." She stood there. "What are you doing?"

"I'm reading."

"Is that how you read? In the dark?"

"I'm taking a break."

"It's so hot," she said. The heat was always a good excuse. The heat was a good excuse for taking a break or going to the doctor or not driving out to the fields for one day in your entire career. The heat was a good excuse for Dad to have spots on his lung. "I guess we could use the air again tonight."

"Come on," I said, "let's have a drink."

I rolled the limes on the counter with the butt of my palm and squeezed them into a pitcher using a fork as a reamer. I added superfine sugar and ice and the vodka and I stirred and stirred. I poured two into cocktail glasses and we drank them quickly and I poured two more. "Is the lime okay?"

"There's something growing in the pool," she said. "I don't mind the lime." With the red nail of her index finger she picked out the thick pieces of pulp settled at the edge of the glass and

wiped them on her cocktail napkin. "Wilson's pool boy is going to stun it."

"Shock it."

"Right, shock it." We both waited.

"Where's Daddy?"

"How did it get so green so fast?"

"It's algae."

Mother said, "It's growing and taking over everything." A lot of the time we spent our lives wishing things to grow so good and fast. Other times, we wanted them to slow down—not just with algae, not just with spots on the lung.

"Why is Wilson sending his guy?" Wilson never parted with money, never even picked up a drinks tab.

"He thinks it's depressing," Mother said.

"It is depressing."

"Too depressing to look at when he sits at this table, I guess." She said, "It's good you're here."

"I'm glad I'm here." I was, sincerely, for once, glad to be home. My ankles burned with bites. I rubbed them, casually.

In the freezer, Mother found the stale end of a yellow cake Anne had brought from Los Angeles.

"Do you know even the garlic couldn't save those peaches?" Dad came into the kitchen wearing his work boots. He wore work boots like they were slippers, because he didn't know what else to wear around the house. He'd never owned any slippers except ones my mother had taken from hotels. "What a waste of garlic."

We had one peach tree out front that Dad called the Family Tree, and we could pick peaches off it and eat them hot from the sun, because instead of fertilizers or pesticides, Dad used concentric circles of garlic, a technique meant to keep the pests away and the soil fertile, but too expensive for real production. You don't know what peaches are until you eat them hot and jammy

right off the tree. I can't eat the hard, cold two-dollar peaches from farmers' markets in Hollywood on Ivar or on Union Square or obviously from Portobello Road. People from central California who've got peach trees in their yards are spoiled when it comes to fruit, and to everything else: prosciutto cured by Mr. Boschetti from his own almond-fed pigs in Firebaugh, raisins still warm and chewy from your grandmother's backyard, cheese made by the Jensen's Dairy daughter just south of Fresno, pistachios oven-roasted from a neighbor's fresh crop. Food didn't taste as good anywhere as it did at the house in Fresno.

"But we have plenty of good garlic," Mom said. No one had bothered to go out and pick the garlic. It had gone all weedy and grasslike. In the garage, we had burlap bags of onions and garlic from the Matheuses, crops they brought over every summer. We never thought of the garlic in the front yard as actual garlic.

"Did Mommy tell you I've got spots?" Dad said.

"It's dust," I told him. Fleas, the bites must have been. Fleas in the dust.

"Dr. Epstein can't fix dust," he said.

"Just go see the doctor, Dad. It's dust and you'll be fine." I put a plate of cake in front of him. "Who's he sending you to?"

"That awful guy," Mother said.

"I wish you wouldn't say it like that," said Dad. He rubbed the back of his hand over his face, over his forehead, wiping away perspiration.

"You know that guy," Mother said to me. "Jane's doctor."

"Oh," I said. "He's fine." No good could come from seeing Dr. Parker. His patients invariably died. I knew from Uncle Felix and Aunt Jane he had a waiting room that looked like a crowded bus station: not enough chairs, everyone standing against the walls, sick relatives crouched next to sick relatives. It was hard to imagine such an office, where patients were paid so little regard

because they were clearly expected not to be here much longer. An office like that could really test your dignity. He got away with this by being the only oncologist in town who took everyone's insurance.

Dad said, "We can't go anywhere else right now."

I said, "Stanford will see you, or UCLA, those places will see you. Why not go there?"

Mom said, "Daddy has the grapes."

"Daddy, I love you, but anyone could look after the grapes. I could look after the grapes." I said this with less confidence than I might have before the fiasco with renting the machines.

Mother said, "Felix should just pick those fucking grapes." Mother never used the f-word. I had heard her use the f-word one other time in my life, when I was sixteen and she said, "The whole fucking bathroom has flooded!" Now it was into the first week of September. He should have at least picked the white grapes. All the Fiestas and Thompsons around Dad's vines were on the ground or being harvested. Everything from Bakersfield to Selma had been picked two weeks ago. Fresno was picking right now. Even Mello was calling their juice, and Mello waited until the very last minute to call the juice. I scratched beneath my socks until blood sunk into my nails.

We ate the cake, and slowly in the heat the buttercream frosting slid off the half we didn't eat. Anne had brought it from the famous bakery in Beverly Hills where you must stand in line. Anne put a lot of faith in shops where people were willing to stand in line for a product despite being in a capitalist country.

"It's just a cough," Dad said again. "Everyone's got spots. You breathe in dirt every day of your life."

"I miss it when we don't have peaches in the ice cream," Mother said.

"Should we make ice cream?" I asked.

"We could get peaches," said Dad.

"I don't want ice cream from Georgia peaches. I want our peaches." She poked at the cake with her fork until it became a neat pile of crumbs.

"Our peaches are the most delicious," I said.

Mother put both hands around her throat, as if she were trying to keep someone from strangling her. "I wish this hadn't been the year the peaches didn't grow," she said.

"Bad timing," I said. "But I rented your machines, Dad."

"You did," he said, and patted my hand. "I knew you could handle anything you needed to."

"Let's use the air tonight," Mother said, lifting the hair off the back of her neck. "I'll close the windows."

I said, "When does the note get called from the bank?"

"Which note?" said Mother. "I can't keep track of all the notes."

Dad said, "They're not going to call my note. Even if they thought about it, Felix would step in." Uncle Felix was on the board at the Bank of the West. "We're still talking to financers."

"What if you don't get the financing?"

"Then we're going to have a tough year," my father said, and chuckled. "We'll get the financing."

"Every year we worry whether or not we'll get the financing." Mother held her glass out to me. Her hand was wrinkled, loose: an old woman's hand. "I can't drink this lime juice, darling. Will you get me a tumbler with wine?" At the house we often drank Uncle Felix's old wine, with the labels written out by hand, when we didn't know what else to pull out of the basement. Sometimes these bottles were drinkable and sometimes they weren't.

I emptied Mother's gimlet into the kitchen sink and closed the window. I clicked the thermostat to cool.

"The windows in the dining room and the bedroom," Mother said.

"She'll get them," Dad said. "Let's just sit for a minute. It's nice to sit."

The cold air came forced in from beneath the cabinets.

"I'll get them," Mother said, making a move to rise.

"I'll get them," I said.

"Don't forget the front door," she said. Every window in the house had to be closed: the bedrooms, four bathrooms, the three sets of sliding doors in the living and dining rooms, the small casement window in the bar off the kitchen, the small pass-through at the top of the front door that Mother had built in so she didn't have to open the door entirely to small deliveries or to men she didn't know.

"We can now be completely refrigerated," I said, returning.

"And pickled," said Mother.

"Don't look sad," I said to Dad.

"I'm not sad," he said.

The cool air at my feet eased the itching in my ankles. None of us drank the drinks in front of us. I had my hair up, and Mother ran her finger along the base of my neck. "You have a line of dirt here," she said.

"I have what?"

"You need to wash your neck."

"That is so rude," I said. "I do not have dirt." I shifted my chair out of her reach.

"I never say the right thing," she said, sending her eyes toward the ceiling. "Everything I say is a mistake."

"That's not true," Dad said, his hand on her hand. She squeezed, and he squeezed her back.

"My daughters hate me," she said.

I said, "Mother, you say these things so I have to declare how false they are, and then I'm just telling you how wrong you are once again, and then you're upset about that, too."

"Stop," said Dad. "Let's stop."

There was more to say, but Dad never gave orders, so when he did we listened. I could see Mother pulsing with accusations. "Did you speak to Anne?" she asked me.

"Earlier." I touched my neck to feel for dirt.

"What did Anne say?" she asked. There was no correct answer to this question. Any answer could be interpreted by Mother as a slight against her.

"Anne says I ought to come be an assistant on the show," I said.

There was a quiet wait.

"At voice-over?" Dad said.

"You should write a play, Ingrid," Mother said, "and the title should be *What to Wear to the Oncologist*."

"It doesn't matter what you wear," I said.

"That's the point. That's why it's funny."

"An oncologist joke," said Dad, flat.

An angry bee knocked itself against the kitchen window. There were bugs everywhere, it seemed. "A job at the show," my mother said.

"Aren't you happy here?" Dad said.

The urge to cry came on like a smack. "I never know when I'm happy until I look back later," I said. It was the truest thing I could say.

"I don't understand what you mean," Dad said.

"I understand," said Mother.

Movement solves every small crisis, even tiny movements, like getting up from your chair and putting your glass in the sink. I put my unfinished gimlet in the sink and poured myself a tumbler of wine, not because I wanted it but because there was nothing to do but to do something.

"Would you like to manage things here," Dad said, without

a question mark. "Just through the harvest. If you can do that for me."

"Are you too tired?" I said. The saucepan we used to soft boil eggs sat on the counter, so I began to scrub the water line from the top.

He said, "I've just got a little pain in my gut."

"But what do I do? I don't know what to do." Baking soda works very well for cleaning old stains off pans.

Mother said, "Of course you know what to do. We all know what to do."

"Most everything is done," Dad said. "You check the water, you watch the vines, measure the sugar."

Mother said, "It doesn't matter if you measure the sugar. Felix will pick when he wants to pick."

"Daddy." I feared if I stayed here much longer, I could do more harm than good, as they say. I would have to wait until Dad felt better to tell him how I'd failed at the rentals.

"You keep the records. It's just a few weeks," he said. "You might be here a few more weeks anyway."

"You think I'm going to stay permanently."

"No," he said, laughing the laugh that turned into a cough. "Get in the truck tomorrow and drive around and talk to people, that's all I need you to do. I can handle the office work."

"People just need to see the truck out there," Mother said. It was true; one of the old rules of farming is that half the work is simply being around, and Dad's truck hadn't been around for days now, not since Phillip quit.

"What would you have done if I weren't here?"

"I'd have asked you to come back."

"But you might have asked Anne," I said. "Anne is so intimidating. She would be better at all of this."

"Oh," Mother said, "Annie doesn't even know which vineyards

are ours." There were close to twenty thousand acres of vines, and I knew them all.

"That pan is clean enough," Dad said. "Sit with us."

I stood at the sink with a dish towel, drying the pot. "I'm here," I said. I'd had to leave when I was thirteen because I hated the "here" of being here so much. But then I had to leave school, too, because I hated the "there." And then I kept leaving places, and now I was back home. I tried to catch myself every time I called Fresno "home."

"Annie didn't say anything else?" Mother asked. Mother had this sense of things. If there was something you didn't want her to know, you would have to deliberately force it out of your head, or else she'd detect it from three thousand miles away and start asking questions.

"Evelyn. You've driven her away from the table already."

"I just think it's funny Annie hasn't called us since she was last here," Mother said. "She calls Inky."

"What are you going to do?" I asked Dad. "How are you going to feel better?"

"I'm going to work softer," he said.

Mother said, "Daddy has spiders in his lungs."

16. "If the guy in the tractor were any smarter than you, you'd be on the tractor and he'd be in the truck." Wilson was full of encouragement. There are wives and children all over the valley who pretend to know nothing about their family's ranch, but if something were to happen to the person in charge, anyone else in the family could take over without having to learn an awful lot. Miguel organized the labor and weighed the grapes and kept Dad apprised of the vines. Then I would show up to look. All farmers really do is look around. "The most valuable thing you can put on your land is your shadow," Wilson said, which I'd heard before, and, "Grapes don't stop growing on Saturday."

I told Wilson, "Thanks for the tips."

"Don't take advice from Wilson," Mother warned me. "If there's something in the field you need advice on, call Mr. Matheus or Mr. Ellison or, if you want to," and she paused here, almost with a wince, "call George Sweet."

"And why not Uncle Felix?"

"Felix has got his own agenda," Mother said.

"Bootsie says George has got bees or something."

"Bees? He might have bees." The Sweets had four hundred acres just north of town. "But he's still got the vines and the pistachios. I think they've got pistachios."

"If you don't trust Wilson to give me the right advice, why have you got him handling your money?"

"You ask too many questions, Ingrid."

"Simple questions."

"Call George," she said. "Wilson's only expertise is telling people he's an expert."

Anne called my mobile. "Have you checked the Brix?"

"What do you think I'm doing?"

"I used to love to check the Brix."

"The grapes to the south are getting high. Way too high."

"Where are you?"

"I'm driving Dad's truck."

"I mean where."

"In Berenda." Berenda was some of Dad's early acreage. Anne knew this landscape well. "This all feels so masculine."

"Masculine," Anne said. "It doesn't have to be masculine. Why is driving the truck masculine?"

"I mean my associations are masculine."

"It doesn't sound at all masculine. Think of Marianela, with all those vines."

"This is not exactly Marianela's operation."

"Maybe you'd be better off thinking of it in terms of how Marianela runs her operation. Just think of twenty acres at a time."

"That's not possible. You have no idea what's going on here."

"You never listen to what I say, and you know, you *know* I'm always right. You're thinking about masculinity, you're already making yourself separate from all those guys, putting yourself in a secondary position. Can you remember the last time I was not right?"

"All right, Annie, then you come home and look after the farm." I unwrapped a stick of hard, waferlike Juicy Fruit I'd found in the glove compartment. Poor Dad had probably bought it expired at the dollar store. Dad loved the dollar store. The gum was crunchy. I put the wrapper in my pocket. Dad's truck was pristine, the worn beige leather of the interior oiled to a shine; never had he left a receipt or pennies or a packet of salt in the console.

"I'm coming home while the show's on hiatus."

"When is that?"

"Tonight, I'm coming home tonight. I'm packing. Do you think I need to pack dresses and things? Are there weddings or anything?"

"I think that's wonderful," I said. "That's the best news ever."

"It's actually very bad news, obviously."

"Come home," I said. "I'll make soft-shell crabs."

"You have to order them from Virginia," she said.

"And I'll find nice wine somewhere."

"Get it from Felix. Just take it from his house."

"How's Charlie?"

"For half our marriage, he's been trying to figure a way to get out of it."

"That's not Charlie."

"I know. He's impossibly charming."

"What's happening at work?"

"I don't think we're getting picked up again. Which is all right. Which means I can go to New York if I want."

"Do you want?"

"It would be nice to actually act for a while. I've been a squeaky-voiced cow for five years."

"Five years," I said.

"Should I not even suggest we go together?"

"What's that mean?"

"I mean we had kind of talked about going together."

"Maybe," I said.

"But you seem very happy doing what you're doing."

"I'm not doing anything."

"Helping out Dad, I mean."

"We would have so much fun," I said.

"So many times things that should have been fun have turned out to be pure dread and terror. I could make you a list."

"Make a list," I said. "I love lists."

All existential problems are solved when you're driving somewhere. Being in the truck, passing the vines and trees and row crops from one end of the valley to the other and back, gave me that feeling of accomplishment movement gives you.

Dad had had the same white pickup for twenty-four years. It's a point of pride among the farmers to drive the oldest truck. The older the truck, the less likely you're in debt.

When I was little, on weekends and in summers, I used to love driving around with Dad in the truck. He'd come home for lunch—he was always home for lunch—and afterward I'd ride next to him while he drove from Fresno to Firebaugh and out to Berenda, checking vines and trees and rows, answering workers' complaints, looking for leaks in the water lines. Coyotes would get to the drip hoses and chew holes through the plastic. When we were teenagers, Wilson and his friends used to shoot the coyotes for sport. One summer they dragged in the carcasses of ninety dogs. The police and wildlife rangers never bothered to stop all that. The farmers and workers and everyone else were grateful, and Uncle Felix paid Wilson and his friends fifty dollars for every dead coyote they brought back with them. That was a lot of money then. Those boys didn't need another summer job, and during college they'd come home on the weekends just to shoot dogs.

I had always been best at spotting leaks in the water lines. I could see a tiny spark of water shooting out from fifty feet away. Dad had one of those old, thick phones wired into the car, and the first leak I spotted I called Miguel. We had always called Miguel for everything.

"Ingrid," he said (he pronounced it *Ehn-greed*), "you're calling me for a leaky pipe? Ingrid! You call José. He's in charge over there."

"I thought you were in charge everywhere," I said.

"Yes, in charge. Call me if you have a dead worker, don't call me for a leaky pipe."

Mom called the phone in the truck. That phone rang like a fire alarm. It startled me every time. "Anne's coming home."

"She told me. I think you should order some soft-shell crabs. You know how to do that, don't you?" I drove slowly past the vines, scanning for leaks but careful not to drive so fast that dust would spray the fruit.

"Do you think something's wrong?" she said.

"Of course nothing's wrong."

"I mean between her and Charlie."

"The thing you have to do is order crabs. Can you order crabs?"

"Of course I can order crabs, Ingrid, what do you think I am?"

"Just get the crabs here, get Dad to pull out some nice wine, everything's going to be fine."

"Your father doesn't have any nice wine."

"All of Dad's wine is nice."

"Maybe we should have that harvest party."

"Maybe we should."

"Why isn't Charlie coming?"

"Maybe he will."

"I mean with her, now."

"Someone has to work in that family." That was my favorite line. "If Dad has any old Mondavi, he should bring that out, or ask Felix to bring his. Anne loves the old Mondavi."

"Oh, Dad's got cases and cases of that stuff." Mother didn't consider old Mondavi nice wine. Mother thought all the really nice wine came from France, and all the nice cheap wine came from California. The plonk came from Germany or South Africa. This is how all the farmers' wives think. The farmers themselves love their California wine. Fortunately, we farm kids learned to drink by drinking everything from the Blue Nun to the To Kalon to the really old Inglenook, because we'd just steal it from our parents' cellars; we'd mix Lodi plonk or Figeac or Lafite with ice and Sprite, not knowing what was what. It's when you have no idea what's what and you drink it all with impunity that you learn a lot about wine, and why some is good and some is not. That old Mondavi is wonderful.

"And just be nice to Anne. Don't interrogate her," I said.

"I would never interrogate. I have never interrogated."

"Order crabs, get the wine."

"I'm going to call Charlie and ask him to come." In the background I could hear the channels switching rapidly on the television.

"If you like."

"It won't be a party without Charlie."

"We'll see."

For the first time since my grandmother was alive, Mother

would have both me and Anne here for the harvest party, but without Charlie, you see, it wasn't a party.

Mother said, "I'm going to call Charlie and speak to him. He just hates driving over that Grapevine."

I said, "All right," when I should have said, "Leave it alone." But I'd been preoccupied, busy looking out for sprung leaks, fallen branches, grapes hanging too low to the ground. I'd been working and half listening, just as my father had been his entire life. Just as everyone else I had ever known had always been. It felt wonderful.

Off Avenue 24 in Madera, between his vines and a vast swath of pomegranates owned by Paramount, I ran into George Sweet. I expected to—I'd practically driven around looking for him.

"I wondered how long it would be before I saw you out here," George said. He wore old corduroys and a white button-down pitted yellow under the arms. Even when I had been in love with him, even for the time we lived together in New York, George's shirts had always been yellow under the arms.

"Today's my first day."

"I mean I wondered how long before you took over." His cigarette voice sounded, as it always had, as if he'd just woken up from a nap.

"It's a favor to Dad. I'm not really taking over."

"You're modest."

"No."

"I'm going to give you unsolicited advice," he said. "Don't be modest. No one in this valley gets anything done with modesty."

He squinted at me. George had never worn sunglasses. "Just brawn and swagger."

"All right. Thank you."

"You're welcome." He smiled. "Fresno's not so bad when you've got work to do all day." He leaned against his truck. We'd pulled up beside one of Paramount's water filtration systems, a gated collection of tanks and pumps half the size of a soccer field. Our trucks were almost exactly the same. The farmers and their white pickups. "I'm going to smoke," he said.

"Smoke," I said.

He had the same lighter, the same plain silver Zippo in his pocket. His father's lighter. George's father had died of heart failure when we were in high school. *Click-clack.* "How long are you staying?"

"Through the harvest, I guess."

"Which harvest?"

"All the harvests."

"You'll stay through the cab?"

"I guess so. I think so."

"Long time, Inky." He inhaled. Even his inhale was the same, as if he were in a hurry. Two hurried seconds while you waited for what he had to say next. "That's a lot of work, you know."

"Dad asked me to."

"I knew from how slow that truck was going that you weren't him."

"I don't want to get dust on your grapes."

"You're polite."

"Anyway, I was looking for you."

"Were you?"

"I was. Mother says if I have any questions I should ask you."

"Your mother said that?"

"She likes you."

"Your mother?" He laughed. He put the cigarette out on his shoe, smashing it until he knew it was out, and tossed the butt into the bed of his truck.

"But this place runs itself," I said.

"Your dad's already sold everything to Felix."

"It's all juice this year."

"No one's getting anything for raisins anyway."

"Where's your juice going?"

"Mello. At least I can predict exactly how they'll fuck me." He took his cigarettes out of his pocket and tapped the package and put them back. "With your uncle Felix, it's always a surprise."

"He's very creative."

"How does your dad feel?"

"He's got a cough, you know." The open heat felt pure, almost as if dust were sterile. "He has to see some idiot doctor."

"No, I mean about having all his juice with Felix."

"Fine, I think." No one felt fine about anything. "I don't know," I said. "Maybe nothing is fine." As always, George gave me that feeling of comfort, the kind of feeling where you end up talking too much.

"It's all right," George said. "No one is fine this year, which means everyone is. They can't foreclose on everyone, can they."

"Pistachios are fine."

"This year, they're not too bad." He scratched the back of his head, another of his mannerisms that was exactly the same. "What question was it you wanted to ask me?"

"No question," I said. "Just an excuse to find you."

"You could ask your uncle Felix questions."

"Or I could ask you."

"I can't see you staying here too long." We'd both tried to get away from this place. We'd tried to get away from this place together.

"Maybe I'll surprise you."

"Your Fresno State T-shirt surprises me," he said.

I had forgotten that, even in the summer, you wear long sleeves on the ranch. Otherwise you come back for lunch burnt up to your biceps and crusty with dirt. That day I started a farmer's tan that wouldn't go away until October. "I might want to ask you when to pick the grapes," I said.

"Oh, Inks," he said, half laughing, "it doesn't matter what I think. You know Felix is going to pick when he wants to."

"But still, I want to learn things. I want to know what you think."

"I'll tell you what I think," he said. "I think you better not let those Fiestas hang one more night. You're going to lose that crop."

I knew that. I knew it. "What do I do?"

"You tell Felix to pick or you'll take all your juice someplace else."

"I can't take it anywhere else. There's a glut, Wilson told me."

"Felix wants that cab, Inky. I'd call his bluff early on if I were you."

"Dad has this thing about contracts. He won't back out of a contract."

George nodded. "That's not going to do you much good this year."

"It never does us much good."

"I'd talk to Felix. If you're asking my advice." He ran his hands through his shorn curls. I knew the tiny dips shaped like oysters at the base of his back. I had to shake those oysters out of my imagination.

"I was. I am."

"You have a little while before you have to think about the red grapes."

He got back in his truck and drove on. People didn't really say goodbye around here. We'd all see each other again the next day, or the day after that.

☒

Anne thought my tan was hilarious.

"You look like a cartoon."

"Why are you always such a bitch?" I had been in the truck nearly all day, and still I had a sunburn and dirt beneath my nails.

"I don't mean you're a cartoon in a pejorative sense."

She was sitting at the kitchen table by the time I got home. She smelled like cucumber perfume and cigarette smoke. She looked tired; her peachy cheeks sagged just a little and she had a line where her dimple usually is. There was a cystic pimple forming beside her nostril, and she kept touching it. The smoking, especially, is how I knew that Charlie and she had decided to separate.

"You don't like my Fresno State T-shirt?" I said.

"We're excited about the Bulldogs," Dad said. "Aren't you excited about the Bulldogs, Anne?" He had a big book about the Vanderbilts in front of him. Dad liked to read about rich families. Earlier in the day he had been to the oncologist, and they had scheduled a small surgery the coming week to look at the spots on his lung. The whole episode felt like air. Just something else happening.

"Go 'dogs," Anne said obligingly.

Mother started to set up the backgammon board. "Who's going to play?"

It was early evening, when out in the country the sound of trucks passing had stopped and the crickety sound of night hadn't yet started. It's quietest at dusk. Soon the harvests would start in the surrounding vineyards and then the grinding of harvesters and tractors and gondolas would fill up the silence.

There was polenta on the stove and sautéed mushrooms— cremini mushrooms dropped off by Clara Masterson in the afternoon.

"Ingrid said to ask you about the Vocis," Anne said to Mother. The Vocis were swingers, which I'd heard at the Vineyard that day during lunch, where I'd eaten quickly at the bar.

"That's not true," said Dad. "It's just not true."

I said, "Do you know Jack McGourty? He's an appraiser. I sat by him at lunch." Jack McGourty would tell you just about anything if you engaged him in chitchat.

"Tell me about them," Anne said.

"Nothing to do but swing," I said.

"It's quite disgusting," Mother said.

"It probably goes on everywhere," Anne said. "This is the only place people actually care to gossip about it."

"Inky," Mother said, "what else have you learned over lunch?"

"The Vineyard is where you go to learn things," I said. "Why didn't you tell me that, Dad?"

"We've learned plenty at the Vineyard," Dad said.

"I didn't know there was more to learn every day."

"Always more to learn," he said. "I prefer to come home for lunch." He didn't take his eyes off the Vanderbilts. "Your mother cooks better than the Vineyard."

"One night Jackie Voci came over here for drinks," Mother said, "wearing a sweater over her nightie."

"Aha," Anne said. "I knew you had more information."

"We're all lazy, though," I said. "I sometimes wear my pajamas in public."

Mother continued, "Then she took off the sweater and said she was too hot. 'I'm having hot flashes,' is what she said. 'Oh, I'm so hot!' she said."

Every day you were confronted with these tiny examples of what the boredom of Fresno could do to you.

"Maybe she had hot flashes," Anne said. She took the dice cup and rattled it. "I'll play," she said.

"Your father shared his drink with her," Mother said, emptying dice across the board.

"That's a good story," Anne said.

"Dad," I said, "you won't even share your drink with me."

"Yes, Daddy, gross."

Dad looked up from his book at the window for a little while and then said, "You know fishing in Alaska a couple years ago, I was carded."

"How many years ago?" Anne said.

Mother said, "He was forty. You were forty when that happened, Neddy. Not a couple of years ago."

"It doesn't seem that long ago," he said.

"What kind of bar was that where you were carded?" Mother said it like she already knew. She tossed out that question like a toy Dad would wind right up.

"That was a bar with naked girls in it," he said. Both of them smiled. They laughed together just briefly, a secret laugh that left me and Anne out.

Anne said, "You let Mrs. Voci come on to you?"

Mother said, "He encouraged it."

"Anyway, your mother doesn't allow me to see them anymore."

We had the television going in the kitchen, a very old rerun of *Three's Company*. All four of us knew the lyrics to the theme song by heart. Anne sang loud and clearly, as if this were an audition. She still needed to show the rest of us how talented she was. Later I would tell Bootsie, "She blow-dries her hair every single morning," and Bootsie would look at me like she felt sorry for all of us, for the whole town, for everyone who'd ever read the news or had parents or needed to leave the house.

Dad said, then, "I got carded because your mother takes good care of me."

I could see Anne vibrate with something to say that she would not say. Instead she said, "Oh, Mother. You do take such good care of us all."

Mother just rolled the dice.

"Such warmth and care," Anne continued, as if to herself.

Daddy read his book. Mother studied the board, visibly counting with the staccato nod of her head.

It took me a long time to realize that Anne's and my estrangement from the place where we grew up wasn't so much the the fault of the town itself—what William Saroyan called "the terrible boredom and stupidity and meanness of Fresno"—but more the repellent magnetic force between our mother and us.

Later Anne came to my room while I was changing, of course. It's like she knows exactly when I'll have no pants on. This is one of the things Anne does to make sure she's in control: she barges in on you at your most vulnerable. Actors are all very cavalier about nudity.

"Your legs go practically up through your head," she said, which is the kind of thing she says to make sure you forgive her for walking in on you.

"You smell like smoke. I can smell it from here."

"I'm not smoking," she said.

"I just thought something might be wrong."

"There is something wrong, Ingrid."

I didn't say anything. Anne always comes up with something smarter than what you have to say. She always wins.

"Is this what you want?" she asked. "You want to come back here and be a farmer?"

You see: she got mean anyway, while I was trying to be nice and quiet. "Did I say this is what I want?" I said.

"I want you to get out of here."

"I'm not you. This is fine for me, for now."

"This isn't you, either."

"I don't know." I was still thinking that I wanted to talk her out of smoking cigarettes. But the real thing is, cigarettes aren't so bad—they're just a good way for us all to feel superior to everyone else. I feel superior to Anne, who smokes occasionally, and she feels superior to Bootsie, who smokes every day, and Bootsie feels superior to George, who smokes first thing in the morning and last thing at night. "Why are you being so mean to me?"

"I am not being mean," she said. "Let's go outside."

"You're being so critical."

"I want you to do something with yourself."

"I want to do something with myself, too, Anne."

"Well."

"For now, I'm going to look after things here."

"Oh, God," she said. "Let's go outside."

Outside, the crickets had started and the heat hadn't wound down. The nighttime heat might not wind down until October, at least. The stone steps were still hot from the day. Anne and I never wore shoes at night in the Fresno summer. You want to feel your toes in the grass, on the pavement, sinking through the dust and dirt. We sat in the old lawn chairs by the tennis court, two terraces down from the house, ostensibly so Mother and Dad wouldn't smell Anne's smoke.

The cigarette was a thing to hold on to as she talked, a point of focus.

"Charlie is moving out," she said.

"I knew something had happened," I said.

"Because you think I'm a bitch."

"I don't think you're a bitch."

"Charlie thinks I'm a bitch."

"You two just need a rest. You just need a little break, Anne."

"I don't know how people stay married."

"I don't know how people even get to the point where they get married."

"Well, we were young. We didn't know yet how stupid we were."

"What's happened?"

"Nothing happened. He doesn't like me." She exhaled and watched the cigarette's smoke. "I'm not sure I like him, either."

"Well, I like him," I said.

"Ingrid, that is not nice. Be on my side."

"I am on your side. This is temporary."

"Everything is temporary," she said. "Except divorce. Divorce is permanent." We heard an owl. Farmers love the sound of owls, which they hope are eating the bunnies and squirrels that ruin the crops. "The smoke looks pretty in the night, against the moon," she said. "Doesn't it?"

"You're not getting a divorce," I said.

"Yes," she said, "I think I am." She started to cry. "And then I will always be divorced."

"Even if you were, being divorced is kind of glamorous."

"Don't try to be funny. You're not funny."

I looked at her, and she watched her hand. She flicked ashes into the air. It had been a long time since I'd seen Anne cry. Even when she scrunched up her face and wiped her nose with the back of her free hand, she couldn't help being pretty. The crying gave her a fragility and softness she didn't have otherwise. "William Saroyan married the same woman twice."

"He divorced the same woman twice."

"All the great women are divorced."

"Is that true? Who?"

I couldn't think of any. "All of them."

"Not Margaret Thatcher."

"She couldn't get divorced for political reasons."

"Mrs. Gandhi."

"Well," I said. "She was exceptional."

"Remember when we thought we were exceptional?"

I scratched the back of her head. "I still think you're exceptional," I told her.

"I just thought of one," she said.

"Who."

"Grace Paley."

I had forgotten Grace Paley.

"Susan Sontag," I said.

"You see," she said. "You *can* have children and still be exceptional. Everything has gone wrong."

Anne refused to ride with me in the truck. "I'm depressed enough," she said. She was in bed, in her stark room, wearing one of my father's large white T-shirts.

"A woman crosses a room," I said. It was just before lunch and I had spent the morning driving around, weighing grapes in my hand, walking through the rows for any sign that the tops of the vines had started to burn. The tops of the vines had started to burn.

"I don't want to play this now." It was a game we had—I started a story and then she gave me the next line, and I gave her the next, and on and on. It was a boring game that had kept us occupied during the long car rides of our childhood.

"A woman crosses a room and falls into a pool," I said.

"Come on, Inky."

"A woman crosses a room and falls into a pool and tries to drown herself but forgets to put rocks in her pocket and keeps popping up."

"This is the most depressing version of this game I've ever heard," Anne said.

"You don't want to just ride with me?" I said. "Don't stay in bed the whole day. The truck has air-conditioning." Mother and Dad were off the air-conditioning again. Even the dried food in the pantry had begun to smell like dehydration. The boxed raisins from last year had turned hard like pebbles.

"I am beginning to understand that you and I are much more different than I thought," Anne said.

"I feel like you mean that in a derogatory way."

"You always think the worst of me. I'm not derogatory, I am just being frank. I could never come back and drive around in that truck, like you have apparently chosen to do, like you are apparently enjoying." All the softness from last night had disappeared.

"You would, if you had to."

"You don't have to, Ingrid."

"Have you spoken to Charlie?"

She became still and emotionless. "I think at some point in the future we're going to have to stop mentioning his name, or anyone called Charlie."

"What did he say?"

Charlie had e-mailed to say he had begun to pack his clothes and books and audio equipment and the contents of his wine collection. He'd taken the first apartment he looked at, near his office on the Westside, on the second floor of a glassy high-rise on Wilshire. "An absolute bachelor pad," Anne said. "Near all the coeds of UCLA."

"Near work," I said.

"It's about as far away as you can get from a pokey house in Beachwood Canyon."

"He's just having a tantrum."

"He's going to find someone else quickly," she said. "He wants to have a family." She pulled the sheet up over her head. From under the covers she said, "I don't feel well."

"Staying in bed all day is going to make you feel worse."

"The heart is a muscle," she said. "It regenerates. It needs rest."

"We could go out and buy underwear."

"I don't need new underwear," she said. "What I need is paperbacks. Charlie is going to take all the books. I know him."

"We could go out and buy paperbacks."

"He's going to take everything he wants with no consideration for the things I'll miss."

"You can buy it all again, Anne. None of that stuff means anything."

"But it means something that he takes it. It's not the objects, Ingrid, it's the gesture, and the lack of consideration. The lack, the lack of love."

"Why don't you speak to him and divvy things up, like everyone else does?"

"I don't want to do that. He should know the things I'll miss. You see, this is the problem."

"Why don't you speak to him, and tell him that, then?"

"God, Ingrid, do you think I'm a moron? Of course I've spoken to him about all this. But it does no good to go on speaking if the other person doesn't listen. It does no good if Charlie can't hear, and Charlie can't hear."

"Hardly anyone can hear," I said. "That's not a failing specific to Charlie."

"It's an epidemic," Anne said. Then, "You know, I read that the brain can't tell the difference between the pain of rejection and the pain of a broken arm. All the same receptors light up."

"I read that, too. That same article." The broken-arm parts of my own brain had started to heal, or maybe had healed almost entirely. Feeling responsible for something, having people rely on you, was a very good remedy for all sorts of pain.

Anne would go back to a house half full of furniture: a bed and two coconut chairs and the Copenhagen dining table, but no sofa and no armoire. Charlie would take the pots and flatware. Anne would keep the everyday dishes, the china, the Saint-Louis crystal. Anne would start smoking indoors, exhaling out windows and leaving ashtrays in every room.

The Karastan rug would be slightly brighter in the rectangle where the sofa had been.

Charlie did take all the paperbacks, and the hardcovers, too. He left the lopsided IKEA bookshelf and the Samuel French copies of all the plays Anne had done in college.

"I knew he would leave the plays," she said later. "They all have my handwriting in them."

17. I found Uncle Felix at the Vineyard. He was at his table in the corner, bent head to head with bald Billy Moradian, both of them eating fried calamari with their fingers. When I was a child, Billy had gone to jail for five years after killing his show horse for the insurance money. I remembered his fat face and broken nose from the pictures I'd seen in the paper. Many of Uncle Felix's friends had been in and out of jail. Felix seemed to admire these characters, men who valued money over integrity, men who did whatever they thought they could get away with, until they couldn't.

"Uncle Felix."

"Inky! Do you know Billy Moradian?"

"Hi, I'm Ingrid."

"Ned Palamede's kid," Uncle Felix told him.

Billy had a fat, slippery mouth, now glistening with grease. He wiped his thick fingers on the edge of the tablecloth and reached to shake my hand. "Billy Moradian," he said. "He's a good guy, your dad. He's got good land."

"Uncle Felix," I began.

"And a good operation," Billy continued.

"A great operation," said Uncle Felix. "Best grapes in the valley."

I had never before heard Felix refer to Dad's grapes as the best. "What about your grapes, Uncle Felix?"

He shook his head. "No grapes compare to Ned Palamede's. Not in the valley. Your dad knew all the land to pick up. He knew what he was doing all those years, your dad."

"All those water rights," Billy said. "Nobody goes broke with that kind of water access."

"Uncle Felix," I said, "I've got some numbers I'd like to show you when you have a moment."

"Have some lunch," he said, pulling the leather armchair from the side of the table, waving to the waitress for another wineglass. "We're drinking the viognier."

"Harry Cline's grapes."

Uncle Felix held up the bottle for me to read. "They call this Napa wine," he said, tapping the label. "It's all grown in Madera."

"The artichokes," Billy said. "Ingrid, I'm going to order you a plate of the best fried artichokes you'll ever eat. You tell your dad I ordered you the artichokes. And you tell him we ate them with the viognier." Billy was the type of man who snapped at waitresses.

"Why are you looking at numbers?" Uncle Felix said. "What numbers?"

"There are some things I want to show you."

"What things?"

"The sugar, mostly. We can talk about it after lunch. I can take you over to the vines if you like."

"Where's your dad?"

"Haven't you talked to Dad?"

"I talk to him all the time," Felix said.

"Oh," I said. "He's at home." I didn't know what else to say. "I'm just trying to learn," I said.

"No one better to learn from than this guy right here," said Billy, hitching his fat thumb toward Uncle Felix.

"What happened to not interested?" said Uncle Felix.

"I'm interested," I said. "I told you if I were interested I'd work for Dad."

The waitress brought my glass. "Drink this," Billy Moradian said, pouring the wine. "Tell me this isn't better than anything they grow up north."

They were right, you know, it was a beautiful wine: sharp and crispy with citrus blossoms. The kind of wine that didn't make you itch right below the ears. (Bad wine makes me itchy right at the jaw hinge.) "Gorgeous." These guys were used to sharing two or three bottles at lunch and then climbing in their trucks to drive around all afternoon, or going back to the office to make deals drunk. "Young and complicated."

"Like you," said Uncle Felix. "Why don't you come by tonight and show me what it is you want to show me."

"I have the dove dinner tonight."

"Dove dinner, huh?" He nodded. He raised his eyebrows. "Dove dinner."

Billy said, "Fucking doves."

"Hey." Uncle Felix held his hand up to Billy. "Watch your mouth in front of my goddaughter."

Long ago, Uncle Felix had used his clout with the Bank of America and then the Bank of Fresno and then Guarantee Savings to refuse young Bint Masterson the loan he needed to build a shopping center over what had been the Masterson family's orange grove. Bint, now the owner of many shopping centers from Fresno to Sacramento, made no secret how he felt about Felix. Felix, for his part, made no secret how he felt about Masterson's destruction of the land. So Bint never invited Felix or Felix's friends to the annual dove dinner. "Can you come after lunch?" I said. "I want you to come by the vineyards and look at them. I want you to see something." The high sugar is what I wanted him to see. The burnt leaves and grapes beginning to shrivel at the top of the vines is what I wanted him to see. "It can't wait too much longer."

"Have some artichokes," he said. "Finish your wine."

"I mean it, Uncle Felix. I'm not happy."

"My girl's not happy?" he said. He gave my shoulder a pat. "I'll follow you out after lunch. Eat those artichokes. They came from Castroville this morning."

"Uncle Felix, you can see the burn from here."

"Yeah," he agreed.

I drained a grape into my little refractometer and showed him the sugar, at 26 percent far too high. "We could do a larger sample, but I don't see the point. These need to be picked right now, tonight."

He pinched a grape between his thumb and forefinger for the feel, the color and texture. Then he took another from the vine and ate it. "Who's the field guy out here?"

"I haven't met him."

"How long you been checking these vines?"

"Just a couple of days."

"You don't know my field guy?"

"You don't have to be out here longer than a couple of days to see these grapes need to be picked."

"Where's your dad?"

"Dad has a cough. He doesn't feel well."

"Your dad doesn't stay in because he has a cough." He ate another Fiesta off the vine.

"Listen. Uncle Felix. I love you, but I'm picking these grapes tonight. If you don't want them, don't take them, but then I'm not selling anything to you. None of it."

"That's not how it works, Inky."

"Don't make me show you I'm serious, Uncle Felix."

"You don't have to show me anything. I'll call your dad and speak to him."

"Daddy's sick."

"Too sick to talk?" He looked truly surprised, truly concerned. "What kind of sick?"

"You can call him, but he's going to tell you the same thing. Pick now. I've discussed it with him. He agrees and he's put me in charge." This was a lie. If I had told Dad I planned on picking the Fiestas and was threatening to pull out of the contract with Felix, he would have banned me from the business altogether. Dad didn't pull out of contracts, he didn't pick grapes without authorization from the buyer's field guys, he didn't make the kind of threat I was making. This was why Dad had a reputation for being such a swell guy; it was why he was in trouble now. I didn't know then exactly how much trouble.

Felix pulled the phone out of his shirt pocket. "Evelyn," he said. "Let me have Ned. You know Inky's out here trying to call shots?"

I waited, grateful Mother had answered the phone. It dawned on me, in that hot moment at the end of the vines off Avenue 14, that Mother may have orchestrated all of this. She knew I couldn't bear to see those grapes burn on the vine. This is why she'd told me to go to George with questions. Dad would have told me to wait on these Fiestas, to wait, wait, wait for the field guy. Dad would do anything to avoid a conflict. There was no way Mother was going to put him on the phone. I waited.

Felix rang off. "Listen," he said to me, "let me talk to my guy. I'll call you tomorrow."

"Not tomorrow," I said. "I'm going to have Miguel call a crew. These grapes needed to come off the vine last week."

He laughed the kind of affectionate laugh you give a mischievous child. "You couldn't sell these grapes anywhere right now."

"I'll go to Mello, Felix. Do you think they'll take this juice if I promise them the cab?"

"Oh, Inky. All right. Don't get upset."

"What are you waiting for?"

"I was waiting for the sugar."

I looked at him.

He said, "You're right, they're past where they need to be."

"Why are you giving me bullshit about your field guy? Do you think I'm an idiot?"

He laughed his kind laugh again. "No one thinks you're an idiot."

"Next we'll have to talk about the Thompsons. Don't make me do this every time." I hugged him, his soft blue vest. His neck was wet and sour with boozy perspiration. He smelled so familiar; the comfortable, yeasty smell I had known since I was small. I hugged him with both arms, relieved there had been only the threat of a rift. "Don't make me get nasty. I love you."

"No dove dinner for you tonight," he said.

"Oh, I'm going to the dove dinner."

"You going to supervise a harvest from the dove dinner?"

"Too hot to pick before midnight," I said. "And they don't need me. I have to eat. I have to make sure those vultures at the club know they can't have Dad's land."

He laughed again and nodded. "You're something," he said, and opened the truck door. "What can I pay you to come work for me?"

"This is an act of love, Uncle Felix. Love!"

"I remember love," he said. "It makes you do stupid, stupid things." He got in the truck.

18. On the first of every September, the Masterson brothers would shoot between thirty and sixty birds, and those birds would get served at their season-launching dove dinner. Lean years, a person could measure his social worth by whether he got an invitation to eat a dove.

"Lucky you," said Anne. She stood at the stove, eating the crispy corners from a pan of lasagna Mother had baked earlier.

"Don't eat the best part," I said.

She said, "But you get delicious yummy doves. Just think of it."

The dove dinner had always been men only. Mother had a lot of complaints about Bint Masterson, from the yellow Ferrari he drove to the rumors that he'd hit Clara in the face to the fact that he'd spent only six months in jail for what was a much more substantial tax evasion, but his no-women policy for the dove dinner was at the top of her list. This year, Mr. Masterson had asked Dad to bring me along. I don't even eat dove.

Anne said, "And you get upset that I'm eating two bites of lasagna."

"The crispy part."

"It's the part I like best."

"It's the part everyone likes best. Sometimes it's like you don't even listen to what you're saying."

She turned away from me, back to the stove. "You should be nicer to me," she said.

As we left the house I said to Dad, "Is this invite because you all think I'm moving back here to run the business? Are they trying to suss me out?"

"You don't know these guys," he said. "You should meet them."

"Are women invited now? Am I going to be the only one?"

"You don't count as one of the women, Inky." He said it as if this were something I should be proud of.

"Do I count as one of the men?"

"Oh, Ingrid," Dad said. "They just want a pretty girl around, and they can get away with inviting you." No one but my father ever called me pretty. The curse of the plain girl is that you can get her to do just about anything by using the word *pretty*. This works even better if the plain girl has an older sister who is always called beautiful.

"I don't know that I want to be thought of as one of the men," I said.

"You're not one of the men," Dad said. There was, in Fresno, and maybe everywhere, a positive glamour in being the farm daughter, and even more in being the daughter who leaves. You don't even have to be pretty. Fresno is so full of irresistible ugliness.

"It's going to make the next couple of months easier on you if you get to know these guys."

"Months?" I hadn't thought of my tenure here in terms of months. I had been thinking more like days, more like until the end of next week. Even when I thought that I might stay through the entire harvest, I had never thought of time in terms of months. "Months," I said. "You make it sound like my whole life."

Dad smiled, and I could see he felt just too sore to outright laugh. "I remember when months felt like my whole life, too," he said. In the past week, he had been out of the house only for doctors' appointments, but tonight, for the annual dove feast, he put on his white linen shirt and his lace-up dinner shoes and his blue blazer with the gold buttons that Mother had bought thirty years ago, maybe in the eighties, from Hiller's in Sausalito.

"Anne's wedding was the last time I saw you dressed up," I said, getting into the passenger seat of Mother's tiny black Jaguar.

"You're never here for the dove feast," he said.

The club was closed for dinner on Mondays. A long table had been set up in the dining room along the wall of glass overlooking the river and the golf course and the droopy willow trees and the rich squares of peach orchards and vines and red barns in the distance. Mr. Boschetti, the almond grower, had brought a platter of his home-hewn gorgeous melty prosciutto, and I parked myself beside it with a glass of white wine that tasted like water. Half the men in the room must have been in financial trouble. More than half.

Everyone I know wants her white wine to taste like water. That is something I should have already mentioned.

That prosciutto pig had eaten nothing but Boschetti's tree-fresh almonds its whole life. The flesh was sweet and nutty. I ate more than was polite. I had the urge to drink more than was polite, too. All these farmers in their durable dress shirts gave me an unmoored feeling of homesickness. I had no place to be homesick for.

Mr. Boschetti, red with wine and conviviality, delighted by how much I loved his ham, pulled up a chair and sat down right next to me. He said, "I don't know anyone in the valley who's not real happy to see a daughter in the truck."

"Thank you."

"That's not a compliment. That's just a fact." He folded a slip of prosciutto. "Have I told you about my son's girlfriend?"

"No," I said, my mouth full. He had told me about his son's girlfriend twice before, of course.

"She cut the fat off!" He looked around, as if the gods should be as incredulous as he was. "She left the fat on the plate!" He shook his head as one shakes one's head when there is only sorrow. "And then she asked for more," he said. He nodded the nod of knowing he was speaking to someone who understood his plight. "She asked for more to take home."

"I'm sorry," I said, holding a piece in each hand.

"I think she's the one, too," he told me softly, with regret. "I'm going to be stuck with an idiot."

That evening, contrary to my expectations, no one treated me like a novelty. I kept waiting for the standard snide remark about the big city, a comment about being a girl driving Dad's truck. That evening, everyone was generous with his welcome, everyone seemed glad to see me. This was, of course, a reflection of how glad they were to see Dad.

"Did you hear about Bill Lewis?" Mr. Masterson asked us.

"What happened to Lewis?" Dad said.

"He shot Emory, the florist."

"I read about that in the paper," I said, a ribbon of prosciutto tucked inside my cheek like chew.

"What do you mean, shot Emory?" Dad said.

"He got tanked up in the Grill, you know how he gets," Mr. Masterson said. Mr. Masterson was like a high school bully all grown up and successful and still acting like a high school bully. "Remember when he leapt across the table and tried to strangle Matheus?" Before their divorce, the Mastersons lived across the street from us. One summer, maybe the only day Anne and I had ever seen the ice-cream truck on our remote farm road, its bells ringing the suburban neighborhood tune we never got to hear, we took twenty dollars from Mother's purse and sprinted out to Avenue 7 to catch the ice-cream man. We had waited for him for years. We got there and, of course, Mr. Masterson was there with his sons. "I'll buy the girls' ice cream, too," he said to the vendor. Quite arrogantly, we thought. We hadn't stolen that twenty dollars for nothing.

"Oh, that's all right," Anne had said casually, as beautifully as an eleven-year-old can say "That's all right."

"I know it's *all right*," Mr. Masterson said. He was angry, sarcastic. "Just be a lady and accept it." He stood over us like a beast. We did, of course, accept the sno-cones, primarily out of fear. But by the time we got back to the house and felt safe enough to open them, they were already formed into hard balls of ice. Whenever I see Mr. Masterson, and sadly I see him every time I return to Fresno, I can think of little else but how nasty he was to Anne that day, buying us ice cream. How old does a man have to be before he doesn't compete with an eleven-year-old girl?

"I don't know," said Dad to Mr. Masterson, trying to remember Lewis strangling one of the Matheus brothers (both of whom deserved to be strangled, in my opinion—I began to feel more and more sympathy for the late, beleaguered Bill Lewis). Dad never remembered gossip. It was one of his personal and professional failings.

"Did you see the cop car waiting outside the gate?" Mr. Masterson said. We had. "They'll be cracking down on us now. Better not drive home after three or four drinks."

That night for dinner I was seated next to a land broker called Chris who had an orange tan and a rope belt. He had been drinking vodka, not the white wine that tasted like water. He was only slightly older than I was, but the years of sun damage had given him tight skin and deep crevices where a smile could have been. "Everyone loves your father," he said.

"He's terrific."

"What do you mean terrific?" he said. "You're supposed to hate your father." His pants had little lobsters stitched into them, which was more than just slightly out of place in the Central Valley. He wore a coral polo and loafers with no socks and the whole look was embarrassing, with the farmers and doctors and insurance salesmen in their boots or lace-up dinner shoes and the short-sleeved linen shirts their wives had bought for them marked off triple at the discount clothing store in the Riverbend shopping center. This Chris obviously didn't realize: in the old Fresno crowd, the less you seemed to care about your wardrobe, the richer and more important people thought you were. He wasn't from around here.

"Oh. I don't, though."

"You think he's just terrific, do you?"

"He is."

"Well, I think you're probably lying. No one can be that loved by everyone and by his family, too." He stirred his drink with his hairless finger. "Why doesn't anyone tell the truth anymore?"

Mr. Boschetti was still talking about Lewis, about the voice mail he'd left. "He was apologetic. He said he'd killed Emory and couldn't live with himself."

No one wanted to hear many more of the details. I kept wondering about the wives: these two widows who now had to live next door to each other, women who had been married to angry, explosive men. Women who in any other circumstance probably would have had a lot in common, but who now had a personal obligation to despise each other. Would one have to sell her condo in this depressed real estate market? I thought a lot about real estate then, and the physical and financial realities of having a place to live.

The dove was served: roasted, with wild mushroom rice. Poor bird.

Chris got drunker and drunker and stopped speaking before the affogato.

"I've seen you at the Vineyard lately," Mr. Boschetti said to me, across the table after our dinner plates had been cleared. "How long are you here?"

"I'm not sure yet."

"Everyone thinks it's nice you're here," he said. He had that straightforward, gruff voice all the farmers have. He could say something so kind and generous as "Everyone's glad you're here," and it came out sounding like an order.

"I think it's nice to be here," I said. He turned back to his friends, and I wished that I didn't sound so very much like a little girl, a songbird. I should have barked a thank-you at him and looked away. I would try that in the future.

At the end of the evening, Dad's friends called this service the club recommended where they drive you back home in your own car. I wasn't the only one who needed to get to their vines that night.

For at least two weeks after Lewis shot Emory, no one drove himself home from the club. The authorities did, in the end, investigate how much Lewis had been served by the club the day he shot his neighbor: they could find no one willing to state they'd seen Lewis drinking, and the club records showed he had paid for just one gin and tonic.

"I wonder what will happen to the dog," Anne said later that night. She stayed up to keep me company while I waited for Miguel to phone. We waited for the night to cool down enough that the sugar in the grapes would be stable and we could pick. He and his crew had driven the pickers and the bins out to the southernmost vineyards this afternoon.

"Mrs. Lewis will keep the dog."

"I don't know if I could bear to keep the dog, after something like that."

"The dog's not to blame."

"Blame isn't reasonable," she said. "If he loved the dog so much, she probably hated it."

"No one hates a dog called Tutu."

"You don't know how irrational marriage can be until you've been in one," she said. "Charlie hated Elroy, and Elroy is stuffed."

After our parents had gone to bed, Anne and I would wander down to the pool, where she could smoke cigarettes undetected. I kept my mobile between us, waiting for word from Miguel. The night was still too hot. "Charlie just hates to see you shower affection on anything that's not him."

"No," she said. "It's because he wants a child."

"What's happening with Charlie, it must be more than just this thing with having children," I said. My entire adult life, my idea of relationships and love and how fidelity could endure was based largely on Anne's loyalty to Charlie, and his love and admiration for her. "One thing like that doesn't change the entire life you've had together." It was a question more than a statement, a question I asked her out of fear.

"The life we've had together, I'm not sure he and I were sharing the same thing. What the priest says about being one, that's not how it is at all, Inky. It's two people, with two different experiences of the same thing."

"Two people experiencing love for each other."

"No." She shook her head. "Not really." She dropped her cigarette into the wine bottle we kept by the pool as an ashtray. "I'm not the person Charlie wants, and he's very angry with me for not being what he expects me to be." When Anne tries to keep herself from crying, her voice becomes very even, like a flat line.

"What does he expect?"

"And I have tried really hard, Inky, to be just so. To be wifely or something."

"I think you're wifely."

She didn't respond. She stared into the algae pool, transfixed. I could see she was trying to keep herself as still as possible. Even her sweepy hair was still. If your body doesn't move, doesn't feel anything, it's possible for you to not feel anything, either.

I said, "I mean wifely in a good way."

"I don't want to be a wife," she said. "I want to do my work."

"And sit with me in the summer. We'll keep each other company."

"For now," she said.

"You don't think I'm good company long-term?"

"I was a much better catch ten years ago," Anne said. "When Daddy was rich and I stood to inherit lots and lots and lots of money."

The night cooled and the sound of machines began. In central California, March through December, something is always being harvested. There are very few silent months, and September is the noisiest. Mile after mile in any direction, all you hear are birds and the gunning of machines.

By the time I reached the vines, Miguel had the harvester well into the vineyard and the bin in the row beside it, catching the grapes. There was a gondola truck at the opposite end. He gave my hand a shake. The air smelled like diesel.

The ground along the vines was wet with grapes that had fallen and been crushed.

"How you got this done, I don't know," he said. "I thought Felix would let this go to rot."

"What do you think he did? Contract to buy too much?"

"He doesn't want to pay for this," Miguel said. "He only wants the cab. There's so much white juice this year. It's going to sit in tanks way past next season."

"He should sell cheaper wine," I said.

"I don't know his wine could get any cheaper."

There were two crews, one at the vineyard here and another a couple miles east.

"It's better if you sleep," Miguel said. "You don't need to stay."

"I'd like to stay."

He laughed the wide, wholehearted Miguel laugh, a laugh full of tenderness and a lot of big teeth. He put his hand on my shoulder. Miguel had strong, sinewy hands with long fingers. He had work hands, athletic hands, musical hands. Well-used hands.

"You can stay," he said, "but you'd better sleep sometime."

"When?"

"It's beginning of summer, Ingrid." *Ehn-greed*. "Sleep, so later you can be sharp."

"Sharp for what?"

"Negotiations. With your uncle," he said.

No one in the valley felt fondly about Uncle Felix. No one but Mother and Dad and me and possibly Wilson. Maybe not even Mother. "He can talk about rot with you, too," I said. "I'm not the only person who knows when grapes are ready."

"Yes, but Felix knows I have no power to pull the cab," Miguel said quickly, naturally. "So you will have these conversations with him from now on, not me. With you, he's afraid. You'll see I'm right."

We stood still for a moment and watched those brilliant

vehicles do all the work for everyone, slice and dice and pick and harvest. The picker moved slowly, almost imperceptibly, down the vine, shaking clusters of grapes onto the trays and into the conveyor cups below, transporting them through fans and magnets to remove the debris, and depositing a cascade of grapes into the catch bins in the next row. Those vehicles didn't exist when I was a little girl—Dad had paid all his workers one by one, in cash. He had checked their identifications himself, in the beginning.

"Afraid of what?"

"Afraid of you. Afraid you'll sell that cabernet to Napa. He wants those grapes because he wants them, yes. But even more, he doesn't want those guys up north to get them."

I patted Miguel's hand, still resting on my shoulder. "He's afraid of me," I said, to hear how it sounded. Uncle Felix was afraid of no one. "And it took just one conversation."

"Not too afraid," Miguel said. "But still, better that you talk about when to pick than me. He knows with me that he's in charge."

"You want him to think that I'm in charge?"

"You are in charge."

Miguel's big open face is soft and says everything before he says it. I get embarrassed by Miguel's big open face. It makes me nostalgic. "I'm happy you came back," he said. "I feel like everything is going to be okay."

It was late and I was full of dove-dinner rice and prosciutto and booze. "Everything is always okay," I said. "You farm people are always hopped up about something."

"You farm people," he said, "is you." The yellow picker came back toward us, and he motioned it to slow down. "Have you been on one of these?" he asked me.

"I have never seen this in action."

He helped me onto the ladder, so that I could climb up the

metal grate to sit with the driver. "Take a look," he said. "I'll meet you at the end of the row."

Miguel got into the truck, and I stood on the small platform behind the young man driving. Over the hills beyond Firebaugh, the ambient light would keep the sky slightly orange all night. Just past midnight, there was a dull orange tracing the waves of the hills to the west.

The picker turned right around and I went back with it, watching that machine crush everything in front of it. So many wasted grapes. I knew then, I know now, it's economical to use those harvesters, and financially unviable to pick by hand. Still, to watch all that lovely fruit get crushed into the dirt—it made me hungry.

Sitting in that picker and seeing Dad's little truck at the edge of the vineyard, I began to feel slightly overwhelmed, the kind of panic that feels a lot like exhaustion. There were how many rows to pick? Thirty thousand? Three million? I had no idea. I had no idea about anything, and here Miguel wanted to put me in charge.

At the end of two rows I climbed off the picker, and there was his familiar posture, his familiar red flannel jacket, his happy teeth. "I don't know what I'm doing here," I said.

"Call me when you don't know something," he said. "You know everything already."

"Everyone says that," I told him. "My mother keeps saying that. But then I get into the picker and I don't know the details. What if I don't know how many vineyards there are? I don't know the names of the new managers. What happens when something goes wrong with the trucks? What if a truck breaks down in the middle of a shift?"

"Just worry about your Felix," he said quietly, handing me a dish towel. My hands had gotten all sticky, hanging on to the railing of the picker.

"He's not mine."

Miguel poured from his water bottle over my hands to get them clean. "Did you see the light in the west?" he said.

"What does that come from?"

"City and smog," he said. He took my palms and scrubbed them with the towel. If you grow up on the easy side of a vineyard, you think you only need to wash your fingertips. Lately every gesture was a small humiliation. "It makes the most beautiful vineyard."

"Dad always got the most beautiful vineyards."

"Why do you talk in the past tense?" Miguel said.

"I'm sad."

"Oh yeah?"

"Sad people talk in the past tense," I said.

He walked me out of the vines, toward Dad's truck. "You don't have a reason to be sad."

I have always had trouble telling the difference between sadness and anxiety, especially when they're my own.

I got back into the truck and Miguel knocked on the window. "Go slow," he said. "These tractors don't look, they just pull right out in the middle of the road. You have to see them first."

"I'll be careful."

"You don't always see them coming, even if they go slow."

"Call me when you're on your way to Griffith tomorrow morning," I said.

"Ingrid. I call you tomorrow afternoon." I didn't even realize then that only the gondola drivers actually go to the winery. "You worry when you don't need to worry," he said.

"Does this face look worried?"

"Go slow," he said again, and rapped his knuckles on the side of the truck. "No one looks out for the other around here."

I drove back to the main road, past the limit of light from the halogens over the vineyard, and headed north. There were no streetlamps, no traffic lights, no painted lines in the center of the road. Just dark country and the thick smell of ripe fruit, like driving through a vat of fresh juice. I drove past acres of dark orchards and vineyards, dark intersections with two-way stops, past closed gas stations and closed bait shops and boarded-up-for-the-night fruit stands. I drove past acre after acre after acre of fields left fallow for the drought, toward home.

Naturally, Felix did not try to negotiate the price, or claim the grapes weren't what he expected. He paid exactly what he said he would, which is what I knew he would do.

I knew Uncle Felix didn't want to appear to the guys in the bar at the Vineyard that he and I were having any sort of conflict. So the next afternoon I stalked him there at lunch.

"I'm going to pick the Thompsons all this week," I said to him and Gale Macpherson over fried artichokes and crispy, over-chilled viognier. "The tops of the vines are shriveled, Uncle Felix, but the juice is going to be sweet and clammy, just like you like it."

"Clammy," Felix said.

"It's going to make you click the back of your jaw," I said.

Gale laughed. "You still got Thompsons on the vine, Felix?"

"I need sugar," said Uncle Felix. He sat back in the red-leather swiveling club chair. He grinned and rocked.

"Because he must add so much water," I said to Gale, smiling. "This is why Uncle Felix makes more money than you."

"There are more reasons than that why Felix makes more money than me," Gale said.

Fresno was the only place I'd ever been—and still is—where the topic of money was not unreservedly taboo. In fact, during lunch at the Vineyard, the topic of money—who had it and who was losing it, how to make it and how to squander it, where it came from and where it was going—provided the center of every conversation. Even in Hollywood, the gossip between Anne and her friends would skirt around money as if money were a snake you didn't want to poke. Here, though, what was the point of talking about anything if you were not going to talk about where the money was?

"Pistachios," Uncle Felix said. "Pistachios are the reason I make more money than you." He kept his hands off the table, patting his big round tummy.

"Why's that, Uncle Felix?"

"Ask Gale. Who gets all your money, Gale?"

Gale shook his head.

"Who does, Mr. Macpherson?"

Uncle Felix tilted his club chair toward me. "The packing house."

Gale shook his head, as if this were not true.

I said to Felix, "You're a packing house, sort of."

He nodded, he rocked. "That's why I make all the money."

We all kind of laughed.

Gale said, "Pick those grapes before they dry on the vine."

"I am!" I said. "The pickers are already parked." I held up my glass of wine, as if to toast.

"Are they," said Uncle Felix, rocking, holding his stomach. The waitress didn't come around to our table once that day to ask how things were.

"I told you, I am picking right now. I'll find someone to buy the juice if you don't want it."

"I want it," said Felix.

"I know you do," I said. "That's why you always buy me artichokes."

Uncle Felix walked me to the truck afterward in the deep, relentless sun.

"You don't know yet all you think you know," he said.

"I know all those Thompsons are frying," I said. And then, "Any other year this would be different. But Dad doesn't need this kind of stress right now." My scalp itched with dust. My fingernails were full of sand. "I don't know why you're pulling this stuff with him. Pull it with other people, but not your brother."

He patted the small of my back and opened the driver's door for me. "You really don't know anything about wine," he said. "And you're trying to make decisions you don't know how to make. I know your father wants you to learn, but this is not the way to learn. You're just lucky, this time, that the Thompsons are ready to come off the vine tonight."

"I'm lucky?"

"You've always been lucky," he said.

I slept early that night, easier now that Mother and Dad were running the air conditioner, and woke at 2:00 a.m. to join the harvest in progress. There was nothing for me to do, really, but make an appearance, drive Dad's truck through the blocks of vines and, as the farmers say, leave my shadow on the land.

The Thompsons were high in sugar, meaning the weight was lighter than we'd planned for, or hoped. We would need to harvest a lot of cabernet, I suspected, to make up for what we lost on the Thompsons. But the cabernet looked ample. The stressed vines had produced a strong crop.

Dad grew thirty varieties of grapes. Getting just the first two off the vine had been trickier than it should have been. *You really don't know anything about wine*, Uncle Felix had said. I didn't want to know that much about wine. My job was to know about grapes.

19. When I was young, we were warned not to go near the canals. Canals were full of corpses and old toys and household rubbish. We were not to ride our bicycles on the banks, and never, ever, were we to consider going swimming. As a child, the canals seemed terrifying, a living evil. I thought about this a lot that year—the perceptions of canals, life and death—as I drove through the vineyards where sometimes the canals carried no water at all.

Anne came back to Fresno quite a lot. "It's such a quiet house now," she said, meaning Beachwood Canyon. "It's too empty. I don't want to live there alone." Anne had gone to the discount shops at Riverbend, where proper department stores sent the items they couldn't sell, and had purchased dozens of pairs of lacy underwear, new flannel pajamas with monkeys on them, and a bag full of soft T-shirts, the kind that are still expensive even when they're on sale. It was teatime, and I'd come home from my rounds, and she was folding gauzy, bright underpants and placing them carefully in her girlhood dresser. "I'll stay here with you and go back when I have an audition."

"When will that be?"

"What I'd really like to do is sell the house and go to New York. I don't want to grow old without having lived in New York."

"You're not growing old."

"Sure I am. It happens while you don't realize it's happening." She clipped tags with a pair of kitchen shears, Mother's kitchen shears with the orange handles, which were actually sewing scissors. "I've been thinking for so long that I'm young and things are just beginning, that I'm in the feather-dusting part of the play, where the maid comes out to the drawing room with the duster and the phone rings and then the action begins. But the phone rang a long time ago. I'm in Act Two."

"I am too, then."

"Maybe not. Returning home to run the family farm usually happens in Act One."

"Or the finale," I said.

The desk beside the window that looked out to the river was strewn with half-used tissues. Anne never blew her nose, only dabbed at it, so her tissues had all these little fingertip imprints on them, a dozen tiny little domes on every tissue. They lay flat on the desk like dry butterflies. Anne wouldn't throw them away until she felt they were all used up.

Anne kept a bottle of regular Tylenol at her bedside. "What do you take this for?" I asked her, holding it up.

"It helps with the pain," she said.

"I should have thought of that earlier this summer."

"You shouldn't take Tylenol with booze."

"Let's get dinner later. I'll take you down to Bootsie's. I have money now, you know."

"The irony. Now you really are trapped here."

"I'm not having a bad time."

"I am," she said. "I am having a very bad time and I don't want to go out and see people in a restaurant. People who are all having a good time."

I'd started reading *Middlemarch* for the third time in six months.

When I lived in London with Newton, I read *Hopscotch* over and over for an entire year. I think this is one of the reasons he broke up with me. At his parents' cold stone house in the south of France, when he shocked me one morning with his declaration that the whole relationship had been a mistake, he said, "I think you must be depressed. You've been reading the same book for a year."

"You have to read it several times," I tried to explain. "To get it all."

Newton shook his head in doubt and sympathy. "I just think you're depressed." There is no explaining *Hopscotch* to a total idiot. Newton was a political consultant. The last book Newton had read was *The Art of War*, and before that, a popular history of importing tulips.

At Bootsie's in the evening, Elliot wore a crisp barman's apron made of blue ticking. He said, "Anyone who reads only one book a year is either an idiot or very depressed."

"But what if it's *Hopscotch* and you have to read it twice or three times, per the instructions?"

"Then you're just depressed. No one actually does that."

He was mixing those lovely frozen mojitos for me. He did them in a big silver mixing bowl, pouring in the steaming nitrogen and whisking it all together until it had the texture of sorbet and then scooping it into a dessert glass. Every time someone ordered one, he would scoop a tiny bit more into the glass in front of me.

"I haven't read anything this year except *Middlemarch* and trashy magazines."

"*Middlemarch* is kind of exactly like a trashy magazine," he said.

Someone waved to him from the front of the restaurant. He nodded back, arms busy whisking. I looked around and saw, by the window, a flabby young couple laughing and greasy with heat and drinks.

"Who's that?"

"A student," he said. "Her idiot boyfriend. They all come in here, they think it's funny."

"Or fun," I said.

"Or fun, maybe."

"They get a kick that you're not really paid anything to teach German? I don't get what's funny."

"I don't, either," he said.

Elliot took his drinks-making job so seriously, with his own belt of tools and a travel iron he kept in the back of the restaurant to make sure his apron was crisp every night; it was hard for me to picture him in front of a classroom, speaking a foreign language, in charge of the poor or lazy rich young people at Fresno City College.

"What do you teach them, exactly? Basic German? German one, two, and three?"

He nodded at the gimlet as he scooped the last bit into my glass. "One and sometimes two," he said. He poured another batch into the bowl. "I'll be paying for my PhD the rest of my life." He used the whisk like a weapon, stabbing and hurling.

This gimlet was thick and froze my teeth. "Maybe Bootsie will pay it all off," I said.

He stopped whisking and looked at me, surprised or horrified or distressed.

I must have been sort of drunk to say something like that.

Bootsie interrupted. "When I get big and fat, I'll have to hire someone to look after this place for me," she said. "Maybe you'll do it, Ingrid."

"I'm already looking after someone's business."

"Your own," said Elliot.

"Right," I said. I hadn't really thought yet of Dad's land as my own business.

"I think we should call the baby Elliot," Bootsie said. "I don't care whether it's a boy or a girl." Bootsie smiled that smile that took up her whole face—she seemed really, purely, joyfully, and excitedly happy. "And I hope it looks exactly like you," she said to him across the bar, "with those dark dark eyes and that big pout mouth."

"You used to make fun of my fish mouth," he said.

"You do have a fish mouth," she told him. "I hope the baby has one, too. A huge wet fish mouth. And your long eyelashes." Bootsie laughed and touched his arm. "Ingrid, do you think Elliot has a delicious wet fish mouth?"

Elliot ripped drink orders from the printer at the bar and lined them up like cards. "I hope the baby is a baby after all," he said.

"What does that mean?" she said.

"It means let's not get too excited until you've been pregnant a while and maybe let's not talk about this at work."

"That's not very nice," said Bootsie. She took a straw to gnaw on. She got the placid, plain look on her face that I knew was hurt feelings. Bootsie's face always had an expression, even when it had none.

I put my hand on her tiny pointy shoulder. "He's being nice."

"Some people don't get preggers at all," she said. "I feel like I'm really lucky."

"You are really lucky," Elliot said.

"We're all lucky," I said.

Then George arrived.

"Ingrid's extra lucky," Bootsie said as George made his way to the bar. George swayed when he walked, that languid way he had about him. He raised his hand hello.

"George," Elliot said. "Are you feeling lucky?"

"I'm not especially lucky," said George.

"You certainly are," said Bootsie. "You have all of us."

"It's true," George corrected himself. "I'll be luckier when I get something to drink and a plate of fritters."

Bootsie turned to the kitchen to put in the order for fritters. Elliot poured George a tumbler of Famous Grouse. "You picked the Fiestas," George said.

"You told me to."

"How did you get him to do that?"

"Just what you said. I told him I'd take the cab somewhere else."

George smiled and shook his head. "Impressive."

"Impressive what?"

"Ballsy. And impressive that he did what you asked."

"My uncle Felix isn't as sinister as all you people think."

George shrugged. "I don't know what to expect most of the time."

"I didn't know what else to do," I confessed. "Those grapes had to come off the vine."

He laughed a little bit. "You know, you're exactly the person your father needs. You're exactly the person he's needed for a long time."

"I'm not staying here, Georgie."

"No one else in this valley can keep Felix in line."

Elliot put another spoonful of mojito in my glass. "No," I said. "I have to go." I meant: I have to go home. I pushed my stool back into its position beside the bar.

"Eat with us," Bootsie said.

Elliot said, "When she says eat with us, she means stay here and get drunk."

Bootsie said, "Stay here and Elliot will get you drunk."

I said, "Someone has to work in this family."

"George has to work," Bootsie said.

"But George has no place else to go," said George, lifting his glass, tilting his scotch from one side to the other. "And no one else to see."

As it turned out, George was getting swindled by Mello, just as he'd predicted. They were threatening to pick before the sugar had fully developed, so the grapes wouldn't weigh quite as much. Plus they wouldn't taste as good as they could, reducing the value of future crop. Mello could get away with this sort of thing; they did every year. If they didn't pick early, they'd pick late. If they picked on time, they'd end up renegotiating your contract to pay less based on the grape glut, the quality of the fruit. Their field guys would find mold where there was no mold. They got away with this because they were big; someday you might need them. "It's predictable, but it's always upsetting," he said. "They could be really nice grapes if they'd just wait."

"Maybe they'll wait," I said.

George resigned himself to the Mello problem by drinking at Bootsie's and by thinking of himself as a gentleman farmer.

"George is writing another book," Bootsie said.

"A spy thriller," said Elliot.

"He's writing a spy thriller that takes place in East Germany," said Bootsie.

I said, "East Germany, George?" George had always known my obsession with East Germany, with how families were divided in the middle of the night.

"It has nothing to do with you," he said. "Except that your obsession became my own."

"You guys act like you're interested enough to have actually studied German," Elliot said.

Bootsie said, "It's a book about a man who knows someone is informing on him, and suspects his wife." She was very good at ignoring Elliot and putting the focus on herself. This is why she was the boss, I guess.

"Why always the wife?" I asked. "Why can't the husband be the informant?"

George said, "It doesn't necessarily turn out to be his wife in the end, Ingrid."

"Well, is it or isn't it?"

"You'll have to read and see."

"I don't want to wait that long."

He said, "When do I get to read your genocide comedy?"

"I think that was the worst idea I've ever had. But I managed to convince someone to give me living expenses for a year."

"Not such a bad idea."

"I don't know. That was a pretty bad idea, too."

"What about coming back home?" Bootsie said.

"Not such a bad idea, as it turns out."

"It's all material," said George.

There was an easiness there, at the bar, with Bootsie and Elliot and George. It was the kind of easiness that caused me to panic.

20. No one was more pleased about the money Uncle Felix paid for the Fiestas than Mother. "We're going to have a party. We'll roast turkeys outside. And we're going to bring Charlie up from LA."

"A fiesta for the Fiestas," Dad said.

"Yes," Mother stopped. "I should have thought of that." She stood at the stove, quickly shaking a skillet of crabs back and forth over a high flame. She had killed them first, spearing their backs with the point of a chef's knife, so that when she fried them, their little legs lay flat.

"I have to go back home soon," Anne said.

"Well, you can come back. Or stay. We can have the party in the next few days. You can stay a few days, can't you? Tell Charlie to get a flight so you can drive back down together." Mother spoke very quickly, in the high, excited voice she gets when she's feeling optimistic. That afternoon she'd had her hair colored at a salon.

Anne said, then, "There is no Charlie."

Mother placed the crabs on a platter and spooned corn relish on top. "If he argues, tell him we'll buy the ticket. Will we buy the ticket, Ned? I know Charlie hates Fresno."

Dad watched Anne.

"He won't argue, Mom." Anne got that flat-line voice. "He moved out of the house."

My mother said, "Why?"

"Mother," I said. "Just— They're having a rough patch. Don't ask questions." I scooped a crab from the platter on the table and placed it in front of Anne. "Here, Annie. Crunchy crabs."

"We should have nice wine with these crabs," Dad said. "Ingrid."

"I think Mom pulled something," I said.

"No, I didn't. I forgot."

"I'll get the wine," Anne said, and as quickly as possible disappeared down the kitchen stairs into the cellar.

Mother stood at the table with the platter of crab. Her hair was perfect: silky and flipped.

"Did you know this already?" Dad said to me.

"I didn't know when she was going to tell you," I said.

"She has to stay here," Dad said. "She can't go back to that house alone. It's in the middle of nowhere."

"It's in the middle of Hollywood, Dad."

Anne came up the stairs with a bottle of the old Mondavi she'd wanted but I thought we didn't have. Anne is like a truffle pig.

"You have to stay here," Dad said. "Aren't you on hiatus?"

Anne said, "I have to face that house." She opened drawers, looking for the wine key. "Daddy, do you want wine?"

"Not by yourself," he said.

"It's just that first moment I'm afraid of, the one where I walk in and it's all empty, he's all gone." In one motion she cut the top and removed the foil.

We were quiet for a moment. Dad said, "No wine for me."

"Think of this as an opportunity," I said. "There are no expectations."

"What does that mean?" Mother said. "It's not an opportunity."

Anne said, "This feels like a dream."

I said, "Maybe that life was the dream, or the fantasy, and this is real life."

"Real life," Anne said.

"Exactly," said Dad.

"I'm an actress, I have a tenuous relationship with real life." She filled my glass and her own to the very top.

"Stay here," Dad said once more.

"We're going to have a party," Mother said.

When Dr. Parker said Dad needed a biopsy of the spots on his lung, Uncle Felix suggested Dad get down to UCLA for a second opinion.

"What second opinion? I can see the spots myself," Dad said.

"We'll take you down in the helicopter," Uncle Felix told him.

Uncle Felix's helicopter had once been Dad's, and Felix had bought it off him during a bad year just a few seasons ago. "I'm happy with Dr. Parker's opinion," Dad said.

"Your father is as stubborn as your mother," Uncle Felix told me. He'd come for after-dinner drinks, something he hadn't done in a while, not since the night he'd dumped his car into the canal with poor Debby inside it.

"It's just a biopsy," I said. "All they do is scrape those dots off." When I was little, I remember that sometimes Uncle Felix's fingers were stained red from squashing grapes on the vine to see if the juice was ready. Dad could hold a grape or taste it, and other farmers would just look at the grapes, or send their men to look at them, and of course most everyone measured the sugar, but Uncle Felix had to squash grape after grape after grape to see which vineyards were ready for harvest. At dinner he would come with purple-red fingertips, but never a bunch of the grapes for us to taste. Uncle Felix didn't believe in the taste of a grape in relation to the wine it would make. He believed in texture. He believed barrels and process affected taste more than the juice. He had many unconventional opinions on wine.

"Just a biopsy," Felix said.

Later, I walked Uncle Felix over the canal and out to the gate. "He's tired," I said. "I think he doesn't want to admit that he's too exhausted to go anywhere."

Felix said, "Let me give you some advice. For the future. When you have a spot on your lung and someone offers you a ride in his helicopter to see a doctor in Los Angeles, accept the offer."

"All right," I said.

Just like the Thompsons, the crop of Fiestas to the north didn't weigh as much as expected. As I knew, as George knew, as we all knew, Felix had waited too long to pick. The grapes shrunk, sugar condensed. White grapes were already down to four hundred dollars a ton, and now there would be even less money than we had anticipated, no matter what the contract said.

"The chardonnay are at their peak. The rest of the grapes look excellent."

Anne and Mother sat together at the kitchen table, Anne in one of my father's discarded white T-shirts and my mother in her gauzy nightgown. They played backgammon without looking up. They had been playing backgammon when I left in the morning and they were still playing now, well into evening. Dad wore a waffled robe over his pajamas, chilled even in the Fresno night heat.

"If Felix picks them," Anne said.

"Don't get down on Felix," Dad said. "We know this is how he does business. We have always known."

"I don't know why you do business with him," Anne said.

"Because he's my friend," Dad said. "And because he's giving me a high price for the cabernet."

"Oh, Daddy," Anne said.

"If he doesn't pick that cab on time, I'm selling it to Mello, contract or no," I said. "Let him sue you, Dad."

"He wants that cab, and he wants it to be good juice. I've been doing this a long time, you know."

Anne said, "You employed Phillip a long time, too. He stole from you for fifteen years."

"If you girls know so much about ranching, why aren't you in the truck so I can retire?"

"I am in the truck," I said.

Mother went ahead with her plans for a party right away, as if she wanted to get her harvest dinner in before the money was gone. "I guess I'll have to do the flowers myself," she said.

Anne said, "A penny saved."

"I save all my pennies," Mother said. "I buy my lipsticks at the drugstore now."

The money would be gone either way, she figured.

I said to Dad, "Tell me what this means, exactly, the payment we're getting for the Fiestas."

"Just work the farm. Let me handle the finances. Just do your job."

"But I won't have a job to do if we don't work things out with the bank." I put bread in the toaster.

"Things are fine with the bank."

Mother said, "Ingrid, don't eat toast for dinner. There's still lasagna in the refrigerator."

"Tell me, then, what the numbers are, what we're looking at," I said. "I like toast, Mom. I want toast."

"The numbers are fine. Everything is fine."

"You say everything is fine always," I said. I leaned against the counter, pressing my back against its coolness. "I have to learn about this part, too, Daddy."

"What for? You say you're leaving once the harvest is through."

"I am."

"So don't worry about the money, Inky. Your job is big enough."

He stood, then, bracing himself thoroughly on the table in order to lift. It was the movement of an old man, a man in pain.

"Go," Anne said. "Don't stay here with us."

"I'm tired," he said. He kissed her head, he kissed Mother's head, he kissed mine. "I love my girls," he said.

"You haven't eaten," Mother said, looking up from her position on the backgammon board. "Stay and eat."

"I had toast earlier. I like toast, too." He creaked back to his room. Tomorrow he'd have his chest opened up, just a little bit, just a dot.

21. What the doctors had originally missed, what the doctors always missed, apparently, in cases like Dad's, was a tiny fungus living inside his lungs, indigenous spores that grow in the central California soil loosened into the air during dry seasons. It's what causes most of the coughs in the valley. Sometimes it turns brutal or fatal and sometimes it doesn't. It could be as harmless as a cold. Stress seems to feed it. Valley fever could seem like a tumor or MS or heart failure or a disintegration of the joints. It could, sometimes, look and feel like bone cancer. There's no cure, only management through drugs. Sometimes the drugs work and sometimes they don't.

We had closed the windows and turned on the air. This afternoon everyone felt very optimistic about the future. "It's the luckiest diagnosis," Mother said. "It's cured with rest and laughing." She emptied the dishwasher with alacrity, handing glasses over to us while we stacked them in the cupboard.

"I don't know if it's exactly lucky," said Anne. "Cancer sounds more manageable."

"Don't say that in front of your father," said Mother. "What he needs is laughing and no stress. Dr. Parker said he's probably had the fungus for twenty years."

Mother served the tea from her old glass sun tea jar. She would put tea bags in the water in the morning, set it on the porch, and by afternoon we'd have smooth iced tea with no trace of bitterness.

Anne had booked a ticket to New York and a swell of auditions. Eight auditions in two days. "You guys think I'm just a cow," she said.

"I never thought that," Mother said.

"I'll show you, though. I'll show you and everyone." Anne said this with neck tall, chin tilted up.

"Annie, no one thinks you're just a cow," I told her. The sun tea jar had a visceral feeling to it—sun tea reminded me of climbing trees—that feeling of stickiness and rough cuts in the palms of the hands and dehydrated blossoms and spiderwebs clumped in my hair.

"I was a good cow, though."

"The best," said Mother.

"Is that an insult?" Anne said.

"You could not be a cow," said Mother. "Because I am your mother."

Anne's neck is long and straight and has no imperfections. My neck has a protruding knob where it meets my spine.

"People love cows," I said. "Sad cows that talk."

Annie would drive directly from Fresno to LAX, bypassing her house. The small patch of lawn in the front had started to go a bit long and wild. Charlie had been the one to coordinate gardeners and chimney maintenance and things like roof repair or tree trimming. The air-conditioning had stopped producing cold air, and Anne didn't know how to contact the climate-control people. Someone had dented the garage door while she'd been away, trying to make a turn in the middle of the narrow hill street, and she couldn't bear the sight of the dimpled door. Rather than figuring out the logistics of having the door fixed, rather than calling a gardener or treating for termites or replacing the picket that had come loose from the fence, Anne had been ignoring the house entirely.

The table grapes were all off the vine. Raisin trays were laid between rows. The landscape had started its seasonal shift from green to gold. The wet ground had gone from orange to yellow— that dry, dark yellow dirt that means the very center of the harvest has arrived.

Wilson came over to play backgammon with Mom. Lately he would come over in the afternoons, around teatime, around the time I came home for a snack. Backgammon was the only thing that could distract Mother from her cards. Mother never played with the doubling cube unless she was playing with Wilson. She nearly always beat him.

"I don't like how he's letting the cab hang out there," Mother said. "It's time to pick them." She gammoned Wilson, who was quiet.

"The sugar's on the low end," I said. "Is Felix waiting for the sugar to go up or the weight to go down, Willy?" I refilled his gimlet while I asked him. It was a trick I had learned from Felix himself—always refill a person's glass as you're asking him questions.

"Felix isn't thinking about anything except the wine," he said.

"The business," Mother said, "not the wine."

"The wine is the business," Wilson said.

"You kids," Mother said. "Everything is easy for you. Why don't you go out there and plant a vine? See how you like working in the dirt."

"I'm working in the dirt," I said.

"You don't know what working in the dirt is," Mother said.

"Like you've worked in the dirt," I said.

"Don't patronize me, Ingrid, I'm your mother. I know more than you do. I've lived longer."

Wilson smiled and reset the game. "I'm going to owe you a lot of money," he said to Mother.

"We're not playing for money."

"Oh yes, for money. Today we play for money."

"What's different today?" Mother said.

"Today we play for money, tomorrow we play for Ingrid's hand in marriage," he said, giving me a sideways wink.

Mother said, "What do I get?"

"We don't place bets in this house," I said.

"In the Central Valley, every day is a bet," Wilson said. It's legal in central California to put your own and your family's and your ancestor's labor on the line in a gamble, but putting nickels into a slot machine is not.

"And the bank isn't gambling on us anymore," Mother said. "What they need is for someone to reassure them what a good bet we are. They need to hear it from Felix, who is keeping his mouth shut. I have never known Felix to keep his mouth shut. Have you, Wilson?" She carefully moved wisps of bangs from her forehead. Mother had been seeing the hairdresser once every two weeks, and she tried to keep her blow-out shape for as long as possible. After a week, Mother's hair still looked all right, but she started to get that stink of an unwashed scalp.

Wilson tossed his dice across the board. "You know Felix doesn't listen to me."

"I don't feel like playing, really," Mother said.

"That was only two games," said Wilson. "I came all the way out here for two games?"

"That's not why you came out," Mother said. "Ingrid, will you pour me a glass of wine? I can't drink the lime in those gimlets."

"I can't afford to be caught gambling anyway," Wilson said. "Every time he stops me, the cop at the corner of the 99 and Ashlan pretends he doesn't think I've been drinking."

"A warning every time?" I said.

"It's the Semper Fi sticker on the back of my truck," he said. "I'd rather not use up all my luck on backgammon." Wilson had bought the truck from an ex-marine.

"You've had no luck in backgammon," Mother said. "You'd better figure out some other way to get Ingrid to marry you."

"I'm not getting married," I said. "I'm a woman of the land now."

"Women of the land get married," said Wilson. "Farmers need families. That's the way it works."

"Families do nothing but split farms," Mother said.

"When you have a family, you have more people dedicated to the same venture. You have a team," said Wilson. He swirled his drink. "I'd like a team."

"You'll have more adversaries," Mother said.

"A family is a gamble, too," I said.

"Not with me," Wilson said. "My family's not going to be like that."

"Like what?" said Mother.

"Splitting things apart," he said. "My family's going to make wine and eat peaches."

Mother said, "That's a very nice thought, Wilson. Where did you get it?" She kept her eyes on the board. She smoothed an eyebrow with her index finger.

"And no one's going to build a shopping center," he said. "Because it won't be as lucrative as wine grapes."

"Right," said Mother.

I filled Wilson's glass with more ice. "I like these notions, Willy." I patted his damp back. "I like your plans."

"I need to find a good girl," he said.

"You will," I told him.

He said, "I already have. But you don't like me back." He filled his mouth with ice and began to make windy sucking sounds.

"Ingrid likes you," Mother said. "But Ingrid can only fall in love with men who have no love in them at all."

She said these things while counting the number of spaces her checker could move. "Thank you, Mother."

She said, "Ingrid doesn't understand a man whose life is ruled by seasons and crops."

"Mother, please stop."

Wilson watched my mother count spaces. He nodded along. He said, "Ingrid's life is run by crops right now."

In two more rolls, Mother managed to lift all her checkers from the board. "Look at that," she said. "Good luck."

22. Beneath the arbor next to the house, beside the vineyard, Mother lined jam jars filled with sunflowers along a rectangular table seating twenty on each side. We used Grandmother's Metlox grapevine dishes, as we always had for harvest parties. Beside the table, set on top of the weeds mown down: a bar with rows of wine bottles and a drinks dispenser full of sidecars. Anne draped white Christmas tree lights across the top of the arbor.

Daddy slept late into the morning while Mother ironed white napkins. On the porch in the back of the kitchen, Miguel assembled and scrubbed clean his old red barbecue and the two we kept in the garage. Dad, with his lungs, wouldn't oversee the roasting of the turkeys, so I'd promised to do it for him. It would give me a reason to sequester myself on the back porch. At parties anywhere, I always preferred to be in the kitchen or a back bedroom or outside with the smokers. I preferred to sort of linger on the edge, where the party really isn't a party. Often I would take off my glasses so that everything was a soothing blur, and in this way people really had to make an effort if they wanted to speak to me. I didn't want to have casual conversations with neighbors and acquaintances about what had brought me back to Fresno, what had happened with that genocide comedy I'd been writing, whether that had been me in the truck last night following the harvester from row to row.

There is little more comforting than following a harvester from row to row, watching all those grapes pour into the bin, watching all that work come to fruition, and all the hope and anticipation of the money that will come.

That day, I had gone to sleep after breakfast and then slept past lunch. This was not my normal sleep pattern, but I had never had much of a normal sleep pattern. The harvest had gone on until seven or eight in the morning, when the day and the grapes began to warm up.

"What are you smoking?"

"Well, God, it's a cigarette." Anne was arranging dozens of white votives between the jars of sunflowers. The brilliant thing about sunflowers is their interminable-seeming life span in the Fresno summer devil-heat. Nothing is more cheerful in 105 degrees than a sunflower refusing to shrivel.

"At nine in the morning?"

"Don't force me to tell you how much I smoke now."

"I have to go to bed."

"You always have to go to bed."

"I haven't been to sleep yet. At one point I fell asleep in the truck and lost the picker." I'd driven up Avenue 7 and found Kappas's pickers, but I couldn't find ours and I had to call Miguel.

"They have drugs for that, you know. Prescription drugs. They give them to astronauts."

"I know," I said, "but you can't drink on them."

Anne dropped the end of her cigarette into an extra jam jar. "You can drink on anything," she said.

Anne's auditions had gone well. She would know in weeks whether to have the air-conditioning fixed in the Beachwood house. She had now begun to think of herself as an Artist and smoked cigarettes before breakfast.

"Mom gets these ideas in her head," I said.

"She's making very little sense these days." She opened a box of votives and began to pull the wicks up straight. "But so little makes sense, having this party doesn't seem like the strangest of all."

That evening, Uncle Felix brought Debby to the party. We hadn't seen her since the night he had dumped her in the canal, and I guess we all assumed he hadn't seen her, either. She didn't look so bad this time: she'd worn a simple cotton sundress printed with blue moths, tied with a ribbon at the waist. She'd shaved down her talons and painted them a muted pink. She wore her curls loose and she looked pretty, almost girlish, and younger than I remembered.

They were among the first guests to arrive.

"Oh!" Mother said, taking Debby's hand in hello. "The manicurist!"

"Debby," said Felix, flat.

"Ned! Felix has brought his manicurist." She winked at Debby. "We thought we'd seen the last of you after Felix tried to drown you!"

Dad gave Debby a genuine hug hello. All Dad's hugs are genuine.

Mother kept on, "I don't think we've ever had a manicurist at the harvest party. A real working girl! Felix loves working girls, don't you, Felix?"

"Evelyn," just saying her name was an admonition.

"I'm just being silly." Mother smiled. "You know that, Felix, I like to tease." Mother kept that bright, delighted smile. Her lips were vibrant red, a glamorous shade called Flame she ordered directly from Sweden and wore only a few nights a year. "We're so glad you could come, Debby. Hands are always very rough in the harvest season. You could be very useful around here tonight," she said, and moved on, giving Felix a quick pat on the arm.

Later, even Mother would wonder why she had been so awful.

The Vocis were there, floozing all over, pretending to be a little bit drunk. Mrs. Voci had worn high heels and wobbled uncertainly on the dirt beneath the arbor, beside the bar, along the vineyard. Bint and Clara Masterson came together, confirming the rumors of their reconciliation, and brought an ostentatious bottle of champagne. (Felix and others would later complain it was in bad taste not to bring a California wine.) That terrible Chris, the angry man in the lobster pants from the dove dinner, had been invited by his golf buddies and wouldn't leave Anne alone. We had to set an extra place for him at the table. He asked for vodka, but Mother told him to drink the sidecars. Eventually he got too drunk and fell asleep in a lounge chair by the pool.

"You'll miss all the small dishes," George said when he found me at the grill, wearing that white wraparound dress my mother loved but that I hated, which is why I was wearing the dress to barbecue three forty-pound turkeys. "And scintillating gossip."

"Someone has to cook dinner in this family."

George and I had hidden from everyone at these harvest dinners since we were fourteen. Then, the harvest dinners were much more elaborate, more densely populated, all the intimidating wine people and farmers had attended, and George and I would hide out on the bench beside the tennis court or down at the river, drinking the dinner wine straight from the bottle.

Tonight he helped me monitor the turkeys, which had been slow-roasting since two. He wore a soft pink linen shirt with the cuffs rolled up to his elbows. His hands were tanned and scarred by injuries I didn't recognize. Bee scars, probably. Vine and tree scars.

"How much tonnage do you think you lost?" he said.

"Oh, George, I don't want to talk about the farm. I don't think either of us has good news to share."

"I'll bet he got you for bunch rot, too, didn't he?"

"George."

"He'll add water to that wine, you know."

"I think Daddy just didn't have the right contract, because it's Felix, and he didn't think Felix would nail him on these things. Daddy's big on gentleman's agreements, and Felix isn't much of a gentleman."

"There was no bunch rot on those grapes."

I turned to him. He sweated slightly from the heat of the evening. Beads of perspiration formed against the hollow of his throat, and I wanted to touch him, to wipe the slick of sweat off his throat, to lick and bite and devour him. Sometimes the thrill of seeing George next to me became so physically overwhelming that I had to step away. I moved back from the grill. "I have this feeling that everything is going to be okay," I said. "The cabernet is gorgeous, I mean really beautiful, plus there's a lot on the vine." Usually it was one or the other: a small yield of beautiful fruit or a large yield of an average-tasting crop. "You've seen the cab, right? I know Felix won't let those grapes hang."

"That's going to burn," he said, pointing to the bird.

"It's not going to burn. I've done this before." I moved one of the turkeys toward the side of its kettle, away from the center of the heat.

"It's like, with these guys, you have to learn the same lesson over and over and over," he said. "But truly, I will never sell to Mello again. I'd rather sell to one of the small guys and wait until April to get paid."

"They're too big not to sell to, George." It was Uncle Felix's line.

"I don't need them. We're not in debt."

I put the lids on the kettles. "We can leave these alone," I said.

George said, then, "Why is it that I'm the only one in my family invited to these things? You never invite my mother or brothers. You never invited Dad, even, when he was alive."

"I think we did."

"No, Inky. And your dad liked my dad. Didn't he?"

"Everyone loved your dad, George." George's father was simple and honest. He liked guns and falcons. He took care of his land, which is the most important thing neighboring farmers can ask.

"My dad liked your dad, I know," he said.

"Our dads are alike. A lot alike."

"Why, then?"

"It's because my mother is a bitch."

He laughed. "I knew that."

"She's the reason we broke up, George."

"I think I was the reason we broke up."

"You were," I said. "But she was insidious."

"Yes. She was." That's when he pulled out his first cigarette.

"No worse than Ellie's mother, though, right?"

He laughed just a little bit. "I love you because you have not changed at all, not one moment, not one molecule has changed." He put his lovely rough hand on my waist.

"Don't use the word *love* with me, really." I moved away.

"I do, though. It's the right word. I know you. I thought we were going to be friends."

"We are friends. While I'm back here, we're friends."

"While you're back here," he said, "is not very friendly."

I adjusted one of the turkeys and poked the coals a bit. "Let's just start here."

He kicked at the dried-up grass. "I'm not going anywhere else."

"How do you know that?"

"Bees," he said. "And trees. I have things to take care of. This is home, I'm happy here."

George had always worn his shoes until they looked like they needed to be taped back together. He brushed his foot left and right over the dirt.

I conceded. "We can be friends everywhere."

He nodded. "I can't believe I talked you into that," he said. "I wonder what else I can talk you into."

Debby wandered over to the barbecues, quite far from the rest of the guests and the lively action of the party. "This smells exciting," she said. Debby had worn terroir-appropriate ballet flats, pale blue to match the moths on her dress. I wondered if she did this on her own or if Felix had given her instructions. So many of the wives who'd come to these parties for years still wore pointy heels that sunk into the grass or slipped precariously over the dirt.

"George, this is Uncle Felix's friend Debby."

"This is where all the chic people are, I see," Debby said.

"All the antisocial people," George said.

Debby said, "The smokers are always the most interesting people." Everyone was always flirting with George.

"I didn't know Uncle Felix had a friend," George said.

Debby stood between us. "Ingrid, Felix tells me you lived in Paris."

"Briefly," I said.

"You'll have to give me a list of your favorite places for when Felix and I go."

"Paris?" I said. As far as I knew, Felix had visited Italy once in his twenties and had never been back to Europe.

"After the crush, he says."

"After the crush," I said. "How did you convince him on Paris?" Mother was going to love this. Love it in a hate sort of way.

Aunt Jane had never been to Paris.

"He convinced me!" she said, her hand fluttering to her chest. She had begun to get those little wrinkles above her cleavage that women get in middle age.

"You tell Felix to take you to the south, to Bordeaux," George said. "He'll be treated like royalty there."

"It's true," I told her. Even Mom and Dad were treated like celebrities in the wine regions of France. French growers and wine makers can't fathom the idea that someone farms twenty thousand acres.

"But he's treated like royalty here," Debby said. "We want to see the Mona Lisa."

"Let's go to Paris," George said to me then. "We never went to Paris."

"We never went anywhere," I said. "Except New York, and you see what happened."

"We should have gone to Paris, then," he said.

"Paris is all pink and romantic, right?" said Debby, smiling those huge socially aspirational teeth.

"I don't know," I said. "I was poor in Paris." Paris was on my list of places that belonged to someone else.

Dad gave a toast, "To friends," he said, "and my girls." In harvest dinners past, Dad had made long toasts with jokes and addressed each guest with personal thank-yous. Tonight he had the strength for five words, which were enough. Anne carved my turkeys. Anne is very capable like that.

There were platters of tomatoes and cucumbers with piles of herbs on top and a large cast-iron pot full of pilaf, the same as always. Bottles of wine outnumbered the guests at the table. The pitchers of sidecars had been emptied. Chris seized a seat next to Anne and poured vodka into his glass from a bottle at his feet. He'd presented the bottle to Mother when he arrived and then had retrieved it from the kitchen counter before dinner started. Anne sat with her legs crossed toward Wilson, on her other side. She gave me long Anne winks across the table.

People laughed. Dinner outside, with the trucks and harvesters going for miles on farms all around, you can only hear the conversations happening right there next to you on one side at a time. You can't hear what's being said two seats down; you can't hear diagonally across the table. But you can hear the laughing from one end to the other.

There was no conversation worth listening to. I knew, by now, real conversations happened over lunch.

For dessert there were Thompsons with Manchego and a big wheel of Stilton you could dig out with a spoon. There were tiny thimbles of port from Ficklin, the winery in Madera, just up the road.

Mother was right: the dinner was good for Dad.

By the end of the evening, there was an unidentified Mercedes left in the driveway. We couldn't determine whom it belonged to until the next morning when Chris, still in his khaki pants and rope belt, ambled into the kitchen for breakfast, contrite, embarrassed, all his anger turned to humiliation.

"I don't know how I ended up down there," he said. He had a

red mark across his face where the criss-cross straps of the lounger had been.

"They're very comfortable lounge chairs," Mother assured him. "Ask Ingrid."

"Your pants are torn," I said.

"I must have stumbled. Yes." Terrible Chris looked as if he might cry. "You have been really kind to me. Thank you for having me last night. I didn't realize it was a sit-down affair."

"But nothing," Mother said. "Just some turkeys." She spoke to him softly, tenderly, in a motherlike voice she never used with her own daughters. "We hope you had a nice time before you went to sleep."

Then, shockingly, he did start to cry. "I'm sorry. You've been so kind. I don't know what's wrong."

"It's a hangover," I said.

"This town has been very difficult," he said. "You know? It's just nearly impossible to live here."

"It's been a particularly hot summer," Mother said.

"It's not the weather," he said. "It's been the people. I can't seem to find a way into this place. Not you, of course. But others."

"People have their old friends," Mother said. "It's like that."

He nodded. He wiped his nose with the back of his hand.

"No one likes an outsider," he said. "Even I don't like an outsider."

"It must be lonesome," Mother said. "A new place where everyone else knows each other."

"I didn't mean to say that," he said. "I don't know what I'm saying. I mean to say thank you, that's all. And I'm sorry I got so lit up last night."

"We like for our guests to get drunk," I said. It was true: we all loved a good drunk party, and last night had been one of the drunkest.

Mother gave him burnt toast and a small glass of pickle juice, her hangover cure.

When I saw him again at the club that fall, Terrible Chris never mentioned sleeping by the pool or his hangover in our kitchen. He never again asked about Anne. He had very pointy incisors, and he was always flashing them at me.

23. By the end of September, growers were burning old vines. We needed sweaters outside at night. The smell of raisins drying had vanished; the valley smelled more each day like fertilizer and tar, the blank smell of the dormant season.

Dad's bedside table became his office, although the illness had compromised his ability to focus for more than a couple hours a day. He rarely left the bed. For valley fever, there was no more treatment than bed rest and fluids. The antifungal drugs the doctors tried at the beginning had no effect on Dad but to nauseate him even further.

He learned to wear slippers. We brought his work to him. From bed, he kept the books.

"It's nice when he raises his voice," Mother said, listening to him make demands on the phone from his room.

"Who could he be talking to?"

"You would know better than I would," she said. "They're all the same people to me. The chemical guys? The truck repair people? What's the difference. It's good to hear him fight for something."

"Dad fights for everything," I said.

What I didn't learn about the harvest season from George, I learned at the Vineyard. Sometimes I didn't even eat there, just went in to see who was there and to talk. Always there was some-one to talk to.

Billy Moradian turned out to be a big gossip and full of good advice on harvest. It was Billy Moradian who warned me to keep on Felix about the grapes. "He's never going to pick those colombards, I don't care what he's telling you." Green grapes that went for eight hundred dollars a ton last year were bringing in about two hundred dollars by the end of the season. In addition to the financial challenge of the grape glut, Felix was letting my grapes shrink on the vine.

I had started to think of them as my grapes.

Billy would give Felix a hard time, too. "Why are you putting this poor girl through this? Pick the grapes." There were always artichokes, regardless of the season. There was always the bottle of lunch white on the table.

"I like my grapes sweet," Felix would say.

"You can add the sugar," I said.

"Sugar costs money. Let the sun make the sugar. We have plenty of that."

Most all white grapes were off the vine. Their weight had been compromised by the delayed harvest, but it wasn't so much the weight that did us in that year as the drop in prices, no mat-ter what your contract said. Napa and Sonoma and all the north-ern counties had gluts, too. It would have been impossible to sell the green grapes for more anywhere else. Felix had given us fair prices for the syrah and the merlot and the barbera, all the black grapes harvested so far, sticking to the number in the contract although he could have easily cut the price in half.

"Poor girl," said Billy.

"She's no poor girl," Felix said.

"You pick when you like," I told him. "That's what the contract says."

"That's what all my contracts say," said Felix. He ate the breading off an artichoke.

"You're like Jack Sprat," I said, eating the artichoke he'd left bare.

"I'll pick them this week," he said. He took the crust off another and this time he ate the artichoke first. "I have been doing this a long time, Inky."

Billy said, "Why do you let him speak to you like you're a little girl?"

"Inky's her name," Felix said. "It's always been her name."

"You should have picked last week," I said. "At least last week and probably earlier. Dad says so, too." The waitresses and most of the other guys in the bar had learned, by now, to avoid the table when Uncle Felix and I sat together. Billy Moradian, I think, enjoyed the tension.

"Where's your dad?" Felix said. "He hasn't joined us in a while."

"Ingrid doesn't get either benefit," Billy said. "She doesn't get the benefit of being your goddaughter, and she doesn't get the benefit of being an arm's-length grower." He poured the last of the viognier into his glass. My grandparents used to tell me that whoever poured the last bit of wine in his glass had to buy the next bottle. No one at the Vineyard abided by that tradition. At the Vineyard, every meal got split individually, and each bottle of wine was charged to whoever had ordered it. Most everyone had an account settled at the end of each month.

Uncle Felix raised his index finger to the waitress for another.

"Wilson's the only one who gets the benefit of being family. Right, Uncle Felix?"

"Because he is," Felix said. "He's what I've got to work with. You won't let me work with you."

"I have to go," I said, and kissed Uncle Felix on his round, dry forehead.

"Stay for one more glass," Billy said.

I shook Billy's hand. I scooted the red club chair back up to the table. "Thank you," I said. "I have a meeting in Berenda. Someone has to work in this family."

Anne had returned to Los Angeles, to her half-empty home, to wait for word on what might happen in New York. Her agent, predictably, was not enthusiastic about Anne's theatrical ambitions. He'd been trying to distract her with a heavier than usual onslaught of auditions, keeping her from escaping.

"I'd rather be in this house alone than stay in Fresno any longer, anyway," she said. "I think I begin to actually smell like Fresno."

"Do I smell like Fresno?"

"It's hard to tell when we're both there. You'd have to come down here and I can tell you."

"I'm enjoying myself here."

"I saw that. It alarms me."

"What's happening with New York?"

"What would you think if I sold this house?"

"I would think that's genius."

She *tsk*ed. "I thought you loved this house."

"I do love your house. But I think you should get out of there. How could you continue to live there?"

"If I sell the house, Charlie will never be able to come back

"Your marriage wasn't built on a house, Annie."

"He won't know where to find me."

"You're being very dramatic."

"I'm going to sell the house and go to New York."

"Now?"

"Come to New York with me."

We would have these conversations while I drove around the truck. I had pulled to the side of the road near one of cabernet vineyards in Madera. I could tell from the road the gra were nearly ready. I walked into a row and tasted one off the of the vine: plummy and tart, but too taut yet. The grapes wo taste and feel like jam by the time they were ready to come the vine, probably a week from now. "I like it here," I said. "A what am I going to do, abandon Dad?"

"I mean after the harvest," she said.

"I might like it here then, too." I went back to the truck to the refractometer.

"No, you won't. Of course you won't."

"I really like grapes, Annie."

"You have an incapacity to stay any one place for too l Your mother made you that way." I could hear her suck on a arette. "I mean, we all like grapes."

"Staying here to run the ranch could be the most rebel thing I've ever done."

"If you did decide to stay, you'd be a grave disappointme your mother."

"She's made that clear," I said.

"Nothing you have ever done has made you happy. W the ranch going to make you happy?"

"Why is New York going to make you happy?"

"God," she said. "Answering a question with a question."

"You are like the personification of a question answered by a question."

"What does that even mean? Have you been drinking?"

"I'm looking at grapes, Anne." The soil in Madera reacted like powder—fluffy and explosive. I stepped lightly.

"You're being very sharp-edged," she said. "You're getting a little hostile."

"I have very little patience these days."

"Well, you need to get out of there. You are, you know, a very patient person by nature."

"I'm not. A patient person is what I am not."

I could hear the cigarette and the tongue suck through my mobile. "Something has made you impatient."

The grapes, though beautiful, had all that powdery dust on them. "I love you, Annie, but you don't know me very well."

She laughed a laugh that said *I know*. "And I know you so much better than I know myself."

I think many people assumed that I would, once harvest was done, move on to someplace else. Annie assumed this, and Mother and Felix and Wilson. I may have assumed this, too, but now everything is harder for me to remember.

Annie did sell that house in Beachwood Canyon. She and Charlie had owned it for ten years. By the end of the year, Anne bought herself a West Village studio, a fourth-floor walk-up on Bethune Street with two double-hung windows and a built-in china cabinet along the length of the entire back wall. "Can you imagine I could have missed out on this?" she said that winter. "I could have spent my entire life in that dull house with that dull Charlie."

"You would have never married someone dull."

"He was dull at the end," she said. "We were both dull at the end." I could hear her heave a window open, to climb onto the fire escape to smoke. "But now I have this, and it's my own, and it doesn't have any of Charlie's furniture."

"And nothing is dull."

"No, nothing will be dull ever again. Now I'm going to be you, and I'm going to run around doing whatever I please."

I could hear the New York sirens far off through the phone, and it did make me itch with a restlessness and a hunger to move. So I got in the truck, and I drove. I drove a lot that winter, aimlessly, not even checking on crops. I drove to Firebaugh and back, or all the way to Merced, and sometimes as far south as Bakersfield, always on the country roads, where all I passed was fallow land and someone else's dormant vines.

George wore a white cotton button-down and sturdy khakis and folded his elbows on the bar. He was freshly clean, closely shaved, his hair still damp from the shower. His hands were smooth with the glycerin cream he kept in the center console of his truck.

I said, "How's the book coming along?" I was still dusty from the fields but I was hungry and anyway I had to go right back out there after dinner, to a small field west of Fresno in Rolinda, where the crews were picking overripe sauvignon blanc.

"Don't taunt me."

"I'm not taunting. I'm asking."

Elliot kept our glasses full. By now I had stopped drinking the frozen mojito and had adopted as my regular drink vodka with a splash of water. I couldn't have gone on drinking that sugary mojito three nights a week. I ate at Bootsie's a lot that season, because I didn't want Mother to be bothered cooking for me and there was no question, after being in the fields all night and all day, of cooking for myself.

"Well," he said. "The idea is to get the book done before we shake the trees."

"How are the trees?"

He smiled at me. He laughed. "The trees are fine," he said. "The crop looks good." In front of him was a bowl of mussels and clams in a spicy tomato broth. "Share this with me," he said, handing me a slice of grilled bread.

"I've ordered the burrata." I had gone back to the kitchen to ask Arturo what to eat. For the burrata, he was roasting tight, dense bunches of pinot noir straight from the vines in Bootsie's yard.

"I'll share the burrata, then," he said.

I tore off a piece of the bread and sank it into the chunky broth. "Thank you."

"I went to see your cab today."

"You did? Where?"

"North Friant." The grapes off Friant ripened the quickest—they'd be the first off the vine.

"What do you think?"

He pulled each mussel from the shell with a smaller mussel shell, like pincers, and arranged the empties neatly one inside another. "I think you'd better start picking."

"We're still trying to get Felix to pick the last of the white grapes. I'm picking sauvignon blanc tonight that looks like raisins."

"Never mind the white grapes," he said. "Focus on what's best now. It's the right time for the cabernet."

"I need the money for those colombards. There are two thousand acres of colombards alone."

"How do you know what money you need?" George said. "You never know until the season is done."

Bootsie said, from the end of the bar, "You never count your money until the dealing's done. No one tell you that, Palamede?" There were only a couple tables full that evening. Bootsie kept her eye on the door.

"Felix was only ever going to pay what he wanted for the white grapes," George said. "I thought you knew Felix." He poured tap water from a tall glass into his scotch.

"I do know him."

"Then you should have known that Felix never intended to pay what he said. He never intended to pay market for those white grapes at all, and I'll bet he doesn't intend to pay market for the cab."

"You're making me feel dizzy," I said.

"Consider it one bad year," Bootsie said. "I'm sure that's what your dad is thinking."

"I'm not sure Dad can afford another bad year."

Bootsie came around to the other side of George and scratched the back of his head. "You should grow out these curls," she said.

Elliot leaned against the back of the bar and polished a polished rocks glass. He watched the glass, as if looking for spots to appear. The restaurant was too quiet; anything could happen.

Bootsie, like beauty itself, couldn't really be trusted. She was the same girl now who'd slept with Hasso, the same callous Bootsie who wrecked sweet Linus, who was telling the truth when she said she could never love someone for more than ten years. Poor Elliot, she had loved him for no more than ten months. Ten minutes. More likely, she had not really loved him at all.

"My curls aren't like yours," George said.

"Better," Bootsie said.

Bootsie's power came from knowing that when her beauty ran out, her money could take over. Bootsie knew loss and sadness and an absence of love, but she'd never known a crisis of confidence.

"How do I make him harvest the cab?" I said. "What do I say?"

"You say what you said last time," George said. Bootsie continued to run her hand through his hair, measuring it. He paid no attention. He pinched one mussel after another, deliberately but with ease, as only George could manage. "You did it once before."

"How could he not have noticed the grapes need picking?" Bootsie said. "He wants those grapes. He needs them to make his nasty wine palatable."

"He uses sugar and oak chips and whatever else for that," Elliot said.

"Not for this wine," Bootsie said. "He's been very vocal about doing something new, stepping it up a bit, and I know he needs those Palamede grapes. I don't think much of Felix, but I think a hell of a lot of his business acumen."

"It's possible he forgot about the Friant vineyard," I said.

"That is in no way possible," said George. "Felix knows every parcel of land your father owns. And even if he had forgotten, he pays people to follow those fields."

I looked at Bootsie. "It's not nice to use the word *nasty*, Boots. That's not necessary."

"I'm not saying your grapes are nasty," she said.

"It's just the word," I said.

"I do think Felix's wine is nasty," she said. "And I think he's a vile piece of work, too."

"Bootsie," I said. "It's not necessary! He's my friend, he's closer to me than you are."

Elliot said, "Come on, Bootsie." He put down his towel and reached over the bar to put his hand on her forearm.

She chewed on a cocktail straw, really gnawing on it. She had stopped smoking, it dawned on me then. "Could one of you boys tell Ingrid that she's in big trouble if she thinks Felix Griffith is her friend? Because she doesn't listen to me. She doesn't think I'm very good at friendship." She slapped the bar and turned away, heading toward the two tables of customers, straw clenched in her teeth, wild hair being wild.

The chef brought the burrata to me himself, because there was almost no one else in the restaurant and because Elliot had failed to notice the dish on the shelf behind the service bar. Tiny roasted wine grapes dissolved into their own sauce beside the cheese. "Taste it right away," the chef said. "Before the grapes cool."

"It's magnificent," I said.

"Is good," he said.

"I need another one," I said. "Because I have to share it with George."

"You don't have to share," George said.

"I want to." I nodded to Bootsie's chef. "I'll eat two," I said.

George pushed his empty bowl away and pulled his scotch closer. He took my fork and ate a bite of the burrata. "Just tell him you're picking. It doesn't have to be complicated."

"It seems all very complicated. I'm exhausted."

"It's harvest," George said. "Half the valley is exhausted."

No one else sat at the bar, and Elliot retreated to the kitchen. Arturo delivered another plate of burrata and we washed it down with our cocktails.

24.

Felix disagreed about the grapes. Red grapes, green grapes. He wanted to wait until the sugar was dense. Every other green grape in the valley had been picked. Every green grape but ours. We had colombards drying on the vine.

Mother said, "Don't tell your father more than he needs to know. This whole thing has made him sick."

"A fungus made him sick," I reminded her.

"No, no. This year has been a disaster." She slapped her playing cards on the table in seven neat piles. "Why do you always disagree with everything I say?"

"It's not a disaster yet," I said.

"You always contradict me," she said. "You will probably stay here forever just so you can blame me."

"What do you mean 'here'? I'm not moving in with you."

"It feels like you've moved in with us." She wouldn't look up. She spanked the cards down.

The oaks along the river had begun to droop. This happens in the California fall: old trees start to look old. Not like in New

England, where fall trees look vibrant. Not like in a proper East Coast winter, where leafless trees look absolutely dead. Fresno's autumn leaves begin to sag and wither, straight from green to brown. It's due to the cool, wet mornings and the hard, hot afternoons.

Mother said, "Marianela says in Bakersfield the leaves have already started to drop from the vines."

"She's exaggerating," I said. "That's not possible."

"I don't know," Mother said. "Anything is technically possible."

"Not bare vines in October. Not even in Bakersfield."

She smacked one card on top of another, looking for matches.

I said, "I'm not moving in, Mom. I thought you wanted me here. I am trying to help."

"I do want you here," she said. "But I don't want you to stay."

I ate toast and grapes. I ate this almost every morning for breakfast, or else a soft-boiled egg I could slurp from its shell in the car.

"You never even see the right matches," I said. "Hold back on the two and there is a jack underneath."

"You should be living your own life far away from here," she said, sweeping all the cards together to shuffle them again.

I planned to phone Felix on my way to the warehouse. But the morning was brisk and cool. Everything I needed to do from Dad's truck I could do walking along the San Joaquin. I followed the gravel drive to the end of the yard, down the terrace, past the Wilson-funded rejuvenated swimming pool, past the sad patch of our squandered tennis court. The river was low and swampy and green, with willow scrub and reeds overtaking the bank.

Our grapes grew for a quarter mile north, where they met the Ellison property. The fruit had been picked two months ago at least, because these vines by the house were favored, they were part of our home's landscape, and Miguel tended them as if they were his own. These were the Thompsons we'd been using to chill our vodka since June, fruit packed by Sarkisian in Fowler and shipped as table grapes all over the country. These grapes were just a very small part of the farm's income, and because of the grape glut, that income had been even smaller.

I walked and kept walking and took a right through Walter's almonds, which looked just fine—no black, no shriveling. There had been a lot of hyperbole about Walter's almond disaster at the beginning of the summer. The almonds would be all right. Fewer than usual, maybe, but you prepare for that kind of bad luck. You save, you buy insurance, you get bank loans. Walter would be harvesting those nuts any moment now.

I crossed the near-empty canals and the farm roads and the morning warmed up and I headed toward Felix's driveway, the same walk I had taken every day when I first came home. I walked in from the road, and through the puffs of dust I could see his truck parked beside the tiny house, everything white and polished.

Felix had a harder time telling me no in person. He had stopped answering his phone when I called.

"I thought a lonely farmer like you might want company at breakfast," I said.

"I could have had ladies here," he joked, clapping my shoulder, ushering me in through the glass-paneled side door off the carport. "And I do want company! I always want your company."

Uncle Felix's tidy little kitchen smelled fresh and waxy, like a display kitchen or a kitchen for dolls. Felix never ate anything at home. His refrigerator, I knew, was empty but for bottled water and white wine and possibly an open can of condensed milk. He put the kettle on and took a jar of instant coffee from the cupboard beside the sink.

"Where's Debby?"

"Debby's got work," he said. "She knows I get agitated during harvest."

I liked Debby fine, but somehow I felt loyal to Mother's hostility. "That's sensitive of her."

He said, sincerely, "She is sensitive."

Felix's house buzzed with the sound of old appliances and a churning air conditioner. His quiet, lonely house could be so loud.

"Why'd you come?" he said.

"I was walking."

"It's good to see you here in my kitchen again. You haven't been walking here so much. I'm old, you know. I need friends."

"I've been working," I said. "It's harvest time."

"Harvest is especially when I need friends," he said.

His house was so cool, chilly enough to need a sweater, well insulated in spite of it being an old farmhouse.

"I want the black grapes off the vine," I said.

"Black grapes are coming off the vine. You have twenty thousand acres, Ingrid. You can't do it all at once."

"The cabernet. The cabernet is what I'm worried about, although you're letting all the red sit out there too long, even the colorinos."

"It's not ready." He tipped a teaspoon of coffee powder into a mug advertising American Grape Harvesters. He poured the water in slowly, watching it, stirring. "You like sugar, don't you?"

"But it is ready. I've tested it myself. From various places in each of the vineyards."

"Sugar and milk, right?"

"They're already harvesting in Merced, Uncle Felix. Merced. I'm not stupid, I know things. Do you think I am so dumb?"

"Do you think I am?"

"That's why I'm confused," I said.

"Where is your father? He's not giving me a hard time." Then he said, gently, "Don't push me on this, Ingrid."

"What's the point of paying the premium if you're going to let them hang?"

He smiled. "They'll weigh less."

"Don't joke."

"I'm not joking." He handed me the mug and sat across the speckled Formica tabletop, his smooth, stubby hands folded in front of him. The table, I think, had been left in the house when he inherited it.

"What is the point of buying Dad's good grapes if you're not going to harvest them at their peak, Uncle Felix? What are you doing?"

"I'm making wine." He spoke to me so patiently, patronizingly, as if speaking to a disappointed child.

"But you're buying these for the flavor."

"I don't make these decisions." The lie was plain, and we both knew it was sitting there between us. "I'll leave the call to my field guy."

I couldn't breathe. My chest seemed to fill with water, my whole body stiff with something between anger and fear. I watched steam come off the top of my coffee. When I looked at him, he looked back directly, anticipating a response. I couldn't open my mouth even to sip from the promotional mug. He waited. He had these enormous hazely turtle eyes, lonely eyes you could trust, if you didn't know whose they were. Already, at eight in the morning, he was wearing his blue cashmere sweater vest and his work boots.

"Daddy loves you. He trusts you."

"I trust him."

"But you've tricked him. You've lied to us." I felt my face go red and hot. I willed myself not to look upset.

"I never lied to anyone."

"Your field guy? You're leaving it to your field guy?"

"If you think that's a lie, you'd better get out of this industry."

I eased the mug of coffee into the center of the table, away from me.

He stood up. "I was going to Salazar's for breakfast," he said. "You want to come? I don't think you've been to Salazar's."

"Why are you doing this?"

"This is business, Inky."

"I don't understand this kind of business."

"Well," he said. "You'll learn."

He leaned against the dry, polished sink.

"You have the money. Just pay Dad the money!"

"If I honored all my contracts during a glut like this, I would have been out of this business a long time ago."

"Dad is your friend."

"I've never had a better friend," said Uncle Felix. "He found morphine for Jane when the doctors wouldn't prescribe her pain medication." He looked at me. "Do you remember that?"

I remembered. Dad had appealed to Dr. Epstein, the orthopedist, when Jane's idiot oncologist wouldn't give her palliative drugs. "Dad is excited about this new thing, this new wine you keep talking about."

"He's right to be excited. He knows that."

"But, Felix," I said, "who else believes in you like that?"

Felix laughed. He came over to thump me on the back. "I don't need anyone but Neddy to believe in me like that." He took his car keys from the counter. "Come on to breakfast with me."

"I'm not having breakfast with you."

He said, then, "You be sure to tell your mother about our conversation. You be sure to tell her Debby thinks she's a delight."

"Is that why you're doing this?"

"Talk to your mother about friendship, if you want to have a conversation about friendship."

I may have managed to say "All right." I did manage to get up from the speckled Formica table. My hands went numb and tingly, as if from cold. Later I remembered that moment as if I had been floating above it, watching myself get up from the table and pass Uncle Felix at the sink, the swishy sound of the kitchen door as I opened it to leave.

There was extra juice all over the valley. The wineries had all the cab they needed this late in the season. No one was calling up to find who had nice cabernet. Even wineries who might have loved to get Dad's juice at an excellent price were now full up, I knew.

Too afraid to call Dad and too ashamed to call George, I phoned Miguel.

"Yes," he said. "I thought this was happening."

"Thought what was happening?"

"I thought," he said. "I had thoughts. I had thoughts about Griffith not wanting the grapes."

"Why wouldn't they want these grapes? The whole point was these grapes, this new wine project. Right?"

I could hear Miguel's deep chest wheeze through the scratchy mobile phone connection. I could hear his stony face and his hands swipe his jeans with the dark stains on the thighs. "I knew when Felix contracted to pay too much. I knew then, in the spring."

"Knew what, Miguel? In the spring."

"Ingrid, I knew he would not buy these grapes. I know you love this man, Ingrid. He is close to you."

"Miguel."

"But you are not close to him. Come see me, come to the house."

"Tell me now."

"There is nothing to tell. Come to my house."

"If I drive this car I will kill someone."

Marianela gave him instructions from the background. Marianela shouted in Spanish, in paragraphs. Miguel said, "Your uncle Felix doesn't want just one crop, Ingrid. He wants the whole thing."

"He wants what."

Marianela picked up an extension. "You come over, Ingrid. No one listens to us."

"I'm listening now," I said.

"Your father has no eyes," Marianela said.

I said, "What whole thing?"

"He wants all of what Jefe has."

My instinct was to run away as long as I could run.

Marianela said, "You have your own life, little one. You don't want any part of this business."

"Let's call a crew and pick it anyway," I said. "They're too ripe to let sit one more day. Don't you think?"

"I think so," he said. "But we have to pay the crew."

"Uncle Felix will have to honor the contract or else we'll just sell them somewhere cheap." I knew we wouldn't be able to sell the grapes anywhere else, no matter how cheap.

He said again, "We have to pay the crew."

"That's fine, we have the money to pay the crew."

"Cash?"

"You want me to bring cash?"

"I think the crew is going to want cash this time."

"Why cash?"

"Or else don't call the crew."

"I don't think Dad's ever paid cash, Miguel."

"They haven't been paid for a while, Ingrid. They won't come without cash."

"Since when haven't they been paid?"

"All this season. I tell them it's coming, but they won't come to work again unless I promise them cash."

"I'll bring the cash."

I carried the news home with me.

Mother and Dad sat at the kitchen table, drinking tall brown glasses of sun tea shiny with condensation. Dad so rarely got out of bed these days. Mother rubbed his chest with Vicks VapoRub in the mornings when the cough was thickest and again last thing before bed, to help him sleep. In between, he sweated, propped up in bed by pillows from the living room sofa, with folders and books piled at the table next to him. There were some days he'd spend so long vomiting that Mother would check him into the hospital just to get IV fluids and to make sure he'd keep the medication down.

Now, before I opened the screen door, I could see them laughing and leaning back in their chairs, as if this were a last strong effort made by each of them to save something.

"Tell Miguel they're getting a check," Mother said, handing me an envelope damp with the impression of her fingers. She waved it toward me. "They can take the check or they don't have to work."

"I think he meant cash, like cash," I said.

"Your father has never written a bad check in his life."

"I'm not the one concerned about the check, Mother."

Dad said, "They don't mean cash, Inky." The wet glass of sun tea had made a puddle in front of him. He had withered this summer, more than just the weight he'd lost. His bones, somehow, seemed delicate. It was good to see him smiling at the table.

Mother said, "Is it nice to be home, Ingrid?"

"You mean home right now or here in general?"

"Both," she said. A small plane flew over the house, interrupting the country quiet. She filled a glass with ice and poured tea from the jar on the counter. "Here."

"Yes." It was a true thing to say. "And I'm glad Dad is with us in the kitchen." This time of year, in the past, Dad would come home to sit in the kitchen with his clothes smelling of ripe fruit. The whole kitchen would smell like caramel.

"Sit," Dad said. "There's no place to go in a hurry. Believe me."

I sat. The three of us watched water pool around our glasses. The sound of the plane trailed off. When I lifted my glass to sip, water drained down my wrist to my elbow and soaked into my white cotton button-down.

"What do you think?" Mother said.

"What do I think about what?"

"What do you think will happen?" she said.

"To what?" I said.

"I'm just talking. I want to know what you think."

"I don't know," I said.

She said, "Do you think we should go get margaritas at Zapato's?"

Dad laughed, so I laughed, and then the three of us were laughing. There was nothing to laugh at. Sometimes there is nothing to do but laugh.

I decided to pick those grapes because leaving the choice to Dad could have killed him, I thought, just then. Already he was so diminished.

———

Of course Uncle Felix didn't buy the cabernet for the price he had promised. He didn't buy half the cabernet at all, and most of Dad's beautiful grapes went to waste. There was no powdery mildew. There was very little rot. Uncle Felix, like many of the wineries in the valley, just stopped buying fruit.

Uncle Felix knew, of course, as I didn't, that without the money for the black grapes, all twenty thousand acres of vines and twenty-five thousand more of row crops and peaches would go back to the bank. Dad might, if the bank was merciful, get to keep the original hundred left to him by his parents.

Uncle Felix had all Dad's financial information because Wilson had provided it to him.

I couldn't deliver those grapes anywhere. Even if a winery could have paid for them, by the time we had picked everything it was the end of October. The wineries were congested. I called the small guys and the conglomerates; no one had any room left in their tanks.

25. The papers relinquishing the ranch had to be signed in San Francisco, at 555 California Street, by the end of the day on the Wednesday before Thanksgiving. The building is that fifty-two-story accordion on California and Kearney with the granite courtyard in front; it looks like a prison. The thousands of bay windows look like thousands of cells. The lobby inside is gleaming gold.

Mother wouldn't go, as if by not going to sign the papers, the ranch would stay in the family, as if not going could reverse anything, everything.

"You go," she told me. The windows were open and for miles you could smell the controlled burns, the damp ashes. A warm wind carried everything with it: across streets and rivers and canals, through orchards, through walls.

"But Daddy needs you," I said.

"Someone has to stay here," she said. "Someone has to watch the house." It didn't need to be pointed out how ridiculous that was.

"What should I say to him?"

"There's nothing to say. Just go with him."

During the three-hour trip, we listened to Joni Mitchell's album *Blue*, and then listened again, and then listened again. Dad wore his dress shoes and a white shirt stiff from the cleaners.

We parked the car in a cheaper lot up the hill and walked to the building. Waiting for the elevator in the shiny gold lobby of 555, Dad looked small, fragile. Just last week he had been in the hospital, getting fluids by IV.

The Bank of America receptionist was pert and bubbly and we didn't wait long. Dad's banker, a rotund man called Worstley, ushered us in to a back room where his secretary waited with a large file full of paper. Worstley had stubby little fingers and a jiggly wattle beneath his chin. His secretary was short, athletic, too enthusiastic, I thought, for the afternoon's situation.

"Have a seat here," Worstley said, pulling his own office chair around to Dad's side of the desk. "It's more comfortable."

"This is fine," Dad said, and sat in the straight-backed wooden chair in front of him.

"I'll take your chair," I said to Worstley.

The secretary pulled out her stack of documents and bent over Dad while instructing him where to sign. She had her thick, abundant hair pulled back in a wide clamp, like a fist. "First here," she said, flipping pages and pointing to where Dad should sign. "And initial here."

Very quickly it was over. Worstley shook Dad's hand as if they'd happily agreed on a deal. In twenty minutes, everything was gone. Everything was over.

"Come over here for a minute, I want to show you something fabulous," the secretary said to us. Dad looked half as large as he'd been an hour ago. "I want you to see this." She motioned us to come to her office. "Look," she said. It was a Tiffany table lamp.

It had blue dragonflies around the bottom of the shade and a base twisted like a vine.

"Isn't it so beautiful?" she said to Dad. "They gave it to me for all the work I've done on your account."

If Mother had been here, she would have shouted at this stupid, vapid, cruel secretary. If Mother had been here, there may have been a cathartic scene. I said, "Why would you show us that?" and Dad and I left the office quietly, as if nothing had happened in the past hour, as if we were the same people we'd been when we walked into this building.

Dad told Mom about the dragonfly lamp later, while we sat eating peanuts at the Fresno State game that weekend, dropping the shells on the ground. Fresno State football smells like home—coal barbecues and spilled beer and wet grass and cleats. Dad had four season tickets, from when Anne and I were young, but these days we used only three. This would be the last year, we knew, for football tickets. There had never been a year previously when Dad had given up the football tickets. The names engraved on the backs of our seats said Palamede Farms.

The evening was cool and we wore our red Fresno State snap-up jackets. Dad had had the same seats since I was small enough to be carried in, and we knew the people who sat around us. When they asked Dad, "How's business?" Dad said, "Okay."

Griffith Wine Company had a large tailgate that afternoon, three open white tents and a string-heavy country band. Mexican food on one side, barbecue and burgers on the other. A service bar made from cases of wine.

"Why do you want to do this?" Mother said.

"There's no point in being angry," Dad said. "It's all done."

"That is exactly the point in being angry," said Mother. "He's done what he's done."

Dad said, "It's not Felix who got us overleveraged, Evelyn."

"It's Felix who wouldn't intervene with the bank. It's Felix who shorted you for your grapes."

"He's in business, like the rest of us."

My mother seemed to shrink with a helpless anger. "Not like the rest of us," she said.

At home games, Uncle Felix would switch his navy blue V-neck for bright red. He came toward us with a glass of wine in one hand and Debby in the other.

Mother turned from him, toward the drinks.

"A little more corporate than your parties, Neddy," Felix said.

"Fancy," Dad said.

"No money to be made in socializing," Felix said. "But the employees like this stuff. I keep everyone happy."

"You do," Debby said, and tilted her head at Uncle Felix to indicate how much she admired him. Debby turned out to be far cleverer than I'd originally thought. She wore an enormous pink sapphire on her left hand. That stone must have been eight carats.

"We went to San Francisco," I said. The band played an old Nitty Gritty Dirt Band hit, a song Anne loved when she was in high school.

"I'd heard something like that," Uncle Felix said.

"You could have intervened," I said.

"All right," Dad said. "All right, let's just have something to eat."

I said, "Why didn't you call them off, Felix?"

"Enough," Dad said. "I'm tired. I'm tired of talking business." Dad turned toward the bar, as if following Mother, but Mother had moved on to the food.

I said, "I don't understand. I don't get where you're coming from." Of course, I did understand.

Uncle Felix smiled and reached to take my shoulder. "Why don't you get married and settle down? Why do you keep struggling like this?" He turned to Debby. "Whenever I look at Ingrid, I see her as this little girl with this messy hair."

Debby said, "Were you a tomboy, Ingrid? I was, too."

"You're so transparent, Felix. I know, we all know." I stepped away from him.

"Then why do you upset your father like that? Why do you need to have a scene?"

"This is not a scene."

"Do you think I got where I am by accident? It's no accident, believe me."

The loss was so acute, it felt like suffocation. In the middle of the tailgate party, all those salesmen and managers and ag workers with their red polo shirts tucked into their khakis milling around with their glasses of wine and game-day joviality, I felt so full of betrayal and homesickness and disgust, I had no room for anything more. "Believe you?" I said. "You're a thief, a liar, a fraud." I tried to think of all the words I could right then to describe him. "Duplicitous, deplorable, disingenuous." Debby stepped away.

"Go on," he said. "You should say everything you want to say."

"You're a poison." Nothing could hurt him. Nothing I could say. "Everything I would call you, someone else has already called you."

"I'm sure that's right."

He was my same uncle Felix, but he seemed like an impostor, a new gruesome incarnation. "I wish Aunt Jane were alive."

"So do I," he said.

"Annie said you're going to take Dad's land. She says this whole thing was about getting Dad's land."

"Someone's going to get it," he said. "Why does that matter to you?"

"Annie says you're the only one who knows every parcel, who knows the full value. You and Wilson."

"What else does Annie say?"

"Annie says this has been a long-range plan of yours."

"That Annie has a big imagination. She should write for television."

"She doubts that land will even go on the market. She thinks you'll snap it right up from the bank before anyone else even knows it's available."

Felix shook hands with a passing employee and turned back to me, casually. "You ought be thinking less about what's just happened and more about your future, if you ask me."

"Did I ask you?" The chitchat and shouting and pop-country music of the tailgate seemed to get further and further away, a one-dimensional din, as if it were happening on film.

"I'm telling you. You should listen to me. I've given you excellent advice in the past."

"In the past I could believe the things you said." Between us were our drinks, the tailgate noise, and the cold beginning of the end of harvest. Between us was not just the past few weeks, but a warm past, a happy past, a lifetime of past tense in which I really had loved my uncle Felix.

"Why's that?" he said. "I'm the same Felix as always."

He did look the same as always. The same tough, round torso, the same laughy green eyes. He caused me that feeling of heaviness, the same broken feeling I'd had at the beginning of the summer, when I'd worried the lining of my heart could be suffering irreparable damage. "I thought you were someone it turns out you're not."

He said, "You have that problem once in a while, I've noticed. Especially with men."

Whatever the various ways it comes at you, grief always feels the same. Always a sort of physical violence.

Wilson sat several rows behind us at the game and he waved at us happily. He didn't come down to say hello. He sat with drunk Chris and with two women I didn't recognize. The women had frosted lips and brittle hair, and I began to get an idea of how Mother had become so judgmental.

After the game (Fresno State over Nevada, 24–21), on our way back to the car, past the pickups and campers in the tailgate lot, Dad was intercepted by Carlo, one of Miguel's handymen who'd worked on the ranch a long time. "Jefe!" Carlo said. "You owe me five dollars!"

Dad turned, and clearly even turning required an effort. "Why's that?" he said.

"At the car wash, I put in five dollars and no change came out."

Dad opened his wallet and gave Carlo five dollars.

He took the money and said, "Jefe, your grapes should be picked already."

"That's all right," Dad said. "You pick them, you take what you want."

Carlo looked at Dad and leaned away, the way you look at someone who may be dangerous. "Thank you for my money!" he said.

We walked on, to the middle of the field where Mother's tiny Jaguar was parked.

"I have to get that change machine fixed," said Dad. "A lot of people in this town are upset with me."

The bank let Mom and Dad keep the coin-operated car wash. They let them keep the original one hundred acres and the house on the river, though it was clear that without the ranch, Mom and Dad wouldn't be able to keep up the house. Still, it seemed unwise to put it on the market while Dad was still coughing. We hoped, then, that the cough would improve, that the fungus would find his body an inhospitable environment.

Nothing about my father was inhospitable.

We kept the farm equipment and the warehouse with the offices in it. Dad would rent the farm equipment from the office on days he felt well, and from home on other days. He carried records in the briefcase that used to carry nothing but the sports sections from the *LA Times* and *The Fresno Bee*. The antifungal drugs had begun to do their work on the illness, but the side effects debilitated him in their own way: dizziness, nausea, a pain in his back that made it nearly impossible to move.

I wanted to stay, to put things in the soil and to care for them and to produce food. I wanted work that had physical value.

"Come work in New York," Anne said relentlessly.

"I don't know what I'm going to do yet."

"What's there for you?" she said. "It's all gone."

"There's a hundred acres here. It's not just a backyard."

"Don't be fantastical," she warned. "Who can make a ranch work with a hundred acres?"

"You can tend bar here," Bootsie offered. "You could manage this place when I have the baby."

"I'm not you," I said to Bootsie. "I'm antisocial."

"No one thinks that but you."

There were two phone calls from Uncle Felix, offering me the same work I did for Dad—managing vineyards, essentially. When Felix called, I let the phone go to voice mail.

"It's just business," Dad said when Felix's name came up. "He did what people do in business."

"That's not what people do in business, it's what he does."

Dad's kind laugh had the wobble of regret. "It's just business, Inky."

"I want to work with you," I said. "I think we should continue working together."

He smiled. I sat on the edge of his bed. The files from the office were still piled beside him. "We have nothing left to do," he said.

"We have a hundred acres."

It's so easy, even for someone as humble as Dad, to forget what you started with.

"Farming isn't the same now as it was then," he warned me. "A hundred acres is less now."

("A lot less," Anne would say.)

"But your acres are good acres," I reminded him. Good acres come with their own water. Good ground has no stones in the soil. The dirt is soft and fragrant. Good acres couldn't help but be fertile.

"It's just business," Dad said when he heard through Bint Masterson at the club that Felix had bought every acre of Dad's land, the grapes along the river and the peaches and nectarines farther to the east. "It's not personal."

Half the cabernet hung through the fall and dried on the vine. Cabernet grapes taste delicious as raisins, but no one buys them. They're small like currants, and no one buys currants anymore, either. Elliot came by to pick some, filling a box with them, and Bootsie made cabernet-raisin ice cream at the restaurant all winter. The grape leaves turned orange and then brown and then fell off and carpeted the rows. Uncle Felix hired most of Dad's crew at much less than what Dad had been paying them. That winter, they shaped and pruned the trees, tied the vines, sprayed their dormant sprays, made the repairs to stakes and crossarms that Dad couldn't afford to make the winter before.

Without being asked to, or discussing it with anyone, Mother started packing her china in bubble wrap, as if packing china in bubble wrap was her hobby, something she did to pass the time, like solitaire. "We don't use it," she said. "We can go to Anne's for Christmas."

"Annie wants us for Christmas?"

"When was the last time you spoke to your sister?" Lately Mother's voice had become quick and hard.

"I guess we didn't talk about Christmas."

"It's time to talk about Christmas," Mother said. She had lined her shoulders with little slips of wrapping tape so that she could easily pick a piece off and use it to secure the bubbles around a teacup. This was also, incidentally, her method for wrapping presents. "I think we should get the hell out of here."

"Annie doesn't even have a dining table."

"Yes she does."

"Well, chairs, then. I can't remember what Charlie took, but he took part of the dining room."

"He left the crystal."

"Yes." I remembered that, too.

"We can find chairs to sit on," Mother said. "I mean, God, are things that bad?"

By Christmas Dad was too sick to go to Anne's. Uncle Felix offered to fly us all to LAX in the helicopter, but Mother would no longer take favors from Uncle Felix. "It's bad enough Dad takes his calls," she said.

"Anyone would have done what he did," Dad continued to say.

No one believed this but Dad.

Anne came to Fresno and we ate Christmas dinner on Mother's casual red holiday plates. Anne made a crown roast and we did the stuffing from scratch, cutting the bread into cubes and toasting them in the oven, shredding fresh herbs. We were a family of orphans, it seemed, with no Uncle Felix and no Aunt Jane and not even silly Wilson to ruin the holiday. Bootsie came, with Elliot and with her brother—three more orphans— and brought sticky toffee pudding and custard for dessert.

26.

"I was too late."

"For what?"

"I've been too late for everything my whole life. But for this especially. Like a couple of years too late."

"Your dad thinks you're a Communist."

"Dad and I don't talk about politics," I said. "He thinks I'm a Communist because I won't speak to Uncle Felix."

George tapped his cigarette on the bar. After Bootsie's customers at the front table were gone, she would lock the door and we could smoke with our drinks. George could smoke. Bootsie had stopped smoking once she began to develop a big basketball tummy. I tapped the glass ashtray on the bar.

"Stop," George said, resting his hand on mine. "You're making me nervous."

It was New Year's Eve. Bootsie wanted to get everyone out by ten, over to Lorenzo's, where they were handing out free tiny glasses of champagne, but there was this one couple by the window too happy with each other to leave. Bootsie had retired to her office in the back. Elliot had left me and George to watch over the restaurant while he and Boots tallied up the tabs for the night.

"It turns out I'm the kind of girl your mother wouldn't even let you marry," I said. "That is what we call, in the business, irony."

"In my business, we call that tragedy," George said. His kind laugh was so much like Dad's.

"Well." I clanked the ashtray on the bar.

"I like being the rich one," he said. "Why don't you write the thrillers and I'll grow the pistachios."

"I want to grow grapes," I said. "Why is everyone so resistant to this idea? There are a hundred acres of Thompsons already planted, right on the river, beautifully maintained."

"I'm not resistant."

"Yes, you and everyone." I ran my hand over my hair and smoothed down what was left of my bangs. After Christmas, Anne and I had driven up to San Francisco for the day, and she dragged me to Warren-Lion and I had my hair chopped off like Mia Farrow in *Rosemary's Baby*. I should have done it at the beginning of the summer. "Also, you're not rich," I told him.

"At least four times richer than you are," he said.

When I went to tuck my hair behind my ear, there was no hair to tuck. "What's wrong with staying here?"

"Nothing." He went back to tapping his cigarette. "I don't know if I can believe you'll stay."

"A hundred acres," I said. "That sounds like a lot."

"It's a lot to start with," he said. "But that's not going to maintain the house and the business both. You have to live like a pauper."

"I am a pauper," I said.

"But your parents aren't."

"No."

"They'll figure it out," George said. George did not need to say what everyone knew, which was that a family does not sell the hundred acres a family's three previous generations had managed to collect.

I had consumed a bottle of champagne over the course of a few hours. "I don't know why you don't want to bite me," I said.

He laughed again and turned his bar stool right toward me. "Ingrid Palamede, you are absolutely not going to break my heart twice."

"Break your heart?" I looked over to the people at the window. "Just light your cigarette," I said to George, which he did. "Break your heart," I said.

"I'm not doing that again," he said.

"I didn't ask you to do anything."

Elliot emerged from the office. "George, the cigarette," he said. He looked toward the couple at the window, the stupidly happy couple. "Do you guys want to join us at the bar?" he said. "We're closing."

"Ingrid wants to make raisins," George told Elliot, stamping out the fresh Marlboro.

"Table grapes," I said. "For tables."

Bootsie appeared and ambled over to the couple at the window. She spoke softly and sweetly. The couple left, smiling with Bootsie until she clicked the lock to the front door behind them. Bootsie turned back to us. "You know why Ingrid cut her hair?" she said. She took a pack of cigarettes from behind the bar and tossed them toward George, a gift.

"Why?" George said.

"I'm asking you," said Bootsie.

"Why," said George.

"Because she decided to be about twenty times hotter than she used to be."

"The hair," I said. "It had to go."

"A lot of change," Elliot said.

"Change in the hair," said Bootsie. "Ha ha."

"You're different," George said. "You can't help but be different somehow, after the year you had." He smoothed down my hair at the bottom, where it curled into tendrils and my neck was newly exposed. "The new hair suits this different you," he said. "You look crazy beautiful."

"Don't say those things to me," I said. "You're confusing."

Elliot and George and I drank a pink Guy Larmandier champagne and Bootsie assembled crostini from what was left in the kitchen. We didn't do a countdown, we told high school stories and Elliot listened, and we didn't notice when the old year slipped into the new.

We decided to cultivate the Thompsons, and to pick them by hand. We partnered with Sarkisian to package the kind of grapes so lovely they had to be sold in a box, one triangular bunch at a time. The Thompsons would give us enough money to keep Miguel employed, although Miguel could have had any management job in the valley.

"I don't want any job," he said. "I want to collect the eggs."

Marianela said, "I collect the eggs. You must work elsewhere."

Above all, Miguel wanted to keep his home and his lifestyle and to take weekends off to see his daughter play soccer.

Miguel and I farmed the hundred acres ourselves, seventeen hours a day, and hired Carlo to help us. None of the people who knew Dad well wanted to work for anyone else. Miguel and Dad and I would split the profits evenly, if there were profits.

"Are we making a living?" Mother asked that spring, over and over. "Are we making a living? How do we live?" This was in March, about the time of bud break. "How do we live?"

Dad's health got worse, would only get worse for a long time. He wouldn't speak much about what had happened that season, and stubbornly refused to place blame on Felix. "Failure is annoying," he said once that winter, after the trip to the bank.

"What failure?" I said. "Whose failure?"

"It only could have been worse if I'd lost the original land."

Dad would spend the rest of his life mistakenly believing he wasn't the greatest of the great farmers.

By June, Mother had taken paintings off the walls, packed all the books into boxes, and sent the dining table and its twelve chairs to a consignment shop. She began talking about a new condo development by the club; she had seen units with open kitchens and glossy wood floors and walls of glass that retracted entirely with the touch of a button. "Won't it be better to have a small house?" she said. "Won't it be better to have new appliances and a warming drawer beside the sink? Wait until you see how tall these refrigerators are."

All I wanted to do was trim vines and watch them mature. I wanted to measure water and weigh brush. I loved my hands all rough from plants and dirt. I loved the focus and exhaustion of real work.

"Are we making a living?" she asked as she browned vermicelli for pilaf, as she folded Dad's undershirts, as she swept orange dust from the kitchen floors at the house on the river.

"Yes," I would say, although I didn't yet know. "Yes, we're making plenty," I promised, and then a while later she would ask again.

"How will we be the same?" she asked.

"You're not the same," I said. "You don't need to be the same."

Dad continued to rent the harvesters and pickers and tractors and every other machine, but neither he nor I knew exactly how to force people to pay us. All that winter and spring and well into June, I made phone calls to farmers who never did pay us for the rentals from the fall, even after my stupidly cheap deals.

I kept thinking of that happy Mr. Singh driving away from the warehouse in one of Dad's machines, waving to me from Avenue 7.

In the summer I drove to the mini-malls of the Central Valley and sold beautifully bunched grapes to restaurants and specialty shops around town. What I didn't sell at a premium would be packaged by Sarkisian. My grapes were full and perfect, as I had known they would be; even the stems were plump and green. They tasted purely sweet and even, no bitterness. The skins were taut and light and seemed to dissolve in your mouth with the meat of the grape. I sold some to the Vineyard, and soon after I got calls from grocers in Madera and Merced asking for my prices.

Growers all over the valley were pulling out their Thompsons and planting almonds, pistachios, walnuts. There had been more and more instances—not just us—of grapes being left in the field; nuts were more reliable. That first year of my own Thompsons, demand was high. Sarkisian paid me an unprecedented five hundred dollars a ton for those grapes.

At the end of that summer, when Mother and Dad sold the house on the river, I rented a two-bedroom Craftsman in the Tower District, just a few blocks from Lorenzo's. I unpacked my books for the first time in a long time. I bought a silly-expensive Scandinavian down comforter and cool, thick linen sheets. Mother had no room in their new condo for Grandmother's Metlox plates with the vines along the edges, so I took them with me.

We were making a living. George came by the vineyard almost daily to cheer me on. Dad kept good books on one hundred acres, just as he had watched his father do. I needed advice from no one but Dad and Miguel. George, too. George knew things about human beings that my father and Miguel had ignored while paying attention to soil and plants.

For four generations, all my father's family had done was make a living, farming. There were a few good years in there. One hundred acres was, for me, then, starting with the same land Dad had, working in the same soil my great-grandparents had somehow managed to pay for, far more exciting than twenty thousand acres could have been. I learned, slowly, how to live.

A NOTE ABOUT THE AUTHOR

Katherine Taylor is the author of the novel *Rules for Saying Goodbye* (FSG, 2007). Her stories and essays have appeared in *The New York Times*, *Elle*, *Town & Country*, *ZYZZYVA*, *Southwest Review*, and *Ploughshares*, among other publications. She lives in Los Angeles.